LITTLE GIRL GONE

BRETT BATTLES

ALSO BY BRETT BATTLES

Jonathan Quinn Thriller Series
     The Cleaner
     The Deceived
     Shadow of Betrayal (U.S.)/The Unwanted (U.K.)
     The Silenced

Project Eden Thriller Series
     Sick

For Younger Readers: Mr. Trouble Series
     Here Comes Mr. Trouble

1

"GET THE girl," the voice whispered once more.

Slowly, Logan Harper opened his eyes. It had been the dream again, always the dream.

Get the girl.

He knew the words wouldn't completely go away. They defined him now. He'd come to accept that. The best he could hope for was to force them to the back of his mind, and make them a distant whisper he could almost ignore.

Almost.

He reached for his cell phone a second before its alarm started softly beeping. 4:05 a.m. It was time to get up, and start pushing the words away.

Creating habits had been the key. He'd developed a strict schedule that allowed him to go from one task to the next to the next. In the two years since he moved back to his hometown of Cambria, California, he'd basically done the same things every day. In the mornings this meant a six-mile run, a shower, twenty minutes reading, then out the door to work.

The reading had been the hardest part. In the first few months, it had been almost impossible to concentrate on the words. His mind would drift back. He'd see things he didn't want to see. Hear things he didn't want to hear. But he kept at it, finally training himself to focus on the page and not on the past.

At 5:55 a.m., he would close whatever book he was reading, and head out. That Tuesday morning was no different.

Cambria was located on the Central Coast of California, almost exactly at the midpoint between Los Angeles in the south and San Francisco in the north. It had been a good place to grow up, but like most teenagers in small towns, Logan had seen it as confining. He couldn't wait until he turned eighteen and could leave, and that was exactly what he did—Army, college, a great job at a defense contractor based in D.C. He was gone fifteen years before everything changed, and the only place that made sense for him to go was home.

Now, instead of small and confining, he would have said Cambria felt right. But that wasn't really the truth. Nothing felt right to him. What Cambria was for Logan was a place where he could just be, and not worry if it was right or confining or safe or any of those kinds of things.

It was a way station between what was and…what? He had no idea.

At his normal walking pace, it was eleven minutes from the front door of his apartment above Adams Art Gallery to Dunn Right Auto Service and Repair where he worked as a mechanic, but only if he was heading straight there. His routine included a stop at Coffee Time Café for a large cup of French roast— black—and a toasted bagel with a light smear of cream cheese.

Tun Myat had owned Coffee Time for nearly two decades. He was a seventy-something-year-old Burmese man who moved to the U.S. in the 1980s, and a close friend of Logan's dad, Neal "Harp" Harper, for nearly as long. He was always smiling, and never had a problem if a regular was a little short on cash. No one called him Tun, though. He was Tooney, even if you'd just met him.

As usual, the lights inside Coffee Time were all blazing when Logan arrived. He pushed on the door, but had to pull up short to keep from slamming into it when it didn't open. He took a step back and looked at the sign propped in the front window. CLOSED still faced out.

Logan was pretty much Coffee Time's first customer every day, and Tooney almost always made sure the door was unlocked before Logan showed up. Peering inside, he looked through the dining area, past the glass cabinet that housed the pastries, and into the visible section of the kitchen. He couldn't see anybody, but Tooney had to be there somewhere. When Logan had run by an hour earlier, the lights had been off.

Chances were, Tooney was just running a little behind, and scrambling to get everything ready. If that were the case, he could probably use a little help, Logan thought. He decided to go around back and see.

Coffee Time was the second-to-last unit in a row of tourist-focused shops on Main Street. Logan headed around the last of the units, then toward the back. Just as he reached the end of the building, he heard a raised voice. He paused, worried he'd almost walked into something that was none of his business, then took a peek around the corner to gauge the situation.

Tooney had parked his old Ford Bronco directly behind the café like he always did, but this morning there was an unfamiliar Lexus sedan sitting beside it. That didn't necessarily mean anything. People had been known to leave their cars back there on occasion.

The door to the café was open, spilling light onto the cracked asphalt. But whatever voice Logan had heard was silent now. It dawned on him that it could very possibly have been a radio with its volume set too loud when it had been turned on.

He rounded the corner, thinking that must have been it, but he only made it a couple of steps before he heard a heavy thud and a short, muffled yell.

Not a radio.

Tooney. There was no mistaking the voice.

Keeping as tight to the wall as possible, Logan moved to within ten feet of the open door.

The voice from moments earlier spoke out again, a man's voice. Logan was close enough now to make out what he was saying. "Nod your head and tell me you understand," the voice ordered. Logan had never heard it before. "Good. Now sit up."

It was clear whatever was going on inside was not just a friendly visit. Logan's first thought was that Tooney was being robbed.

He glanced at the Lexus, automatically memorizing its license number. He knew the car could hold several people, which meant it was very possible the speaker wasn't alone.

Crime in Cambria was rare even at the worst times. For law enforcement, the town relied on the sheriff's department stationed out of Morro Bay nearly twenty minutes away. Logan pulled out his phone and started to dial 911, knowing they would never make it in time, but the sooner they were en route, the better.

He'd barely punched in the first number when Tooney's voice drifted out from inside. "Please. Just don't hurt—"

There was a hard slap.

Logan shoved his phone back in his pocket, knowing he couldn't waste time making the call, then glanced around, looking for something he could use as a weapon.

"You open your mouth again, and it'll be the last time. Understand?"

Silence.

"Good," the voice said.

Logan spotted two three-foot-long metal rods, in a small pile of wood along the back of the building. Both had double lines of slots running down one side. Screw them to a wall, then insert hangers in the slots, and, bingo, instant shelving unit. Or grab one in each hand, swing them around—instant clubs.

He chose option two.

As he moved toward the door, he heard the sound of something moving or sliding inside.

"...too much, and apparently doesn't..." the man with Tooney said, the first part covered up by the noise, while the last seemed to just fade out. This was followed by a solid, metallic click and everything went silent.

Logan stepped into the doorway, and looked quickly around the room, ready to help his friend. Prep table, food storage racks, sink, dishwasher, stove, walk-in refrigerator, a stack of empty milk crates, Tooney's small desk.

But no Tooney, and no man. No anyone.

As silently as possible, he walked to the doorless opening that separated the kitchen from the front of the café. But there was no one there either.

Where the hell—

He heard a voice, muffled and indistinct, to his left. He whirled around, his arms cocked, ready to strike. But there was no one there.

As the voice spoke again, Logan realized it was coming from *inside* the walk-in refrigerator.

He raced over and yanked the door open. A flood of chilled air poured over him, but he barely noticed it. Three feet inside, Tooney was kneeling on the floor, facing him. Between them was a man in a dark suit, pointing a gun at Tooney's head.

Before the man could turn all the way around, Logan wacked him hard in the arm with one of his improvised clubs. The man let out a groan of pain as he sidestepped past Tooney, and moved further into the refrigerator, away from Logan.

Logan slashed at him again, hitting the man's shoulder and scraping the end of the metal rod across the man's neck.

"Son of a bitch!" the guy yelled. He twisted to the right so he could bring the hand holding the gun around toward Logan.

In a quick, double motion, Logan swung the rod in his left hand at the man's head, then struck downward with the one in his right at the gun. The man leaned quickly back to avoid being gashed across his cheek, but doing so caused his gun hand to drift upward a few inches, right into the area Logan had aimed at.

Just as the rod hit the gun, the man pulled the trigger. A bullet raced by Logan's hip, then slapped into the wall of the refrigerator. Logan struck at the man's hand again until the pistol, a Glock, tumbled to the floor.

Unarmed now, the man staggered back, bleeding from both his neck and his hand.

Logan stood in front of him, ready to strike again. "Tooney," he called out. "Can you get up?"

"I think…" Logan heard a foot scrape across the floor. "Yes…I can."

"Go call 911," Logan told him.

The would-be attacker laughed. "You're not going to do that, are you, *Tooney*?"

Logan sensed the café owner hesitate. "Tooney, now."

That seemed to break the trance, and Tooney shuffled out the door.

"Who the hell are you?" Logan asked the intruder.

"Why don't you ask Tooney?"

Logan stared at him for a second. "Get comfortable. It takes the sheriff a little while to get out here, and you're going to be pretty damn cold by then."

The guy began to smile. "I can handle a little cold. Can you?"

The last word was barely of out of the man's mouth when he charged. Logan whipped a rod through the air, smacking the man in the side of the head, but it didn't stop him. With another step, the guy had moved inside the range of the clubs.

Logan quickly let go of them, then grabbed the man by the shoulders and tried to guide the attacker's momentum past him, not through him. He was only partially successful, though, deflecting the man away from his chest, and into his shoulder.

The man staggered, then started to go down. Reaching out, he latched onto one of Logan's belt loops, and they both ended up tumbling to the floor.

Logan found himself on his back, with the man on top of him. He threw a quick punch into the man's ribs. But instead of responding in kind, the man shoved Logan in the shoulders, and pushed himself up.

As soon as he was on his feet, he started searching the floor, obviously looking for the gun, but Logan spotted it first. He kicked the man in the hip, knocking him sideways into a stack of egg crates, then got his foot on the gun, and kicked it toward the open door.

The moment it passed through the opening, Logan realized that was a mistake. He jumped to his feet, but the man raced outside first.

Almost immediately the door began to swing shut. The guy was doing to Logan what Logan had been planning to do to him.

Logan pressed his hands and arms against the door, trying to stop it from shutting. But the man had the leverage, and the door kept getting closer and closer to sealing Logan in. Then, with just a few inches to go, it suddenly jammed to a halt. For several moments, the man continued pushing, trying to close the remaining gap, but the door wouldn't budge.

There was a grunt of frustration, then the pressure from the other side ceased. Logan pushed the door open just in time to see the man grab Tooney and throw him into one of the storage racks, then race outside.

Stepping quickly out of the refrigerator, Logan spotted what had kept the door from closing. The Glock had caught between the door's lower lip and the refrigerator frame. He scooped it up, and started for the rear exit, but a moan stopped him before he could get there.

Tooney was trying to get off the floor, but wasn't having much luck. There was blood on the side of his head, and a dazed look in his eyes.

"Stay down," Logan said as he knelt beside him. "I'll call for an ambulance and let the sheriff know what's going on."

Tooney jerked under Logan's hand. "No," he said. The look in his eyes wasn't fear. It was terror. "No police. No ambulance. I be okay."

Outside, the sedan's engine started.

"Tooney, you're hurt."

Tooney sat up. "I'm okay. Just cut. Can clean myself. No problem. No police. Please, Logan. Don't call them."

Logan stared at the old man, confused.

"Please," Tooney said again.

Though Tooney was injured, nothing looked fatal. Logan thought for a moment, then grabbed the keys he'd spotted earlier on Tooney's desk, and headed toward the back door.

"What are you going to do?" Tooney asked.

But Logan was already outside, so even if he had an answer, Tooney wouldn't have been able to hear it.

2

THERE WERE only two ways out of town—either north or south, both on the Pacific Coast Highway. North was the tourist direction, the scenic route. It went past Hearst Castle and then up a long, winding road through Big Sur to Monterey. It was a slow drive with few outlets for a hundred miles or more. The one to the south led to Morro Bay, then over to San Luis Obispo and the 101 freeway. From there, the whole country opened up.

Logan barely paused at the red light before turning south. It was the only way Tooney's attacker would have gone. Once on the highway, he jammed the accelerator to the floor, then pulled out his cell phone. But as hard as it was not to, he didn't call the sheriff or an ambulance.

"Jesus, Logan. What time is it?" his father asked, sounding half asleep.

"Get over to Tooney's café right away," Logan told him. "Have Barney drive you. He used to be a doctor, right?"

"Why? What's going on?"

"You'll need a first-aid kit."

"Logan, what happened?" Whatever sleep had been in Harp's voice was gone.

Logan hesitated. "Tooney's had an accident."

He could hear his father throwing back his covers. "My God. Is it bad?"

"He didn't think he needed an ambulance." Logan knew it wasn't exactly answering the question, but it was the best answer he could give.

"I'll call Barney. Wait, aren't you there?"

"Not anymore."

"Why not? Where are you?"

"Just hurry, Dad," Logan said, then hung up.

Nearly four minutes passed before he spotted the Lexus's taillights climbing up the other end of the valley past the tiny town of Harmony. At least he hoped it was the Lexus. It was about the right distance away, and he couldn't see any other lights farther along.

He did his best to close the gap, but the other guy was driving a late-model sedan, while Logan was trying to get all he could out of Tooney's old Bronco. Still, he was able to trim the sedan's lead to less than a mile by the time the other car disappeared over the lip of the valley.

After that, they entered a stretch of the road that wound through the hills toward the ocean, making it almost impossible for Logan to keep track of the other car. Every once in a while he would catch a glimpse of lights ahead, but that was it.

As the miles passed, night began to finally lose its grip on the land. On most days he would welcome the dawn, but not today. The taillights that had been easy to spot in the darkness were becoming harder and harder to pick out. Then, as the hills on the right fell away to reveal the bay, there were no lights ahead at all. Logan knew the guy still had to be up there somewhere, so he kept going, driving through Morro Bay, then inland to San Luis Obispo.

But not once did he see the Lexus again.

A block from the entrance to the freeway, he reluctantly

pulled to the side of the road. There were just too many directions the man could have gone from there.

Logan had lost him.

For several minutes, he sat motionless, feeling the weight of his failure in his chest. He'd done it again. No matter what his intentions had been, he'd failed.

Finally, he put the Bronco back in gear, turned around, and headed for home.

Just as he passed the San Luis Obispo city limits, his cell rang, the display screen simply reading: DAD.

"Where are you?" his father asked.

"SLO, but I'm heading back now." *SLO* was local slang for San Luis Obispo.

"Don't."

"Why not?"

"We're coming there."

It wasn't until that moment that Logan noticed the distinct hum of tires coming from the other end of the line.

"Why?"

"Barney talked Tooney into letting us take him to the hospital." Cambria was too small for its own hospital. The closest was in SLO. "He's worried Tooney might have some internal bleeding, and he doesn't want to take a chance. Me, he says I only need a few stitches."

That last part was such a matter-of-fact add-on that Logan almost missed it, but the second it sunk in, he hit the brakes and pulled to the side of the road. "What do you mean, stitches?"

"I'm fine. Don't worry about it."

Over the line, he could hear Barney yell, "He knocked his head against a storage rack when he tried to help Tooney stand up."

"Dad! What the hell?"

"What the hell *what*?"

"What the hell were you doing trying to help him up? You're

eighty years old!"

"I'm not eighty for three more months!"

"Dad!"

"What was I supposed to do? He couldn't get up on his own."

Logan rubbed a hand across his eyes. "How many stitches?"

"None yet."

"I mean, how many does Barney think you'll need?"

"I have no idea."

Logan knew there was no use arguing with him. "Which hospital?"

3

LOGAN WATCHED from the window of the Hamilton Memorial emergency room as the others arrived. But it wasn't just Barney, Tooney and his dad like he expected. The rest of his father's buddies—Will Jensen, Jerry Kendrew, and Alan Hutto—walked in right behind them. They referred to themselves as the Wise-Ass Old Men, or WAMO. Which, of course, didn't make sense to Logan at all since the M and the O should have been reversed.

When the nurse at the reception desk saw Tooney enter with Harp under one arm and Barney under the other, she called out to one of her colleagues, who rushed over and took charge. Soon Tooney was sitting in a wheelchair, being rolled toward the back with Logan and the WAMO troupe following right behind.

One of the orderlies asked, "Can someone tell me what happened?"

Logan was about to speak when his father, sporting a large square of gauze taped to the side of his head, blurted out, "He was mugged," then shot his son a look that was clearly telling him to keep his mouth shut.

"Mugged? Where?" San Luis Obispo County was a far cry

from being the crime capital of California.

"Cambria," Barney said.

"He was on his way to work," Harp quickly added.

"Cambria?" the orderly said, even more surprised.

"Probably one of those tourists," Will said.

"Did anyone see it happen?"

Again Logan's father glanced at him, then shook his head and told the attendant, "I was going in for an early coffee and found him in front of his café. Barney here's a retired doctor. He was close, so I called him."

"I thought it best if we brought him in right away," Barney explained.

The automatic door to the examination area slid open as the group neared, but the orderly held up his hands, stopping everyone except his two colleagues and Tooney. "I might have some more questions later, but you're all going to have to wait out here."

"Hold on," Logan said. "What about my father?"

"Your father?"

Logan grabbed Harp by the shoulders, and turned him so that the gauze on the side of his head was clearly visible. The orderly stepped over and pulled the bandage back.

"What happened to you?"

"He fell trying to help our friend get up," Barney told him.

The orderly frowned, then waved for Logan's dad to follow him. "Let's clean that out and stitch you up."

The rest of them stood there until the orderly and Harp disappeared inside, and the door closed again.

Turning to Barney, Logan said, "You want to tell me what that was all about?"

"Harp should tell you," Barney said.

"But he's not here."

"I'm sure he won't be long."

Before Logan could ask anything else, Barney and the others

headed to the front corner of the waiting room and sat down. Instead of joining them, Logan took a seat right next to the examining area door, and waited.

Growing up, he had always been close with his dad. Working at Dunn Right, camping on the beach, watching football all day on Sundays—these they did together right up until Logan left home. It was Logan who actually caused them to drift apart. As he became more and more involved in his new life, he lost touch with his old one. His relationship with his parents became a monthly call at best, and then, after his mother died, that call became holidays only.

When he moved back home, he expected Harp to be less than excited to see him. But that wasn't the case at all. His father treated him like he'd never been gone. It was exactly what Logan needed, and it had made him feel all the more ashamed. All those wasted years when he had forgotten what a good man his father was. Better than himself, for sure. He knew he could never— *would* never—let something like that happen again.

That's why his father's actions that morning were so confusing. What were his dad and his WAMO buddies up to? It just didn't make sense.

It was about twenty minutes before the doors opened again, and Harp reappeared. A nice square portion of his head had been shaved, and in place of the missing hair was a new bandage. He took a couple of steps out, stopped to adjust his shirt, then started up again, walking right past Logan without noticing him.

"Dad?"

Harp turned, surprised. "Did everyone else leave?"

Logan shook his head, and pointed to where the others were sitting, then said, "You want to tell me what that was all about?"

"The stitches?"

"Don't play dumb, Dad. You know what I'm talking about."

Harp sighed, then nodded toward his friends. "Let's sit over there."

"I think maybe you and I should talk alone, don't you?"

But his dad was already heading across the room, so he reluctantly followed.

Once they joined the others, Logan said, "You lied to that attendant, Dad. What's going to happen when he tells the police what you told him, and it doesn't match the truth?"

"Who's saying it's not the truth?"

Logan stared at him for a moment. "Me. I'm saying that. I was the one who was there, not you. Remember?"

His father looked uncomfortable. "If we all tell the same story, it *is* the truth."

"If we *what?*"

"Tooney doesn't want to make a big deal of this."

"I don't care what Tooney wants. It is a big deal. That guy was *not* trying to mug him."

Harp took a breath. "He'd just rather not have the police involved, that's all. I would think you, of all people, would be sensitive to that."

"Excuse me?"

Trying very hard not to look at his son, Harp said, "It's just…it's over. He wants to move on."

There were nods all around, the wise men suddenly existing in some kind of alternate universe from the one Logan inhabited.

"You told that guy Tooney was mugged. Mugging's a crime, too, Dad. The hospital's probably already called the cops."

"We had to tell him something," Barney said. "He looks like he was in a fight."

"That's because he was!" Logan told him, surprised once again. "For God's sake, you're a *doctor.*"

"Retired," his dad threw in.

"I don't *care* if he's retired," Logan said to him, then turned back to Barney. "Aren't you morally obligated to do the right thing?"

Barney glanced at him for a second, then looked away. "In this case, I believe that we are doing the right thing."

Logan sat back, and took in the lot of them. "Have you all gone senile?"

"Hey, that's not funny," his father said.

Logan didn't care if it was funny or not. At the moment, he almost meant it. "You know what? You and your buddies can do whatever you'd like, Dad, but I know what the guy looks like, and I got the license number of his car. I'll tell the police myself."

He started to get up, but his father put a hand on his shoulder. "Logan, you can't."

"Really? Why not?"

"Because that's not what Tooney wants."

"We're going in circles here, Dad." This time he did stand. "I'll check in later to see how he's—"

"At least do me this much. Wait and talk to Tooney first. I'm asking you as a favor."

Logan closed his eyes for half a second. His father almost never asked for favors. He stood for a moment longer, thinking about it before he gave Harp a single, terse nod, then sat back down.

Harp patted his knee. "Thanks, Logan. Thanks."

The others looked relieved, too.

They waited for thirty minutes before the man who'd asked them the questions earlier finally returned. Turned out his name was Mayer, and he wasn't an orderly. He was one of the doctors on duty.

"Mr. Myat wanted me to give you an update," he said. "The good news is that there doesn't appear to be any internal bleeding. What he does have is a minor concussion, a cracked rib, and some cuts and bruises. We'd like to keep him overnight, but he's insisting on going home." The doctor paused. "He told me he lives alone. I would feel more comfortable releasing him if there were someone he could stay with for a few days."

"I got plenty of room," Harp said right away. "He can stay with me."

The doctor looked skeptically at Logan's father, his eyes glancing briefly at the new bandage on the side of Harp's head.

"What?" Harp asked. "It's just a cut. You saw it yourself." He tapped the bandage with his hand. "See? Doesn't even hurt."

"Harp's fine," Barney said to Dr. Mayer. "But I'll check in on both of them a few times a day, too."

"Okay," the doctor said, looking only semi-reassured. "I'll have him released. He should be out in just a bit. But…"

"But what?" Harp asked.

The doctor paused, then said in a tone even more serious than before, "It's procedure for us to report crimes of violence."

Logan shot his dad a quick told-you-so look.

"Since it happened in Cambria, I understand that falls under the sheriff's jurisdiction," Dr. Mayer went on. "They're sending someone over, but I don't believe they're here yet. So we'd appreciate it if you could hang around until they can talk with Mr. Myat."

"Of course," Harp said. "No problem. But, uh, Tooney doesn't have to wait in back until they show up, does he?"

The doctor smiled. "Not at all. I'll send him out as soon as he's ready."

"Thanks, Doc. Appreciate it."

After the doctor left, Harp eyed his son nervously. Logan was content to remain quiet, knowing it wasn't helping his dad's state of mind.

Tooney was wheeled out ten minutes later. Everyone smiled and told him he looked great and was going to be fine. The second part was hopefully true, but the first wasn't even close. With a nasty bruise on his cheek and a couple of cuts—one on his nose and one near his temple—Tooney looked like a man in a lot of pain.

As the reunion ebbed, Logan caught his father's eye, silently suggesting that now might be a good time for that talk he promised. Harp sighed, then nodded and said, "Tooney, Logan's having a hard time understanding the…uh…mugging issue. Thinks we probably should tell the truth when the sheriff's department shows up."

"Not probably, Dad," Logan corrected him.

His father frowned, but continued to look at his friend. "I thought it might be better if you explained to him…you know…"

Tooney gingerly turned his head in Logan's direction. "Logan, thank you so much for helping me this morning."

"I'm just glad I was there," Logan said.

"I want you to know, I understand your concerns. But this matter…personal. A…mistake."

"A mistake?"

"A miscommunication, that's all." He hesitated, then added, "Please, Logan, for me, say nothing."

"Tooney, he was going to kill you."

"Please," he said, his eyes pleading. "I beg you. This most important to me. Say nothing."

A glance at Harp told Logan that his father, and probably the rest of the WAMOs, knew whatever it was Tooney was unwilling to share. Apparently, it was enough to convince these old men to lie to the authorities for their friend.

Behind Logan, the door to the outside opened. Given the way Tooney and his father tensed, it didn't take a genius to know the sheriff's deputies had arrived.

Tooney glanced at Logan again, panic now joining the fear on his face.

"I really don't understand," Logan said, then hesitated. He was confused by the fact the six men in front of him, men whom he respected, were asking him to do something that didn't make any apparent sense. But respect was one of the things his father had stressed to him growing up, and it was hard to go against that, especially with this group. "I know I'm going to regret this, but if that's what you want, fine."

Without another word, he stood up and left before the sheriff's deputies could be directed their way. Apparently, he didn't have anything to say to them anyway, because, according to the others, he wasn't even there when the incident happened.

4

"AFTER DROPPING Tooney's Bronco off behind his café, Logan headed over to the Dunn Right, getting there just past 9 a.m.

Since he was usually the first one in every morning, he took some ribbing from the other guys for oversleeping, but didn't correct the misperception. Soon they were all elbows deep on their own projects, and talk was restricted to the occasional joke or comment about something the DJ on the radio said.

At noon, as Logan headed out to grab some lunch, Alejandro, Dunn Right's head mechanic, pulled him aside. "Harp not coming in?"

Logan's dad had yet to show up, which, in Alejandro's eyes, was unusual. Harp had seldom missed a day in the forty years since he'd bought the place from a guy name Alan Dunn. He'd kept the name because, as he always liked to say, "Dunn Right sounds a hell of a lot better than Harper Right."

"He had some things he had to take care of," Logan said.

"He's feeling okay, though, right?" Alejandro had been at Dunn Right for twenty-one years, and had developed a close relationship with Harp.

"He's—" Logan stopped himself. Those stitches on the side of his dad's head were going to be very visible, so just saying he was fine wouldn't cut it. "Actually, he fell down this morning. It's nothing serious. Just a cut on the side of his head that needed a few stitches."

"You weren't going to tell me about that? What was it? The stairs? I keep telling him that he needs to move someplace that's only one story."

"It wasn't the stairs," Logan told him. "He was…helping a friend, got pulled off balance and fell. Just an accident. Could have happened to you, too."

"But he's going to be okay?"

"He's already okay."

"You going to go see him now?"

"There's no reason to. I'm just going to go get some lunch."

"Maybe I should go check on him."

"Alejandro, he's fine. He might not even be there."

"Where would he be?"

"I don't know. Probably out with one of his WAMO buddies."

That seemed to placate Alejandro enough so that Logan could leave.

The afternoon was split between working on the fuel pump of an old Chevy Blazer, and fending off more questions from Alejandro when it became apparent Harp wasn't going to show up at all.

At a quarter to five, as Logan was cleaning off a day's worth of grease and getting ready to go home, his cell phone rang.

"I ordered pizza from Round Up," his father said. "Can you pick it up and bring it over?"

"Isn't one of those high school kids around? Have him pick it up for you." Harp lost his license the year before Logan moved back, and had gotten into the habit of hiring local high school kids to chauffeur him around.

"Gave them all the day off. Besides, I bought enough for you, too. This is me inviting you to dinner."

Logan hesitated for a moment, then said "Sure, Dad. I'll be there in a bit."

Not feeling like walking all the way home just to get his car, he decided to use the old Isuzu Rodeo they kept around the shop. When he arrived at the Round Up, he found not just one pizza waiting for him, but three. All large. Apparently, he wasn't the only one joining his dad and Tooney for dinner.

Harp lived on Princeton Lane in the Marine Terrace section of town. His place was on the down slope of the hill that led to the beach, and had a near 180-degree view of the Pacific Ocean. Years ago, before Logan's mom had died, and when land prices were still relatively cheap, his parents bought the property behind theirs so that no one could ever build on it and obstruct their view. Logan was willing to bet most of his father's neighbors wished they'd done the same.

The house was two stories, but because of the slope, the front door opened onto a foyer between the two levels. From there, stairs led up and down. On the bottom floor were Logan's old room, the guest room, and his father's home office. Up, though, was where Harp spent most of his time. That's where the kitchen, the combo dining room/living room, and the master suite were all located. The top floor also had a deck off the back where the WAMO guys liked to enjoy a glass of wine as they watched the sun go down when it wasn't too cold.

When Logan pulled up, he wasn't surprised to find several other cars parked out front. It looked to him like the whole damn gang was there. He guessed they probably wanted to make sure he wasn't going to blow their lie.

Before he even climbed out of the car, he decided he'd only stay long enough to have a slice or two, then get the hell out of there. He still wasn't sure how he felt about what had happened that morning, and he thought it better to just make a quick exit than get annoyed.

"Thank God," Jerry Kendrew said as he opened the door to let Logan in. "Come on, come on. I'm starving."

"Sorry. I didn't realize I was on the clock."

Upstairs, the others were all sitting in the living room. The TV was on, but no one seemed to be paying it any attention. On the screen was a selection menu for one of Harp's video games.

Bowling night, Logan realized.

Harp had told Logan each of his friends had purchased game consoles so they could rotate locations from week to week. "Kind of like the Pro Bowlers Association," he'd said. A bunch of old men eating pizza and playing video games—Logan had no idea what that said about society.

"Food's here!" Jerry called out as Logan set the boxes on the table.

The others stopped talking, and pushed themselves up, some with more dexterity than others.

"Thanks, Logan," his father said as he walked into the kitchen. "Who wants a beer?"

Three of the guys said yes, while Will Jensen asked for water.

"Logan, what about you? A beer?"

Logan shook his head. "Water's fine," he said, then looked around. "Where's Tooney? I thought he was supposed to be here."

Harp jerked his thumb toward the master bedroom. "On the phone."

The dining table looked pretty full with the six of them around it. For the first few minutes, they ate in silence, Logan because he wanted to finish and get out of there, and the others because they seemed nervous to talk to him.

Finally, Logan asked, "How's he doing?"

His dad shrugged. "Sore, but he'll be okay."

"Glad to hear it. What about you?"

Harp touched the bandage on the side of his head. "Going

to tell everyone I was in a bar fight. The chicks will dig it."

That just made Logan want to eat faster.

As he neared the end of his second—and last—slice, his dad said, "Logan, we…uh…want to talk to you about Tooney."

Damn. So close.

Logan leaned forward. "Don't worry. I'm not going to say anything. If you guys want to lie to the sheriff, then have at it."

His father's face scrunched up, his brows dipping so low his eyes became slits. "What are you talking about? Of course you're not going to say anything. You already promised us that. That's not what I meant."

That wasn't the response Logan was expecting. "Okay, what then?"

Harp looked around the table at the other men, then turned so that he was fully facing his son. "Tooney needs help." He paused. "And I, well…*we* thought maybe it was something that you could, you know, do for him."

"If he's in trouble, he should call the sheriff. That's their job, Dad." Logan looked around the table. Along with Barney the retired doctor and Jerry the retired accountant, there was also Alan the retired teacher, and Will the retired scientist. "What in God's name has gotten into you guys? You're acting like this is some kind of game. If your friend has a problem, then he *needs* to *get help*. And if he won't do it, you need to do it for him."

"What do you think we're trying to do?" Harp asked. "We're asking you."

"I don't mean me. I mean from someone official. Like, you know, the sheriff's department?"

"If we do that," Barney said almost in a whisper, "they'll kill her."

"What?" Logan was sure he'd misheard him.

"Are you sure you don't want that beer?" his father asked.

"No, Dad. I don't want a beer. I want to know what the hell you guys are talking about."

"Whoa. Calm down. No need to get all up—"

Suddenly a tired voice called out from behind them. "I…I could use a little help."

5

LOGAN TURNED.

Tooney was standing at the end of the short hallway that led back to the master bedroom, leaning against the wall for support.

Harp and Jerry were the first out of their chairs, but Logan was the first to reach him.

"Shouldn't you be lying down?" Logan asked as he put his arm around Tooney, allowing the older man to lean against him.

"I lay down long enough already. Besides, I'm hungry."

"We can bring you some pizza to the bedroom," Logan suggested, then tried to turn Tooney around, but the older man showed surprising strength for a guy in his condition, and didn't budge.

"I want to eat in here."

"Bring him over to the table," Harp said.

Logan wasn't so sure that was a good idea, but it seemed to be what Tooney wanted, so he carefully led him over, and helped him into a chair. As soon as Tooney was settled, Barney had him open his eyes wide, asked him a few questions, then declared him healthy enough to eat. Sometimes it paid to have a doctor around, Logan thought, even a retired one who was apparently okay with lying to the authorities.

"Any news?" Harp asked.

The rest of the men stopped what they were doing, interested in the answer. But Tooney shook his head. "Tried five times. Same as before."

Logan felt the tension level in the room rise a notch. "Somebody want to tell me what's going on?"

There were shared looks, then Harp leaned toward Tooney. "I think we should do what we talked about. Logan can be discreet."

Tooney sighed, then nodded. "Okay. I don't know what else to do."

Logan prepared himself to once again direct Tooney to the sheriff's department. He was so expecting to hear something like "please find out more about the guy who attacked me this morning" that he only partially heard what Tooney really said.

"What?" he asked, his focus returning to the here and now. "Say that again."

"I want you to find my granddaughter."

Logan took a second to let his mind adjust. "Your granddaughter's missing?"

"I don't know. I think so, yes."

"You think so. Look, I hate to sound like a broken record, but if she's missing, you should call the police."

"No," Tooney said quickly. "I…I might be wrong. And I don't want to cause any…problems."

"Well, when did she go missing?"

"I do not know if she is missing. She supposed to arrive this afternoon."

"Here? In Cambria?"

Tooney nodded. "She goes to college in Los Angeles. She was coming up to spend a few days of spring break with me. But she not show up."

"Well, you're here," Logan pointed out. "Maybe she's at your house right now."

"Alice and Glenda are over there," Barney said. Glenda was Barney's wife, and Alice was either Alan's or Jerry's, Logan couldn't remember which. "They'll call us if Elyse shows up."

"That's her name? Elyse?" Logan asked Tooney.

He nodded.

Logan looked at the clock on the wall. It was only a few minutes after six. "It's early. She's probably still on the way."

Tooney looked unconvinced. "She supposed to leave at ten this morning. Even if she stop for lunch, she here by three."

Glancing at the others, Logan asked, "Has anyone checked traffic? Maybe there was an accident on the 101 that slowed everything down."

"No accidents," Alan said. "We also checked hospitals, just in case."

That was going to be Logan's next question.

"I been trying to call her all day," Tooney said, "but only get her voicemail."

"All day?"

"He wanted to tell her about this morning," Harp explained quickly. "Didn't want her to be surprised when she showed up."

In Logan's experience, people liked to delay news like that so as not to worry them, especially if the other person was traveling.

"We were thinking," Logan's dad continued, his voice now tentative, "maybe you could pop down there tonight. See if she's home. You know, make sure she's all right."

Logan felt an uneasy tingling under his skin. "Go to Los Angeles?"

"Well, yeah."

"Dad, I've got work tomorrow."

"But I'm the boss. I'll just have Alejandro take care of anything you've been working on. And whatever expenses you have…" He looked around the table. "We're going to split them among the group."

"I would probably just pass her on the way down," Logan argued.

"Great, then that would mean everything's fine," Harp said. "We're only asking because Tooney wants to go himself. So far we've been able to talk him out of it. If you don't do it, I'm afraid he won't listen to us anymore."

A thousand thoughts swirled through Logan's mind. Thoughts about his routine and the dream and the past. He looked at Tooney, whose eyes were full of desperation, and then at his father, whose eyes were full of hope.

"What's her address?"

6

LOGAN WENT home to exchange the Rodeo for his own car, a 1969 electric blue Chevrolet El Camino. It was more vehicle than he needed, but it was in a hell of a lot better shape than the SUV.

He went up to his apartment, and found his travel bag at the back of his closet. He stared at it for a moment before taking it out. It was a backpack, small enough to be a carry-on, but large enough to hold everything he needed.

The thing was, it was part of his old life, back from when he'd been on the road all the time, before his ex-wife had walked out on him, and when his best friend had still been alive. He kept the bag pre-packed with things he knew he would always need: a couple of changes of clothes, paper, pens, batteries, passport, toiletries, and a few other odds and ends that had always come in handy. And though he hadn't gone anywhere since moving back to Cambria, the bag sat ready to go if he ever needed it.

Stay, a voice in the very back of his mind said. *Let someone else find her. You'll just screw it up. Better to stay. Better to keep to your routine.*

A year ago, that voice would have won out, maybe even six

months ago, or three, or perhaps one. But when he grabbed the bag, he realized the balance had tipped at some point, even if just a bit. What that meant, who knew? Before he could dwell on it, he stuffed his laptop in the bag, and headed out to his car.

It took him forty minutes to reach the 101 freeway. Once he was cruising south, he pulled out the picture of Elyse that Tooney had given him at his dad's house. It was a high school graduation shot, a couple of years old, but Tooney had said she looked the same. She had a warm smile, and intelligent, caring eyes, and was cute in that geeky, Comic-Con kind of way. She'd never be elected homecoming queen, but fanboys would have done whatever she asked if it meant they could hang out with her.

"So where are you?" he asked.

Not surprisingly, the picture didn't answer.

He reached the outskirts of L.A. just after 10 p.m., but didn't pull up in front of the apartment Elyse shared with three other students until a few minutes before eleven. It was located in Westchester, near the Los Angeles International Airport. Tooney had told Logan Elyse was attending Otis College of Design, less than a mile away, where she was studying to become a motion graphics designer. Tooney wasn't completely sure what that meant, and neither was Logan, but it probably wasn't important.

As he climbed out of the car, it didn't even dawn on him that he'd been up for nineteen hours already. He was focused on Elyse. He wanted to find her quickly, and set Tooney's mind at ease before something could go wrong. Hopefully, she was just sitting in her living room, having totally forgotten today was the day she'd promised to visit her grandfather. As for the phone, Logan could think of a dozen reasons why she hadn't answered it.

Her apartment was in an older, two-story building with outside walkways and staircases. A quick glance at the numbers on a couple of the first-floor doors told him her place, number 17, had to be up the stairs.

The doors to each of the second-floor apartments opened onto the walkway. On either side of the doors were windows. Most of them had their curtains pulled shut. But while a few of the apartments were dark, the majority had at least some lights on.

He found number 17 near the back, just beyond an apartment where a TV was on and several people were laughing. The curtains were drawn across the windows of Elyse's place, but the lights were on, leading Logan to think someone might be home and awake.

He pushed the button for the doorbell and waited. When no one answered after half a minute, he pushed it again, and added a knock this time.

Nothing.

Tooney *had* said it was spring break. What if all four of the girls who lived there had gone out of town, and the last one out had forgotten to turn the lights off? It certainly wouldn't be the first time that had ever happened.

Before he'd gotten out of the car, he'd slipped the small notebook from his bag into his pocket just in case something like this happened. He ripped out a sheet, and wrote a note asking whoever got it to give him a call regarding Elyse. He then stuck it in the crack between the door and the jamb, just above the knob.

As he started to leave, a guy stepped onto the walkway from the neighboring apartment where the TV was on. Tall and lean, and dressed in a pair of plaid shorts and a green T-shirt, he looked like another student.

When the guy saw Logan, he said, "Sorry, man. We'll try to hold it down." He looked back at his apartment. "Hey, turn the volume down!" The sound from the TV dipped.

"Play it as loud as you want. I don't really care," Logan told him.

The kid took a longer look at him. "Oh. Thought you were the guy from downstairs. Don't think he likes us very much."

Logan gestured down the walkway. "I was looking for your neighbors in number 17, but no one's home. Do you know if they're still in town, or have they all gone away for the break?"

The guy stepped back into the doorway of the apartment. "Angie, someone wants to talk to you."

"Me?" a girl inside said.

"Yeah, you." He looked back at Logan. "You want Angie, right?"

"Yes. Angie."

A few seconds later, a short, blonde girl wearing sweats and holding a bottle of beer joined the guy in the doorway.

"I don't know you," she said.

"No, you don't," Logan replied. "I'm here about your roommate."

"Which one?"

"Elyse Myat." Tooney had said native Burmese didn't have last names, so Elyse's parents had decided to stick with the one Tooney had taken when he moved to the States. Logan could tell there'd been more to it than that, but that was all Tooney had said.

The girl hesitated for a moment, then her eyes narrowed. "What about Elyse?"

As if mirroring her, the look on the face of the tall kid beside her grew suddenly serious.

"Maybe we could talk alone for a moment?" Logan suggested.

"I don't think so."

"I'm only trying to find her."

"Well, you're not going to find her here," the guy told Logan, drawing to his full height. "Now I think maybe you should just leave."

It had been a few years, but Logan had taken down men a foot taller and a hundred pounds heavier, so the kid didn't scare him.

"Did I say something wrong?" he asked.

"You're giving Angie the creeps, okay?"

Keeping his voice calm and disarming, Logan said, "Look, I'm a friend of Elyse's grandfather. He asked me to—"

"I don't care who you say you are," the guy said.

He started to close the door, but Logan pushed it back open.

"Buddy, there's no reason to be rude," he told the kid.

Several people rushed over from inside, and soon there were two more girls and another guy standing behind Angie.

"What's going on?" one of them asked.

The plaid-shorts guy was staring at Logan. "You leave now, or I call the cops."

The only explanation Logan could come up with for the guy's reaction was that he was grandstanding for the girls. "I'm not trying to cause a problem, I just want to ask a few questions."

"All right, I've had enough." The kid stepped out of the doorway and into Logan's personal space. "Get the hell out of—"

Logan could see the fist coming from about two blocks away. As it sailed toward him, he easily guided it upward with his hand, then slipped under the kid's arm, whacking his shoulder into the idiot's chest.

The kid's feet flew out from under him, and he landed, ass first, on the walkway. Shoving him all the way onto his back, Logan placed his leg across the boy's clavicle, then stared down at him.

"If I lean forward just a little bit, that bone's going to snap in two, and that's going to screw you up for quite a while. Do you want that?"

The kid shook his head.

Logan took a look at the doorway. The others were still

standing there, their eyes wide in surprise. To the kid, he said, "How about we start over? Why don't you tell me your name?"

A pause, then, "Ryan."

"All right, Ryan. Here's what we're going to do. You're going to answer a few questions for me, okay?"

Ryan nodded. "Okay."

Logan didn't move. "Are you going to invite me in? It would be a lot better to sit down than do it like this, don't you think?"

"Yeah, uh, please, let's go inside."

"Thanks, Ryan. Now I'm going to get up. So don't try anything stupid. Again, I mean."

7

THE APARTMENT'S décor screamed college student—a hand-me-down couch, mismatched chairs and tables, and a stack of empty pizza boxes near the kitchen. There was even a leopard-print beanbag chair in the corner.

Logan made sure everyone was seated before he pulled over one of the chairs from the dining table and joined them. There was no denying that he was feeling a little annoyed. Not just with Ryan and Angie, but with himself, too. He couldn't figure out what he'd done to cause their reaction.

Putting on his best non-threatening smile, he started off by getting the names of the other three kids. The girls were Maria and Joan, roommates in the apartment directly below Elyse and Angie's place. The guy's name was Kenny. He was Maria's boyfriend, and lived a few miles away.

Still smiling, Logan repeated who he was and why he was there. Joan and Maria seemed to be the first to relax. Kenny was still a bit guarded, but Logan could tell he was also coming around. Angie and Ryan, though, continued to look unhappy.

"You all know Elyse?" Logan asked, focusing most of his attention on Joan, Maria and Kenny.

"Sure," Maria said. The other two nodded beside her. "She's a friend of ours."

"Do you really know Elyse's grandfather?" Angie asked, more of an accusation than a question.

"I really do."

"What does she call him?" Joan asked. Unlike Angie, she seemed to genuinely want to hear the answer and give him a chance.

"I don't know," he said. "I've never met her before. But back home we all call him Tooney."

"Yes," she said. "Grandpa Tooney."

"You could have just guessed that," Ryan said.

Glancing at each of them in turn, Logan said, "Look, she was supposed to visit Tooney today, but she didn't show up. He tried calling her. She didn't answer. So he asked me to come down and make sure everything's okay. That's it."

No one said anything for a moment.

"She…she did tell me she was planning to visit her grandfather today," Maria offered.

"When did she say that?" Logan asked.

"A day or two ago. I can't remember exactly."

He considered this for a moment, then said, "She told Tooney she was going to leave at ten this morning, and be at his place in the afternoon. Does anyone know if that's when she left?"

Maria shrugged and shook her head.

"I didn't see her at all today," Joan said.

Kenny was also shrugging. "I just came over this evening. Wasn't even around this morning."

Logan turned to Angie. "You're her roommate. Do you know if she left this morning?"

She looked torn, like she wanted to answer and keep her mouth shut at the same time. Finally, she said, "She…she didn't come home last night."

"She didn't come home?"

"It's not that unusual." She turned away, her gaze momentarily falling on Ryan. Logan wasn't sure, but it seemed like some message passed between them. "Sometimes she spends the night at her boyfriend's place. I assume that's what she was doing, and she just left from there."

"Boyfriend?" Maria said, surprised. "When did that happen?"

Angie looked uncomfortable. "Not that long ago."

"What's his name?" Logan asked.

Angie hesitated, then said, "Aaron. Aaron Hughes."

"Aaron?" Maria stared at Angie in disbelief. "I thought she said she wasn't interested in him."

"I guess she changed her mind," Angie told her, shrugging. "I mean, we didn't really talk about a lot of things, so I don't know for sure."

"Do you have his address? Maybe a phone number?"

She shook her head. "Sorry."

"I know where he lives," Joan offered.

Everyone looked at her.

"*You* know?" Maria asked.

"What?" Joan said, unable to completely hide her embarrassment. "He was hanging out around here a lot. He's kind of cute, he asked me out, so I said yes. Not a big deal."

Maria couldn't hide her distaste. "You went *out* with him?"

"Just a couple times. You spend all your time at Kenny's. I get bored."

"Where does he live?" Logan asked, trying to get her back on track.

"Over in Venice Beach, right on Pacific Avenue. He's got a little bungalow kind of thing. Tan with a flat roof. You can't miss it. It's about a minute's walk north of Washington Boulevard."

"Do you know the address?"

"Hold on." She pulled out her phone. After a moment, she

smiled and nodded. "Yeah, I guess I do." She read it off, and Logan jotted it down in his notebook. He then asked if she had Aaron's phone number, and she gave him that, too.

"Thanks," he said, then turned back to Angie. "Her grandfather said she has three roommates. Where are the other two?"

"Laura and Carrie?" Angie said. "They went home for the break."

"Thanks," he told her, then looked at Ryan. "See how easy that was? All you had to do was be nice from the beginning, and you'd still have your pride."

"Whatever," Ryan replied.

"I'm sure he didn't mean anything personal," Maria said. "There've been some strange men hanging around the building lately. The guys have taken to watching out for us because of it."

That would certainly explain why Ryan tried to shut him down so quickly. "What do you mean, strange?"

"You know, they show up every once in a while, walk around a little, then just leave," Joan said. "Kenny tried talking to them once, but they just ignored him."

"The same guys every time?"

The two girls looked at each other, then Joan said, "There are four of them, I think."

"Yeah, but never more than two around at the same time," Maria added.

"That's true," Joan said.

"Describe them for me."

"There was one black guy, and the rest were white," Joan said.

When she didn't add any more, Logan asked, "Age?"

"I don't know. In their thirties, maybe."

"Anything else? Height? Weight?"

"Around your height, I guess," Maria told him. "And in good shape. Other than that, nothing stands out."

Interestingly, it was pretty much the same general way he

would have described the guy who'd attacked Tooney that morning. He filed that thought away for later.

Tearing a few pages out of his notebook, he gave each of them his number. "If any of you hear from Elyse, or think of something that might help me, please give me a call right away."

He then had them each write down their number.

"Thanks," he said as he stood up. "Sorry to have interrupted your evening."

"Shouldn't we call the police?" Joan asked.

Logan couldn't miss the instant karma of having the same thing he'd said to his father and Tooney thrown back at him. "We don't even know if there's anything wrong yet. If there is, I'll be the first to make the call."

8

PACIFIC AVENUE was just two blocks from the beach. Logan located Aaron Hughes's place in a walled-off compound on the east side of the street. The wall was about six feet high, with a red wooden door right smack in the center, locked by a deadbolt. Judging from the addresses listed out front, there were five units inside. There was no intercom, though, so he guessed people had to call ahead to be let in.

Logan tried the cell number Joan had given him.

One ring, then, "Hi, this is Aaron. Leave a message and I'll—"

He hung up, then put his ear right next to the gate, listening for any sound from the other side. Dead quiet, but not surprising for near midnight on a Tuesday. Undoubtedly, everyone on the other side of the wall was asleep. But if Aaron was home, Logan didn't want to wait until the kid woke up in the morning to talk to him. He wanted to do it now.

He checked both ways down the street, making sure no one was around, then grabbed the top of the wall, and swung his legs up and over. He found himself in a dim courtyard. To his left was a square standalone building that seemed to be a single unit.

Since one of its sides made up part of the compound's outside wall, it had been the only building he'd been able to see from the street. There were a couple of other structures on the property, too, but from Joan's description the front one should be Aaron's place.

Logan confirmed this a moment later when he saw the number 4A mounted on the wall beside the jamb, the same number Joan had given him.

The place appeared dark, so he guessed Aaron was probably already asleep. Not for long, though.

Logan rapped lightly on the door, so as not to wake up any of the neighbors. Receiving no response, he chanced a louder knock.

This time he did hear something. Only it wasn't tired footsteps shuffling toward the door. It was the clear and unmistakable echo of his own knock.

Immediately, he moved over to the window on the right and pulled out his keys, turning on the small flashlight attached to the ring. What he saw on the other side was exactly what the knock had made it sound like—an empty room.

Moving to the window left of the door, he peeked in again. The room on the other side was a small kitchen. While the appliances were all there, the counters were completely bare. At the side of the house, he found a third window that looked into what was probably a bedroom, and found only bare floors.

What the hell?

He returned to the front door and tried the knob. It was unlocked, so he pushed it open. Even before he stepped over the threshold, he noticed the smell.

Clean.

Disinfectant, bleach, cleanser clean.

Slowly he walked through the small building, checking each room, but the place was as empty from the inside as it had appeared from the out.

Aaron, if he indeed had been living there, was gone now, and the place had been scrubbed down. There wasn't a speck of dust or a scrap of paper anywhere. And by the strength of the smell, Logan figured the cleaning had occurred within the last day and a half at most.

He pulled out his phone and called Joan.

"Hello?"

He couldn't hear a TV in the background, so he guessed she'd gone home. "It's Logan Harper. The friend of Elyse's grandfather."

"Oh. Hi." He could tell by her tone she hadn't expected to hear from him again so soon.

He read off the address she'd given him, then said, "I just wanted to confirm that's the same one you gave me."

There was a few seconds delay while she checked. "Yeah, that's it."

"You mentioned you'd been to his place before."

"Once."

"How long ago was that?"

"I don't know. Three or four weeks ago, I guess."

"Just to be sure, is it an apartment or a house?" he asked.

"I already told you that. A bungalow, you know, a little square house. Tiny. I think Maria and I have more room in our apartment."

"Can you describe how you get into the property?"

"Umm, yeah, I guess so. There's a wall out front. You've got to go through this wooden gate. And—"

"What about furniture?"

She paused. "I don't know. The usual stuff. Why are you asking me all this?"

"Did he ever say he might be moving?"

"Moving? He never said anything to me, but I haven't talked to him since about the time I was there. Why?"

"Okay. Thanks. I'll—"

"What are you doing in here?"

Logan whirled around. Outlined in the doorway was the dark shape of a woman.

To Joan, he said, "I'll call you if I need anything else," then hung up, and headed toward the door. "I'm sorry. I was looking for the person who lived here."

"Does it look like someone lives here?"

He could see her better now. She was wearing sweats and a baseball cap, and was a good ten years older than he was.

"When did Aaron move out?" he asked as he stepped outside.

The use of the name had the desired softening effect. "You're a friend of his?"

Logan paused. "Not really a friend. He…does some work for me on and off. Supposed to come over earlier this evening but didn't show up. Couldn't get him on his cell, so thought I'd come over and check."

"Sorry. I think you're out of luck. He moved out this morning."

"This morning?"

"Gone by nine."

Logan glanced back inside. "You got the cleaning crew in there fast."

"Aaron arranged that himself. Said he didn't want to leave a mess for someone else to clean up. Wish everyone was like him." She paused. "He must have gotten his dates with you mixed up, though. He told us a week ago he was moving back east today."

As Logan climbed back into his car a few minutes later, he felt numb. There was no way to deny it. Something odd was definitely going on.

He stuck the keys in the ignition, but instead of turning them, he called his father. It took five rings before the call was answered.

"Hello?"

"Dad?"

"No. It's Jerry."

Jerry? Apparently his dad was hosting a slumber party.

"You want me to get him?" Jerry asked.

"Please."

A few seconds later, Harp came on the line. "Did you find her?"

"Not yet. Did you check the hospitals again?" Before Logan had left his father's house, he'd suggested they call around one more time.

"Yeah. She's not at any of them. I also did another check with the highway patrol. No major accidents on the 101 tonight."

Logan paused. "Dad, I think it's time we talk about calling the authorities, and telling them what's really going on."

Harp was silent for a moment. "What happened?"

Logan told him what he'd learned so far.

"That doesn't necessarily mean she's missing."

"The definition of a missing person is someone you can't find," Logan told him. "I've checked the places she should be, and she's not at any of them."

"We...we can't go to the police."

"Why not?"

"We just can't."

"That's not good enough anymore."

"It has to be good enough!" his father yelled.

"How can I know that? You guys obviously aren't telling me everything. If you did, maybe I'd understand."

His dad hesitated, then said, "I can't tell you. I made a promise. But I can guarantee you that involving the police would be exactly the wrong thing to do. Please, Logan. You need to trust me on this."

Logan shook his head in disbelief. "What do you want me to do? Ignore what I've learned?"

"Of course not," he said. "I want you to find her."

9

LOGAN HAD met Carl Stone in the Army while in the middle of his three-year, post-high-school stint. Carl had already been in for four at that point. It was one of those situations where their personalities clicked the moment they met. Even after Logan left the Army for college, their friendship didn't falter, and they stayed in constant touch. It was as if they had grown up together. Nothing could ever separate them.

The summer after Carl got out of the Army, he took Logan—a junior at Fresno State by that point—to visit his family in Scottsdale, Arizona. That's when Logan met Carl's sister, Trish. In many ways, Carl was even happier than she and Logan were when they got married.

"Now you're legally my brother," he had said.

By the time Logan finished college, Carl was working at Forbus Systems International in Washington, D.C. The company was a defense contractor involved in a ton of different things. Carl's job was training and assessing its private security forces. These forces were mainly tasked with guarding war-zone bases so that military personnel didn't have to.

"Don't even bother looking for a job," Carl told Logan a

month before graduation. "I'll take care of it."

Logan was never exactly sure who Carl talked to, but within two weeks of getting his diploma, he was offered a job working with his best friend at a salary he couldn't refuse.

In retrospect, he knew it would have been a hell of a lot better if he had. Carl might still be alive, and Trish wouldn't have blamed Logan and walked out on him.

But Logan *had* taken the job. And Carl *had* died. And Trish *had* left.

It wasn't the dream that woke him that morning in L.A. It was the cruel memory of his wife lying quietly beside him. He could see her hair on the pillow, the curve of her body under the blanket. He could almost smell her, too, the faint odor of almonds and wildflowers and...

As his eyes parted, the illusion faded. Trish was three thousand miles away, not lying next to him. That would never happen again.

He threw back the covers and sat on the edge of the bed, knowing he needed to go on a run so he could drive the memories from his mind. But in his haste to leave Cambria, he'd left his running gear behind. The only choice he had was to take a vigorous walk up Sepulveda Boulevard, where his motel was located, and hope that would do the trick.

It was only partially successful. While he was able to put Trish and Carl back into their respective boxes, he was unable to let his mind go completely blank. The void he'd hoped to create was quickly filled by thoughts of Tooney and Elyse.

It was obvious to Logan that there was a lot more going on than he'd been led to believe. Part of him wanted to jump in his El Camino and drive back to Cambria to find out from his father and Tooney what was really going on. But what about Elyse? If something had really happened to her, Logan couldn't afford the time the trip would take. As it was, he'd had to force himself to find a place to sleep only because it had been too late to get anything else done.

Now the world would soon be awake again, and he could get back to looking for her. As much as he wanted his other questions answered, they would have to wait.

He figured his best bet was to find out more about Aaron Hughes. Logan wasn't buying the coincidence of Aaron moving out of his place the same time Elyse disappeared.

He stopped at a coffee shop near the motel and had a light breakfast. When it got close to seven, he grabbed his bag from his room, then went down to the El Camino and made a call.

"Hello?" By the way Angie grunted the greeting, he could tell he'd woken her.

"It's Logan Harper."

"Who?"

"From last night. About your roommate?"

"Oh." She paused. "What do you want?"

"Just a couple questions. Aaron Hughes. Did he go to Otis, too?"

When she answered, her tone had turned guarded. "I, uh, think he was out of school. Had a real job."

"Doing what?"

"How should I know?"

"You didn't talk about these kinds of things?"

"Elyse and I are just roommates. We don't hang out. Now, if you don't mind, I'd like to go back to sleep. I'm on *vacation*."

She clicked off.

Logan stared out the window for a moment. He wasn't sure if she was just socially awkward or trying to hide something. Better to err on the side of the latter, he thought, adding a stop at her apartment to his list of things to do. It was a lot harder to hang up on someone if they were standing right in front of you.

He called Joan next. Though he'd woken her up, too, her demeanor was considerably less annoyed than Angie's.

"Did you find her?" she asked.

"Not yet."

"Oh, God. Maybe something really did happen to her."

"I'm not willing to say that just yet, but I do have a question or two, if you don't mind."

"Sure. Whatever I can do to help."

"I get the impression you and Elyse are friends. Is that right?"

"Yeah, I guess. I mean, we don't go and do a lot of things together. But when we're both here, we'd hang out, watch some TV, talk."

"Other than this boyfriend, Aaron, who—"

"I gotta tell you, I don't think she *was* dating him. I know that's what Angie said, but I'm sure Elyse would have told me that."

"Well, I was wondering if you knew of any other friends she might hang out with?"

"Her best friend's a girl named Lara. And then there's this guy. What's his name?" She was silent for a few seconds. "Anthony, I think."

"Last names?"

"I think Lara's is Mendonca. Anthony's, I have no idea. You can check at the school. They're both in the motion graphics program with Elyse."

"Thanks," Logan said.

"If you find her, will you please call me? I want to know she's okay."

"I will."

One more thing for his to-do list: Contact Otis administration.

He checked his watch. Seven-fifteen. Too early for anyone to be at the school yet. He could go pay that visit to Angie, but if she was sleeping, she'd hold for a little while. There was one other thing he could do first.

He started his car and headed back to Venice Beach so he

could take another look at Aaron Hughes's place in the daylight, and see if there was anything he might have missed.

On the way over, he'd started thinking about the guy who'd attacked Tooney the day before. Sure, his father had said it had nothing to do with Elyse, but just like how Logan was skeptical about the coincidence between her disappearance and Aaron's sudden move, he was equally skeptical about there being no connection there.

There was one way he could find out a little more information, but it meant making a call he wasn't sure he was ready to make. He debated with himself for a full five minutes before he pulled out his phone, and punched in the number. It was already mid-morning in Washington, D.C., so he knew there was a good chance she'd be there.

"Forbus Systems International. How may I direct your call?"

Hearing the words, he hesitated.

"How may I direct your call?" the voice said again.

"Uh, Ruth Bobick, please."

"One moment."

He was put on hold, and subjected to fifteen seconds' worth of Forbus promotional propaganda, complete with patriotic music and what sounded like the crackling of fireworks.

"Ruth Bobick."

He hesitated again hearing the voice of his old friend, knowing he could still hang up if he wanted to, but instead he said, "Hi, Ruth."

"Who is this?"

"It's Logan."

There was a long pause. "Oh, Christ. Are you trying to get me into trouble or something?"

When Logan had worked with Carl at Forbus, Ruth had been their main contact whenever they were out in the field leading training sessions. She and Logan had always gotten along well. When the powers that be took him down after Carl was killed, it would have been easy for him to drag Ruth along with him, but he hadn't.

"I don't want to get you into any trouble."

"Well, you know you're not exactly on the top ten most popular list around here."

"It's been more than two years. I would think everyone had moved on."

"You'd think, wouldn't you? Unfortunately, some people have long memories." She paused. "How are you doing?"

"I'm okay. You?"

"Fine." Another pause. "Are you still in…"

"Cambria? Yeah."

"Working at the garage?" she asked, as if the question itself was ridiculous.

"Yep."

"You know, if you're looking for something else, I've got friends around the industry, and could probably pull a few strings. It wouldn't be what you've done in the past, but it would be better than working in a garage."

"I like the garage, Ruth. But thanks."

Neither of them said anything for a moment.

"So, are you calling just to say hi?" she asked.

"I'm calling because…" He paused. "Because I need a favor."

"You are trying to get me in trouble."

"It's not a big deal. I just need a license plate checked."

"That's it?"

"Yes."

"Someone piss you off and you're trying to track them down?"

"Something like that."

"What's the number?"

Logan gave her the plate number of the sedan he'd chased out of Cambria, then told her his cell number since it was different from the one he used to have.

"Mine's still the same," she said. "But don't use it unless it's an emergency, and, please, don't call me on the office phone again."

"In other words, don't call you?"

"It would be better if *I* called *you*."

"I understand. I appreciate the help, Ruth."

"You're welcome." She paused, then said, "I'm…I'm sorry I haven't been in touch."

"I haven't been in touch either."

"Yeah, but…well…sorry."

He could sense she wanted to say something more, but before she could, he said, "I'll wait for your call," and hung up.

10

TRAFFIC BEGAN building up on Washington Boulevard as Logan neared the ocean. It seemed strange to him. As far as he could tell, the area was mainly residential, so he figured most of the cars at that time of morning should have been heading in the other direction. But the closer he got to Pacific Avenue, the more congested it became. Then, two blocks short of where he'd been planning to turn, he came to a complete stop.

After the car in front of him made a U-turn and headed back in the other direction, he decided to do the same, then turned on the first side street he saw and parked. From there, it was only a few minutes' walk to Aaron's place.

Before he reached the intersection with Pacific, the reason for the delay became clear. Two police cars were pulled across the road, blocking off Pacific Avenue north of Washington.

Logan felt a tingling sensation at the back of his neck, and picked up his pace. When he reached the corner, he spotted several emergency vehicles parked just down the block. He could also see half a dozen firefighters rolling up hoses and packing equipment back onto their trucks, their work apparently done.

Like the street, the sidewalk that ran in front of Aaron's

place was also blocked, but the one on the other side only had a small area taped off directly across from the fire trucks. Some people were gathered along the part that was clear, watching the action, so Logan headed there.

In his gut, he already knew what he was going to see, and he wasn't disappointed. Where Aaron's little house—his bungalow—had been, there was now a charred pile of debris. The side that had once been part of the property wall was gone, leaving a gaping hole. Logan could see the rest of the property through it. Though it looked like the fire had spread, the other buildings appeared to have received only minor damage.

Apparently, just cleaning the house hadn't been enough for Aaron. He'd decided to burn the place down to make sure there was no trace of him left. Logan had no proof of this, of course, but once again, he wasn't buying the coincidence.

Moving further down the sidewalk to get a better look, he could see that there was no part of the bungalow left untouched by the flames. If Aaron had left anything behind that could have helped Logan find Elyse, it was completely destroyed now.

Logan's phone vibrated in his pocket. Expecting it to be Ruth, he was surprised to see DAD on the display.

"What?" he asked, not in a particularly talkative mood.

"What was Elyse's boyfriend's address? Don't think you gave that to me."

Logan's eyes narrowed. "Why?"

"Well…em…when I told Tooney what you said when you called last night, he wanted to come down and see it himself. We couldn't talk him out of it."

"So you let him go?"

"Of course not. He's in no condition to drive. We came with him."

Logan whipped his head around, looking at the crowd on the sidewalk. "Where are you?"

"Sitting in Barney's car."

"Dad! Where specifically?"

"Oh, we're stuck in traffic on…"

Barney spoke up in the distance. "Washington Boulevard."

"Washington Boulevard," he repeated. "Down by the beach. Venice, I guess."

"You guys should have just stayed at home," Logan told him.

"I'm sorry! You tell Tooney that."

Logan closed his eyes for a second. "Never mind. Just…just tell Barney to pull over and park anywhere he can. I'll meet you in a few minutes."

Harp's voice became distant. "Logan's here. Says for you to find some place to park and he'll meet us."

"Call me when you've found a spot and tell me where you are."

Logan hung up and headed back to Washington, arriving just in time to see Barney's Volvo make the same U-turn he had earlier. Only instead of parking on a side street, Barney pulled into the lot of a strip mall, and found a space there.

Logan weaved between the cars and crossed to the other side. Just as he was walking up to Barney's car, his cell rang again.

His dad was in the front passenger seat, phone to his ear, so Logan tapped on his window. Harp turned in surprise, then smiled and hung up.

"Hi, son," he said as he opened his door.

Logan gave him a quick hug.

"Have you found her?" Tooney asked. He was stretched out on the backseat, a grimace on his face.

"Still looking," Logan said, wishing he had a better answer.

"Scoot, scoot," Harp told his son, shooing Logan out of his way so he could get out.

Once his father closed the door behind him, Logan said, "Tooney shouldn't be traveling. What were you guys thinking?"

"He was coming with or without us. Better with, don't you think?"

"You couldn't have done *anything* to stop him?"

"He was very insistent."

On the other side of the car, Barney was helping Tooney get out. Harp used this as an excuse to end the conversation, and headed around the car to join them. Logan watched his dad for a moment, then followed.

Looking out at the traffic, Barney said, "This is why Glenda and I moved out of the city. Where are all these people going?"

"The road's blocked up ahead," Logan said.

"Accident?" Harp asked.

"Something like that."

A ten-year-old Cadillac pulled into the lot, and stopped right next to them. The driver's window rolled down, and Logan could see Jerry behind the wheel and a few others inside.

"Jesus, I thought we'd lost you," Jerry said.

Logan looked at his dad. "What? Did you bring everyone?"

"Just Barney and Jerry," he said. "The rest of those guys are protection."

"Just park right there," Barney told Jerry, pointing at an empty spot two cars down.

"Protection?" Logan asked.

His father shrugged like it was no big deal.

Jerry and the three guys who'd been riding with him walked over a few moments later.

"Logan, this is Nick, Jack and Dev," he said.

They were big guys, tough-looking, like Hollywood's idea of a biker gang, if the members of that gang were all over sixty. As Logan shook their hands, he said, "I think I've seen you guys around town."

"Probably," Dev said.

Harp leaned over and whispered, "They're in the VFW. Marines in 'Nam. They know what they're doing."

"And what exactly are they supposed to be doing?" Logan asked, not lowering his voice.

"Later."

Before Logan could push any further, Tooney said, "I want you to show me where this boyfriend lived. I want to see what you saw."

"I'm not exactly sure he *was* her boyfriend."

"What do you mean?"

"I mean there's a little confusion between her friends about that."

Tooney looked at Logan for a moment. "This boy, his house is near, though."

"Well, yeah, but—"

"Show it to me."

"That's going to be a little difficult."

"Why?"

"The reason the street up there is blocked off? The house he lived in burned down sometime in the night."

"What?" Tooney, Jerry and Barney all said at once.

"But you were there late last night. That's what you told me," Logan's dad said. "What time was that?"

"Around midnight. A lot of hours between then and morning for someone to light a match."

They all fell silent, then Tooney said, "I still want to see it."

Logan frowned, but nodded. What choice did he have?

He led them back to Pacific Avenue, glancing over his shoulder a couple of times to make sure he wasn't walking too fast. They were keeping up just fine, his dad and Barney at the head of the group and Jerry at the rear. Tooney was in the middle, surrounded by the Cambria Marine Corp.

Some of the excitement on Pacific had dissipated by the time they reached the spot where Logan had been standing earlier. Two of the fire trucks had left, and it looked like the police was getting ready to open one of the traffic lanes.

"Don't tell me that's it," Harp said. He was staring at the pile of burned wreckage across the street.

"I did say it burned down."

"But you said you were inside it last night. That it was empty."

"What part of this aren't you understanding, Dad? Do you see the fire engine? Do you see the police? This only happened a few hours ago."

"So you *were* able to get inside," Barney said.

"Do you guys think I was lying?"

"No, of course not."

"Definitely not," Jerry added.

Logan looked at his father, waiting.

When Harp finally felt his gaze, he said, "What?"

Logan shook his head. "Nothing."

Tooney hadn't said a word since they got there, his full attention on what was left of the bungalow.

Logan squeezed by one of the Marines, and stepped beside him. "You okay?"

"There was nothing inside?" Tooney asked.

"No. It was spotless."

"Do you think this fire could have been an accident?"

"No way to know that for sure."

Tooney turned to Logan, his eyes suddenly hard. "I did not ask what you know. I ask what you think."

Looking back at the house, Logan said, "It seems kind of convenient to be an accident." He could feel Tooney's gaze a moment longer, then the older man turned away.

"What are you going to do now?"

Logan took a breath, and let his eyes drift along the perimeter the police had set up. It was like a big, half circle jutting out from the properties neighboring the scene of the fire, and curving across the street to their side. It was marked off with yellow tape held in place by police cars strategically parked in the middle of the road.

"I got the names of two of your granddaughter's friends.

I'm going to see if either of them might know anything helpful."

"Who are these friends?"

"A guy named Anthony, and a girl," Logan said, then paused to recall her name. "Lara Mendonca."

Tooney nodded.

"You know them?"

"I've heard Elyse mention them before."

"Do you know Anthony's last name?"

Tooney's nod turned into a shake. "No. If she say, I don't remember."

That would have been helpful, but not the end of the world. "I was thinking I could get it from their—"

Logan fell silent as he caught a glimpse of a man in the crowd across the street, beyond the taped-off area on the far side.

"Tooney," he said. "How's your eyesight?"

"My eyesight? It's okay."

"Very casually, I want you to look at that group of people on the other side of the emergency crews. There's a man near the wall, wearing a dark sports coat." Logan waited until Tooney was facing the right direction. "Do you see him?"

There was no immediate response.

"Tooney," Logan urged.

"I see him."

By the tremble in his voice, Logan knew Tooney had also made the same connection he had.

"Get back to the cars," Logan said loud enough for them all to hear.

"What's going on?" Dev asked. He seemed to be the Marine in charge.

"Take them someplace where they can get some breakfast," Logan whispered. "But make sure no one follows you."

"Trouble?"

"Possibly."

Dev nodded. "Let's go, guys."

Harp looked at Logan. "Why? We just got here."

"I don't have time to get into it," Logan told him. "Just do what Dev says."

"What are you going to—"

"Dad, do it!"

His father's eyes opened wide in surprise. "Okay. Sure. If you think we should."

As soon as they walked off, Logan glanced back at the man across the street. The same man who'd held a gun to Tooney's head the previous morning.

11

THERE WAS only about ten feet of sidewalk blocked off on Logan's side of the street. He moved over to the tape, then checked the man again. The guy was focused on the emergency crews, and had apparently still not noticed him. As soon as Logan was sure no cops or firemen were looking in his direction, he ducked under the tape.

"Hey, you're not supposed to be in there," a woman in the crowd said.

Logan ignored her, and moved with purpose across the short bit of no man's land to the tape on the other side, then ducked under and joined the handful of people standing there. He then checked to make sure Tooney's assailant was still in the same place.

He wasn't.

Logan stepped off the curb, searching the crowd where the man had been standing. Suddenly the assailant emerged from the back of the crowd, took a quick look at Logan, then sprinted away down the sidewalk. Logan swept around an older couple watching the action from the middle of the road, then rushed after the man.

It was immediately apparent the guy had not chosen the best escape route. There were no cross streets or driveways on the east side of Pacific Avenue in that area, so he and Logan were hemmed in between homes and apartments on the right, and a near solid line of parked cars on the left. And while the man may have been in pretty good shape, it was doubtful he was a runner like Logan. With every stride the distance between them shrank.

Forty feet, thirty-five, thirty.

Then, just a little ahead of them, a pickup truck pulled out from the curb, creating an opening in the wall of parked cars. The man seized the opportunity and shot through it into the street, crossing at a diagonal to the other side where there were plenty of cross streets to choose from.

As Logan neared the opening, the gate of one of the properties opened, and a woman emerged, stepping directly into his path. He twisted to his left, grazing a parked sedan at the curb, to get around her.

"Hey, watch it!" she yelled.

Having lost some of the ground he'd gained, Logan raced through the opening as fast as he could. Crossing the street, he noticed a police car speeding down Pacific, its lights flashing. The job at Aaron's place apparently done, some other crisis in the city was in need of the cops' presence.

Ahead, Tooney's attacker ducked off Pacific onto what turned out to be a block-long pedestrian-only street with houses lining either side. Logan dug deep, attempting to once more close the gap, but was only halfway down the wide walking path when the man turned to the right at the end of the block, and moved out of sight.

He turned just barely in time to see the man veer onto a narrow walkway between two of the houses on the left, and disappear again.

Logan followed right behind him, closing the distance between them to twenty feet as he burst out onto the concrete pathway of the Venice boardwalk that ran along the front of the houses. On the other side of the path was a strip of grass, then the wide sandy beach.

The man had gone to the right, so Logan did the same. Unlike the roads they'd been running on, there were other people around now—joggers and walkers and people with dogs. Logan weaved in and out, anticipating those in front of him, and trying not to get tangled up in any leashes.

To Logan's left, the grassy strip that separated the path from the sand gave way to a mostly empty parking lot. Ahead, he could see the road that led into the lot, and thought there was at least a fifty-percent chance the man would turn down it and head away from the beach. But when the guy got there, he kept going straight.

That was fine by Logan. The fewer turns they took, the quicker he would catch him.

As he swung around a middle-aged man walking a border collie, intending to cross the street and continue down the concrete boardwalk, a police car pulled across his path and slammed on its brakes.

Logan cut to the right to run behind it as the doors flew open on both sides, and two officers jumped out.

"Stop right there!" one of them yelled.

Logan continued around the back of the car, not interested in whoever they were after.

"You! Stop now!"

Just as he realized the words seemed to be meant for him, the officer from the passenger side rushed forward and tackled him to the ground.

"Don't know how to listen, do you?" he said in Logan's ear.

Logan had to fight the instinct to struggle to get free. As much as he wanted to catch the guy who'd hurt Tooney, he knew enough not to mess with the cops.

"I think you've made a mistake," he said.

"Really? So you *weren't* the one running away from the crime scene?"

Are you kidding me? Logan thought. But he didn't respond to the question, knowing it would be better to keep his mouth shut.

The officer pulled Logan's arms behind his back. "Sorry, can't hear you." When Logan still didn't say anything, the cop snickered.

After Logan was cuffed, the cop and his partner got him to his feet, and guided him into the back of their squad car. Once the door was shut, he looked out the window in the direction the other man had run, but wherever the son of a bitch was, Logan couldn't see him anymore.

So damn close.

As they rode away, Logan still had no idea why the cops had stopped him. It was hard to believe they would have come after him just because they'd seen him running. He could easily just have been someone late for work, or out for a jog.

They turned down Pacific and took him all the way back to the taped-off area in front of Aaron's house. Without a word, the cops got out and headed onto the property, leaving him sitting there alone.

As he waited, his thoughts turned to the man he'd been chasing. One thing he knew for sure now was that what happened in the back of Tooney's restaurant and whatever was going on with his granddaughter were related. There was no other explanation for why Tooney's attacker had shown up at the home of Elyse's boyfriend—or friend or acquaintance or whatever Aaron was.

Just as Logan was beginning to wonder how long his new police buddies were going to leave him by himself, they reemerged through the gate of the damaged property with two other officers, and a man in a suit walking next to a woman in jeans and a red turtleneck sweater.

As they neared the car, Logan recognized the woman. The last time he saw her, she'd been wearing sweats and a baseball cap, but she still had the sleepy look on her face that she'd had when she found him in Aaron's bungalow the night before.

One of the cops opened the door and hauled Logan out.

"Is this the man?" the guy in the suit asked her.

She looked at Logan, then nodded. "Definitely."

12

"SO WHY were you running away from the scene of the fire?"

Logan found out the suited guy's name was Baker, and he was an LAPD detective. He'd kept Logan waiting in a windowless room at the station for nearly an hour before he finally showed up and started asking questions.

"I wasn't running away from anything."

The man raised an eyebrow. "Really? Several people saw you. Including me."

"I didn't say I wasn't running. I said I wasn't running away from anything."

"Okay. Then why were you running *to?*"

"My friend was mugged yesterday," Logan said. "I thought I saw the man who did it, and chased after him."

"Convenient, don't you think? Him showing up at the aftermath of a fire you set."

"Whoa. Hold on. I did not set any fire."

"My witness says you were the last person other than herself in the burned down house."

"The last person she *knows* of. There was obviously someone else, because I didn't do it."

"So you are saying you were there."

"Absolutely."

"And why was that?"

Logan could hear his father's voice in his head: *Involving the police would be exactly the wrong thing to do…trust me.* And Tooney's after he'd been attacked: *I beg you. Say nothing.*

As much as he thought he should tell Detective Baker what was going on, he felt he should let Tooney know first. So he said, "The guy who lived there, Aaron Hughes, he's dating the granddaughter of a friend of mine."

"Another friend, huh?"

Logan hesitated. "The same friend, actually."

"Well, that makes things easy."

"I can't help the truth."

"You still haven't told me why you were there?"

"My friend's been concerned about his granddaughter," Logan said, trying to keep things as close to reality as possible. "He's her nearest relative, so he feels responsible. He wanted me to check on her, check out her friends, and make sure she's not having any problems."

"You some kind of private detective?"

"Not at all. I'm just someone helping a friend."

"So, you went to the house…"

"To see if I could talk to her boyfriend."

"My witness says you were there around midnight. That's kind of late for a chat, isn't it?"

"Not for a kid his age."

"Did he know you were coming?"

"I tried calling, but was sent straight to his voice mail."

"So that meant it was okay to go inside his house and check?" he asked.

"No," Logan said, calmly. "I knocked, a couple times. Then I glanced through the window and noticed that it looked empty inside. Not exactly what I expected. I tried the knob. It was unlocked, so then I went in to check."

"Do you try people's doorknobs often?"

"It just seemed to me there was a good chance no one lived there anymore, so if I could look inside, I could confirm that. Which is exactly what I did."

"You weren't planting some kind of device to burn the place down?"

"No. I had never heard of Aaron Hughes until yesterday. Last night was the first time I'd even been to his place. I was only doing a favor for a friend. One that did not include burning down a house."

"Who, exactly, is this friend?"

Logan didn't know how many times they went through everything—three? four?—before Detective Baker finally let him call his father. As they were going through things yet again, an officer came in and whispered something in Detective Baker's ear. The detective then excused himself and left the room. Logan assumed that the WAMO splinter group had arrived.

His concern now was that Tooney would say something that didn't back up his story, but it turned out the reason the detective left the room had nothing to do with Tooney or his dad at all.

Baker walked back in with several pieces of paper that looked fresh from the printer. He took his chair again, placing the papers face down on the table between them.

"Mr. Harper, you have a bit of a history."

Outwardly, Logan remained calm, but inside his guard went up tenfold.

"Mind telling me about it?" the detective asked.

"My *history* is none of your business. It has nothing to do with what happened at the house, because I have nothing to do with what happened at the house."

The detective turned the papers over, but held them up so

that Logan couldn't see what was on them. "Seems you had some problems with the Pentagon."

"I never had any problems with the Pentagon."

"That's not what it says here."

"Then whatever you're looking at isn't correct."

Detective Baker's gaze moved back and forth across the page. "Hmmm, I guess you're right. Your problem wasn't officially with the Pentagon. It was with a company called Forbus Systems International. Looks like you were charged with embezzlement. Oh, and there was talk of a manslaughter charge."

"A—there was no manslaughter charge," Logan said, fighting hard to keep his cool. "And B—the embezzlement accusation was false. That's why the case got dropped before it ever went anywhere. Again, none of this has anything to do with your fire."

"Did you know your file's flagged?" he asked.

Logan didn't know he *had* a file, at least not one that could be accessed by the LAPD. He remained silent.

"Says if your name comes up in connection with any unlawful activities, a Special Agent James Hall is supposed to be contacted. Are you familiar with him?"

Logan was pretty sure his blank expression cracked just a little bit. He was familiar with Special Agent Hall all right, but it had been a while since he'd heard the name. Again, he said nothing.

"Naturally, I had to give him a call. He says you're a sneaky bastard. Says the only reason you weren't brought up on manslaughter charges was because they were unable to locate some key evidence. I asked him if he thought you'd be capable of burning down a house. Know what he said?"

Logan continued to stare at the detective.

"He said, yes, you'd be capable, but that you'd need a really good reason to do it. And that you wouldn't be so sloppy as to return to check things out the next morning."

That was a surprise. Special Agent Hall was far from Logan's favorite person on the planet, and Logan was far from his. Hall had been the man in charge of the investigation after accusations that Logan might have been responsible for Carl's death began circulating. Hall had made it very clear he thought that Logan was guilty, to hell with the fact there was no evidence and, therefore, never even a trial. For the first six months after Logan began his self-imposed exile in Cambria, Hall would call each week to let him know he was still out there, and to remind Logan that if he made a mistake, Hall would be all over him.

Logan had been sure the agent had forgotten him by now. Apparently not.

But Hall saying something that might make the police believe Logan? Definitely a surprise.

Detective Baker leafed through the papers, then looked at Logan again. "One of my colleagues also had a conversation with your friend, Mr. Myat. He showed up with a man who says he's your father about twenty minutes ago. Lucky for you, he confirmed what you told me. But that still doesn't give you a solid alibi for around the time the fire started. And if you think for one moment I'm going to blindly believe what some FBI agent says about you, you're mistaken."

The detective's frustration was showing. At first he must have thought he'd hit the jackpot, and had reeled in the arsonist without having to do any legwork. But then it turned out that Logan wasn't as golden a suspect as he had at the start. A few seconds later the detective said, "I need you to stay in town until I tell you it's all right to leave."

Fifteen minutes later, Logan walked into the lobby, and found his father pacing back and forth near the front desk. The moment Harp saw his son, he rushed over.

"You all right?" he asked as if Logan had been locked up in a KGB torture cell for the past month.

"Yeah, I'm fine." Logan looked around. "Where's everyone

else?"

"Outside. Tooney wanted some air."

"Let's go, then. I need to talk to both of you."

Instead of moving, his dad stared at Logan's face. "Did they hurt you?"

"No, of course not."

"But…" He reached up and pointed at Logan's cheek. "What's that?"

Having no idea what he was talking about, Logan raised his hand and touched the spot. It was rough, and stung slightly when his finger brushed against it. "Just a scrape, Dad."

"They did this to you?"

"Technically," Logan said, remembering being knocked to the ground on the boardwalk. "But it wasn't on purpose."

"Wasn't on purpose? When we get home, the first call we make is to Lloyd Falon." Lloyd was his father's lawyer.

"We're not calling anyone. Now come on."

13

AFTER RETRIEVING the El Camino, Logan, the members of WAMO, and their auxiliary Marine arm drove over to a café on Main Street in Santa Monica and found a couple of tables in the back, away from the other guests.

The moment the waitress had taken their orders—coffees all around and fries for Jerry—Logan looked at Tooney and said, "If you really want me to help, you need to tell me everything. I've just lied to the police for you, and nearly went to jail. That man I was running after? We both know who he was. So don't tell me what happened yesterday has got nothing to do with your granddaughter."

Tooney stared at the table, his head bowed. "I am sorry, Logan. I should have never let your father talk me into involving you. It was a mistake. It's better to just leave things alone."

"Are you serious? Someone tried to *kill* you yesterday. And it's pretty clear you were right about Elyse being missing, too. Those aren't the kinds of things that just go away if you ignore them."

"You misunderstand me," he said. "It's not that I don't want to do something. I think it may be too late."

"You think she might already be dead?" Logan asked, not quite sure what Tooney meant.

"No," Tooney said quickly, shaking his head. "She is not dead. She would be no use to them dead."

Logan leaned across the table, and asked in a very low, steady voice, "Do you know who has her?"

Tooney pressed his lips together and looked away.

Harp touched his son's arm. "Can we...?" He nodded sideways toward the front door.

Logan glared at him, not moving.

"Please," his father said.

Logan remained motionless for a few more seconds, then pushed himself up and walked outside.

There was a little patio area in front for customers who wanted to eat al fresco. Currently it was empty, so Logan took a seat at the table farthest from the door. His father exited a moment later, and joined him.

Before Harp could open his mouth, Logan said, "I don't know what the hell is going on, but I do know that Tooney's making a huge mistake. For God's sake, his granddaughter is *missing!* If it was your grandchild, you'd do anything you could to find her." He paused. "We both know how I feel about the FBI, but Tooney needs to call them *now*. You need to convince him of that."

His dad looked resigned as he shook his head. "He'll never call them."

"Then *you* need to do it."

"I can't."

"Why not?"

"I...I promised him."

"So the hell what? This is a girl's life we're talking about." Logan leaned back. "Dammit, I'll call them myself, then."

"You can't, either."

"Sure I can."

"No. I also promised him you wouldn't."

"I don't care. *I* didn't promise." Logan pushed up from his chair.

"Logan, sit back down."

Logan looked at his father, but remained standing.

Harp sighed. "If the people who have her get even a hint that the FBI, or the police, or any other organization, for that matter, is looking for them, they will kill her for sure."

"Do you know what's going on, Dad? Did he tell you?"

"Most of it."

"Then tell me."

"It's not my place."

"Then I have no choice."

Logan pulled out his phone, and punched in the number for information. Once the connection was made, he hit the speaker button so his father could hear how serious he was. The first automated prompt asked him for the city. "Los Angeles." Then the name. "Federal Bureau of Investigation."

Harp pleaded with his eyes for his son to hang up.

The voice gave Logan the number, then asked if he'd like to be connected. "Yes."

Before the phone on the other end even began to ring, his dad said, "Logan, please."

"Are you going to tell me?"

It took two rings before his father finally nodded.

"Federal Bureau of Investigation. How may I—"

"I'm sorry," Logan said, cutting off the voice that answered. "Wrong number."

He sat back down, and set the phone on the table, making sure his dad knew how easy it would be for him to pick it up and call again.

"Give me three minutes," Harp said, then stood up. "I need to talk to Tooney. He really should be the one to tell you."

"Dad…"

His father held up his hands to stop Logan from saying anything more. "If he doesn't, I will. Okay?"

Logan hesitated, then nodded. "Okay."

It took him five minutes, not three. When he returned, the whole group was with him, each carrying a cup of coffee, Jerry with an additional bowl of fries in his other hand.

Harp and Tooney were the only ones who came over to Logan's table. Barney and Jerry grabbed a table at the other side of the patio, while the Marines all remained standing, covering the edge along the street.

Logan's dad had brought out two cups of coffee. He set one in front of Logan, then sat in the same chair he'd been in before. Reluctantly, Tooney took the chair next to him.

Instead of waiting, Logan decided to start. "I know this is difficult, but unless you convince me otherwise, I can't just sit here and do nothing. I hope you understand."

Tooney gave him a humorless smile. "Of course, I understand. But, please, can't you just trust me?"

"It's not a matter of trust. I believe you think you're doing the right thing, but when it's someone close to you who's in danger, people often don't think straight. If your granddaughter's in trouble, we need to get help."

"If we do that, she is as good as dead."

"Yeah. Dad said the same thing, but you can't know that for sure."

Tooney's shoulders moved up and down as he took in a deep breath. "I can."

"How?"

Tooney gave Logan's dad a pained look as if he were hoping there was some way he could be spared from having to say anything more.

"Tell him," Harp said. "That can't hurt her."

Tooney carefully touched his hand to his bruised face. "But what if even after I do, he call the police?"

"He won't. I promise."

"But what if he does?"

Harp looked at his son. "Then he's not the man I thought he was."

Logan let that one pass. He knew his dad was trying to guilt him into cooperating, but there was potential guilt on the other side, too, the guilt of inaction if it turned out a phone call could have saved the girl.

Tooney didn't move for several seconds. Finally, he lifted his head and looked Logan in the eye. "I was one of the lucky ones."

14

YOU KNOW that I am from Burma, yes?" Tooney said.

Logan nodded.

Tooney's gaze grew distant, lost in a memory. Finally, he looked back at Logan. "When I escaped, I was able to bring most of my family with me. Many were not so blessed. My younger sister, my brother, my wife, my two daughters, we were all together. The only ones who could not come were my father and my older sister. He too old to travel, so she stay to take care of him." He paused again, but only briefly. "It was not easy to leave without them, but we had no choice. My wife had been...*vocal* in her concerns about the government. One day we were warned by a friend that soldiers would be coming for us that night, so we knew it was time to go." He shook his head. "Thirty minutes after they tell us this, we gone. The only things we bring were clothes and food. Everything else we leave behind. All memories of our life.

"Friends hid us in cars and drove us into the jungle in the hills to the East. From there we walk for five days, hiding when we hear patrols, until we cross into Thailand. This was 1984. Already there were refugee camps along the border with thousands of other Burmese. We were just six more.

"Then, for a second time, we were lucky. We stayed in camp for only one year. A church in San Luis Obispo sponsored our whole family. That's how we got out of Thailand. That's how we come to California."

He took another pause. This was a lot more about Tooney than Logan had ever been aware of, but by the knowing nods from his father, the story wasn't new to him.

"My oldest daughter, Sein, did you know her? She several years older than you, but we not move to Cambria from San Luis Obispo until after she graduate high school, so maybe not."

Logan shrugged. "I saw her around a few times. But I don't think I ever spoke to her. I knew Anka a little, though. She was two years behind me, I think."

Tooney gave him a half smile. "Anka, my American child. She born in Burma but it like she never lived there. She teach high school English now, and she married to white boy like you. He's a good man, though."

"As opposed to me?"

Tooney shook his head. "You not bad. But you lonely man. You need someone to warm your heart."

Logan let the instant psychology session, as unexpectedly accurate as it was, pass without comment.

"Sein, she meet Burmese boy at camp in Thailand," Tooney went on. "His name Khin. She tell me all the time she love him. Khin's family sponsored, too, but by group in North Carolina. So he far away. Did not stop them, though. As soon as he out of high school, he come to California for her, and marry her. He good man, too. Very much love her. They have first baby 1988. My first granddaughter, Yon. Then one more in 1991, Elyse." He drifted again. "My wife never see Elyse."

"She was born after your wife died?" Logan asked. He only had vague memories of Tooney's wife. As far as he could recall, he never saw her after his first or second year in high school.

He'd heard later that she'd passed away, but he didn't know the family very well at the time so the details didn't stick with him.

"No," Tooney said, an undercurrent of anger in his voice. "Thiri, my wife, she died in 1994. In Burma."

"Burma? But I thought you said she came here with you."

"She did," he said. "Do you know Burma history?"

"A bit."

"Aung San Suu Kyi?"

Logan nodded. She was the daughter of Aung San, the popular Burmese general who was assassinated when she was still a young child. Later, she became a symbol of freedom in a country that had come to be run by a ruthless military dictatorship.

"In 1988, Aung San Suu Kyi return to Burma, and help start NLD, National League for Democracy. Thiri believe Daw Suu Kyi—that's what we call her—would save our country from the evil that was running it. Thiri want to sneak back into Burma to help. 'For us,' she told me. 'For our families. Burma will always be our home.' We fight so much about this, but I knew I could not stop her. In '89, Daw Suu Kyi was put under house arrest. But Thiri still free, and help spread the word about the NLD, and Daw Suu Kyi's beliefs in a Burma without fear. In 1990, there was a nationwide election, and NLD won by large amount. It should have been moment of my country's freedom. But it was not. The generals void the election and send out troops. Thiri know she could no longer stay, so headed for the Thai border, same trip we had make together six years before. Only she not reach it this time. She caught and taken to prison. After her arrest, I never talk to her again."

"I'm so sorry," Logan said, knowing the words were inadequate. He had no idea that the man who poured his coffee every morning had lived such a tragic life.

"After the election and the crackdown, we not know if Thiri alive or not. She send message to me that she was leaving the country. But that was it. Months went by without a word. She just disappeared. Then my sister in Burma found out Thiri arrested."

Tears glistened in Tooney's eyes as he fell silent for a moment. "It was very hard on our daughters. They handled it very different. Anka was still in high school. She focused on her studies, and began working hard to lose the little bit of accent she still had. She wanted nothing to do with the country that would imprison her mother.

"Sein went the other way, and follow her mother's example. She became more involved in the democracy movement. Doing what she could from over here, taking over where my wife left off. When we learned Thiri had died, Sein got even more involved, speaking out, organizing, doing whatever she could. Now she is a powerful voice outside of Burma, calling for removal of the generals who rule over our people. She travels around the world, talks to groups wherever she can." He took a deep breath. "Thiri would be very proud of her."

"I'm sure you're proud of her, too," Logan said.

"I am." There was wistfulness in his voice, a sadness that confused Logan. When Tooney saw the look on his face, he said, "Sein blame me. Not much for her mother's death, but for not going back to Burma with my wife and helping the movement. Maybe if I went, maybe Thiri would still be alive. But Anka was in school. I had to stay. Thiri made me promise to watch over the girls." A tear finally rolled down his cheek. "Sein and I not talk much anymore."

Tragedy on top of tragedy. Logan gave him a moment, then said, "I'm still not clear what all this has to do with Elyse's disappearance."

Tooney looked at him. "The man yesterday morning, he told me Elyse taken to shut up her mother. If Sein cooperates, they will let Elyse go. There is a human rights conference in London in two weeks. Sein is supposed to give important speech there. They don't want this to happen."

"But who are they?"

"The Burmese false government, of course. The generals of *Myanmar,* as they have decide to call our country."

"Wait. You think the Myanmar *government* is behind your granddaughter's kidnapping?"

The look on Tooney's face said it should be obvious. "Who else? They are crazy. They are not like other countries. Believe me, I know."

Logan let this sink in for a second, but found it hard to believe a foreign government was kidnapping people in the U.S. "The man who attacked you wasn't Burmese. He was Caucasian."

Harp scoffed. "Probably just hired for the job."

"I don't know. It sounds too—"

"Crazy?" Tooney asked.

"But why kill you?"

"Elyse is the important one. Not me. Maybe I was just in the way."

Logan hesitated. "What about the rest of your family? Has any of them been attacked, too?"

"They can't get to Sein. She is in Europe with Khin and oldest daughter, Yon. The foundation that she work for give her with excellent security. Besides, Burma would want to quietly shut her up, not kill her. Her death would be international news and focus *more* attention on the country, not less."

"Have you called her and told her about Elyse?"

"I wanted to know for sure he was not lying to me first. That's what I've been telling myself, anyway. But the truth is that I know Sein won't answer even if I do call."

"You're going to have to try to get a hold of her somehow."

He looked ashamed. "I know."

Logan paused for a second. "If Sein's death would focus more attention on Burma, wouldn't killing her daughter do the same thing?"

Tooney shook his head. "Elyse is not high profile like Sein. Her death could be made to look like anything. An accident, suicide, whatever they want. Besides, Sein would never let it come to that. They know this. Our children are always our weaknesses. She will do what they want so Elyse will live."

"And if we call the police?"

"They will kill her now. Make her disappear so they can claim zero responsibility and avoid creating international incident. No one will ever know what happened. It is the only thing they can do."

"What about your other daughter?" I asked.

"Anka's married to an American. She has an American last name. That's her protection. They would not want the kind of trouble they think might happen by hurting her."

"Elyse is an American, too. Hurting her is going to cause just as many problems."

"They won't see it that way. To them, she is one hundred percent Burmese, like her mother, and her grandmother."

Logan leaned back. "There's no guarantee they won't kill Elyse anyway."

Tooney paused, then locked eyes with him. "One way is for sure, the other is…unknown."

15

LOGAN DIDN'T call the FBI.

He didn't promise Tooney he wouldn't, but he did say he would think about it and let him know what he was going to do. But he knew even then that he wouldn't make that call.

He wasn't ready to buy the whole story yet. The idea of Burma—or Myanmar, as the leaders there preferred—reaching its hand all the way into the United States to pluck a twenty-year-old college student off the street just didn't sound right. Unless things had changed since he last checked, Burma had shown little interest in the world outside its borders. Would they even have the resources to pull off something like this? He had his doubts, but they weren't strong enough for him to test the theory by calling the FBI.

Which meant he needed to find out what was really going on.

While Logan spent his morning at the police station, his dad and the others had unexpectedly done a little work for him and found the address of Elyse's friend, Lara Mendonca. They hadn't, however, been able to further identify her other friend, Anthony.

Lara lived just south of LAX in an area called El Segundo. Her apartment was on the third floor in a generic box of a building, a block off of Imperial Highway.

Logan knocked, half expecting no one to answer. It was afternoon, and though Lara would be on spring break, he thought there was a good chance she'd be out and about even if she were still in town.

The door opened, and a woman about Elyse's age wearing a Starbucks Coffee uniform looked out. "Yes?"

"Lara Mendonca?"

"Yeah. Who are you?"

Logan tried not to let his sense of relief show as he said, "Logan Harper. You're a friend of Elyse Myat's, right?"

She looked at him warily. "Yeah."

"I'm a friend of her grandfather, Tooney."

She continued to stare. "So?"

"Can I ask you a few questions?"

"It's almost time for me to go to work. What kind of questions?"

"Well, Tooney's concerned about her. She was supposed to visit him yesterday, but she didn't show up. And now we can't find her anywhere."

The suspicion on her face immediately turned into concern. "Are you serious?"

Logan nodded. "When was the last time you talked to her?"

She looked away in thought. "The night before last. Yesterday she was supposed to go up to…" She looked at Logan again, testing him.

"Cambria," he said. "To visit her grandfather."

"Yes."

"She didn't make it."

"Oh, God. Did you check the hospitals? Maybe she was in an accident."

"We checked. No accident," he said. "Could I come in for a

minute? Might be easier than talking out here."

She hesitated only a second, then nodded, and moved to the side so he could enter.

Unlike Ryan's apartment, Lara's place was furnished in a much more finished, post-college style—real paintings on the walls, furniture that didn't look twenty years old, and no smell of stale pizza.

As soon as they were seated in the living room, he asked, "What was her mood like when you last talked?"

"Mood? Uh, fine, I think," she said. "She was looking forward to getting out of town."

"Any clue that she might have been thinking about going someplace else?"

"Not that I can remember."

"Any problems with her boyfriend?"

"Boyfriend?"

"Aaron Hughes."

She snorted a laugh. "Aaron's not her boyfriend. Who told you that?"

"Angie."

Her laugh this time was even louder than the first. "I don't think Elyse would ever talk to Angie about her love life. She and Aaron went out once, I think, but that was it. She thinks he's kind of odd, and not in a good, Jesse Eisenberg kind of way. Elyse does sometimes spend the night *here*. Maybe that's what Angie was thinking."

That pretty much confirmed what Logan already suspected. Aaron was not Elyse's boyfriend, and Angie was not trustworthy. "How long have you known Elyse?"

"Three years this coming summer. We started school together."

He looked around the room. "You live here alone?"

"Why?" she asked, her guard coming back up.

"Sorry," Logan said quickly. "Just curious. That's all. You

don't have to tell me."

She allowed herself to relax a little. "My sister. We share this place. She's a CPA."

He smiled. "I was wondering how you could afford to furnish your place like this on a student salary. It's certainly nothing like Ryan's apartment."

She gave him an odd look. "Ryan?"

"Elyse's neighbor?" he said. "That's where Angie was when I went by last night."

She shook her head and shrugged. "I guess I've never met him, but we don't really hang out much over there. Not since Angie showed up, anyway."

"How long has she been there?"

"She moved in over winter break. Three months now, I guess."

Only three months?

"Thanks," he said, feeling the sudden need to have his talk with Angie as soon as possible. "I appreciate you giving me a little time."

"Hold on," she said as he started to rise. "You haven't told me what's going on. Is she really missing?"

He tried to sound reassuring. "I think her grandfather's probably being a little over cautious. I'll bet it turns out she decided to go someplace like Vegas or San Diego on a whim."

Lara looked less than convinced, but she didn't argue the point.

Logan wrote his number on a page from his notebook, and gave it to her. "Please call me if you hear from her."

"Can I use your pen?"

He handed it to her.

She tore the page in half and wrote her info on the blank piece, handing it back to him when she was done. "And you call *me* if you hear from her."

"I will," he promised. "One last thing. I understand that

Elyse had another friend, a guy named Anthony? Do you know who that is?"

"Sure. Anthony Hudson. We're all friends." She was quiet for a moment, then her eyes brightened. "Hey, they were supposed to have dinner the night before last. *He* would have seen her."

"Do you know where I can find him?"

"His apartment's maybe a half mile from Elyse's."

He gave her back the piece of paper, and she added Anthony's address and cell number to it.

"Thanks again," he said.

Logan found a parking spot almost directly in front of Angie and Elyse's building, then ran into the courtyard and up the stairs to the second-floor breezeway. He was almost to their apartment when he suddenly stopped, the soles of his shoe screeching against the concrete surface.

There were no curtains covering the windows of Ryan's apartment. The ratty furniture, the television, even the pizza boxes—all gone. The place was as spotless as Aaron's place had been the night before.

Logan stared inside for a moment, then sprinted the rest of the way to Elyse's place. The curtains were closed, which he took for a good sign as he pounded on the door. When no one answered, he knocked again, then tried the doorknob. Locked.

Angie must have gone out.

He thought for a moment. Anthony's place was only a half-mile away. Logan could see if he was home, and probably be back in less than thirty minutes. Maybe by then, Angie would have returned.

It took him longer to find a parking spot than it took to drive over. Anthony's apartment was at the back of his building on the first floor, off an interior hallway. There were no windows, so Logan couldn't see in.

He rang the doorbell, then knocked several times. But, like at

Angie's, there was no response.

He contemplated what he should do, then decided to go around back and take a peek through Anthony's windows, just to make sure it wasn't another empty apartment.

He found an exit, but was surprised when he had to take a staircase down to reach the back alley. The reason for this became clear as he stepped outside. The building had been erected on the side of a small rise. The architect had used this to his advantage, and built a carport into the lower part of the slope, below the first floor. Unfortunately, this meant he couldn't simply walk up to Anthony's window and peer in.

He examined the back of the building. The last foot of the carport stuck out like a lip just below the first floor. If he could get on that, he could work his way over to Anthony's windows. The question was, how to get up there?

The simplest answer turned out to be his El Camino. He drove it around, then backed it most of the way into one of the empty parking spots, leaving the hood sticking out from under the carport. Carefully, he mounted his car, then pulled himself onto the lip.

Making an educated guess as to which windows belonged to Anthony's place, he inched his way over. There were no curtains over the nearest of the target windows, but when he looked in, he saw with relief a very lived-in living room.

As he moved down to the next window, he noticed that the screen covering it was hanging loose in one corner of its frame. Somebody had cut a triangle flap large enough for a person to fit through.

Logan looked inside. It was a bedroom. And unlike the living room, it was occupied. There was a man lying on the bed, his right arm flopped on the pillow beside his head. But what caught Logan's attention was the Beretta pistol lying inches from the guy's hand, and the impossible-to-miss hole in the side of his head.

He would have preferred it if the place had just been empty.

He thought it was a pretty good chance the dead man was Anthony. According to Lara, he'd been the last to see Elyse. Did that mean she was in the apartment, too? As much as he'd rather not, Logan knew he was going to have to check.

He pulled the sleeve of his jacket over his hand, then put it through the cut in the screen, and up against the window. With just the slightest of pressure he was able to slide it open. He then looked both ways down the alley to make sure no one was watching, then slipped inside.

Immediately, he started to gag.

The smell of rot and death hung in the room like a thick fog. He threw a hand over his nose, and quickly ran into the hallway.

The stench was there, too, but not quite as strong. He did a quick sweep of the rest of the apartment to see if there were any more bodies, but, with a definite sense of relief, he found none.

Returning to the bedroom, he took a couple of T-shirts out of the dresser. He used one to cover his nose and mouth, then wrapped the other around his hand so he could pat down the body.

The dead guy had a wallet in his front pocket. Logan worked it out, then carefully opened it. A driver's license sat behind a clear window in the front. The name on it read: Anthony Hudson. Logan put the wallet back.

The position of the gun, Anthony's hand, it all pointed to suicide, but with the way things had been going, suicide was not a conclusion Logan was ready to jump to. Besides, the unlocked window and cut screen bothered him.

What surprised Logan most was that no one had heard the shot. In most of the apartment buildings he'd lived in, someone was always complaining about hearing their neighbors through the walls. A gunshot from the Beretta should have been heard not just by the people next door, but also by people in the buildings that lined the alley. And since this was the middle of a big city, no matter what time the trigger had been pulled, someone would have been home. But by the look of the wound and the smell, Anthony had been lying there dead for at least a day, if not more.

Logan scanned the room, looking for a note somewhere, but there was none.

Death could be made to look like anything. An accident, suicide, whatever they want…

Was this not what it appeared? There was no way for Logan to know for sure, but it certainly felt that way.

Instead of going out the window, he used the front door, circled around to the alley like he had before, and got back into the El Camino.

He knew he should call the police. But if he did it from his cell phone, they'd record his number, and know who he was. He couldn't have that. He'd lose too much time down at the station trying to explain why he'd found the body, and given the suspicions Detective Baker already had, it was possible they would even lock him up for a few days. He could always find a pay phone, but those were few and far between now, and you never knew where a security camera might be aimed.

There was a third option.

He started the El Camino, and pulled out of the carport.

16

LOGAN'S PHONE rang as he was driving back to the motel. The number on the display had a D.C. area code.

"Logan?" It was Ruth.

"I thought you'd forgotten about me."

"I tried. Trust me." She let out a little laugh. "My contact couldn't run the plate number until after hours, and I wasn't about to call you back from any of my phones."

"Uh...thanks?"

"What? You want me to give them a good reason to fire me? I've got a family, remember?"

He didn't say anything. He'd had a family once, small as it had been.

"Sorry, that was...unnecessary," she said. "It's just if anyone looks at the phone records they'll already see that you called me at the office. One call I can play off, tell them I told you to get lost, but two? Especially if I'm the one initiating the second one? Not so easy to ignore."

"Don't worry. I get it." And he did. Her cell phone and, of course, her office phone were both paid for by Forbus. They would know exactly who she talked to. "What did you find out?"

"Nothing that you're going to like, I'll bet. The car's registered to a Cameron Jackson in Burbank, California. Unfortunately, Ms. Jackson filed a stolen vehicle report yesterday. It seems when she headed out for work in the morning her car was gone."

There was an airport in Burbank, one that was a hell of a lot easier to use than LAX. Fly in, walk a few blocks, steal a car from in front of a home. Easy. No doubt, in another couple of days, the police would find the car, but wouldn't be able to pursue the case any further because there would be no prints.

"Thanks, Ruth."

"I said you weren't going to like it."

"You're right, but I'm not surprised." He hesitated a second. Things had changed since they'd last talked. There was information she was uniquely positioned to provide him. He didn't want to push, but he had to. "Listen, what kind of intel do you have on Burma these days?"

"Burma? I thought we were talking stolen cars."

"Separate subject."

"What's important about Burma?"

"It's for a friend. He…used to live there years ago."

Ruth said nothing for several seconds. "What have you gotten yourself into?"

"Nothing. Just getting some info for a friend. That's all."

"And the stolen car?"

"I told you, unrelated. It dinged my dad's car in a parking lot. But if it was stolen there's not much we can do about it." They both knew he was lying, but if Ruth was ever asked about it, she could honestly repeat what Logan had just told her. "So…Burma?"

The pause went on for several seconds. He could imagine her shaking her head in resignation as she finally spoke. "As far as I know we don't have much going on in that part of the world at the moment. A little contract work in Singapore, emergency response training, but that's it."

"You still get the daily brief, right?" The daily brief was a breakdown of what was happening in the world by country and region. Forbus wanted its top people kept up to date in case an opportunity suddenly presented itself.

"Hell, Logan, I don't really pay that much attention to Burma. As far as I remember, it's pretty much the same as always. A group of old, asshole generals not wanting to relinquish the power they don't deserve. Nothing stands out, though. No new protests or anything."

Logan hesitated, then said, "I need another favor. I need the latest Burma assessment."

"Are you serious?"

"I wouldn't ask you if I wasn't."

"I hate you sometimes, Logan Harper."

"Is that a yes?"

"That's a maybe."

"Thank you, Ruth. I mean it."

He pulled into the motel parking lot a few minutes later, and saw that the cars the Cambria contingent had ridden down in were all there. He called his dad.

"What room are you in?"

"Thirty-five."

"I'll be right there."

Dev and Nick were standing just outside his father's door like they were protecting the Oval Office.

"Everything all right?" Logan asked.

"Everything's fine," Dev said, then knocked on the door.

"Good. Thanks for being here for them."

"Always like to help a friend."

A moment later, Barney opened the door and let Logan in.

Tooney and his father were sitting on one of the two beds while Jerry stood nearby.

"We were going to order some Chinese," Jerry said. "Want

some?"

"We need to talk."

"Did you speak with Elyse's friends?" Tooney asked.

"I talked to Lara, but…" Logan hesitated only a second. There was no use sugarcoating it. "Anthony's dead."

Stunned silence.

"Did you say dead?" his dad finally asked.

"Lara gave me his address. Said that he was supposed to have had dinner with Elyse the night before last, so I went over there. I found him in his apartment."

"How did you get in if he was already dead?" Barney asked.

"I just did."

"Did someone kill him?" Jerry asked.

"The way it looks, he shot himself through the head."

Harp leaned back, surprised again. "Suicide?"

"That's the impression."

"What do you mean, 'impression'?" he asked.

"With everything that's been going on, I'm not willing to believe suicide yet."

"So what do you think happened?" Jerry asked.

"I don't know. Could be he *did* kill himself. But if he did have dinner with Elyse, he would have been one of the last people to see her before she disappeared. Maybe he was with her when they grabbed her. Wrong place, wrong time."

"Oh, no, no," Tooney said, burying his eyes in the palm of his hand. "We should have called the police yesterday."

"I don't think it would have made a difference," Logan told him. "I'm pretty sure he was shot before that guy even came to the café to try to kill you."

"But the police are going to know now anyway, aren't they?" Barney said. "You must have called them after you found the body."

Logan hesitated. "No. I didn't."

"No?" his dad said.

"They almost got Tooney," Logan said. "They probably *did* kill Anthony. The first sign that anyone tries to involve the authorities, I think you might be right. Whoever has Elyse will kill her, too. As far as Anthony goes, the police will know, but it can't come from me. Not if you still want me to find Elyse."

"We can't just let him lie there, can we?" Barney asked.

Logan shook his head. "No, we can't." He walked over to the front door and opened it. "Dev, can you come in here for a minute?"

"Sure," the ex-Marine said.

Once they had rejoined the others, Logan asked his dad, "How much does Dev know?"

Harp shrugged. "Maybe not all the details, but pretty much everything."

Good, Logan thought. It would save him some time.

Vets who'd seen serious action usually went one of two ways: they'd either wall off what they'd gone through and try to forget, or they'd remember and gravitate toward people they'd served with or who'd had similar experiences. Logan had a feeling Dev and his buddies fell into the second group. "You have any local friends you can call on for help?"

Dev cracked a smile. "A few."

"Can you get them in a hurry?"

"Shouldn't be a problem. Why?"

"Tooney's granddaughter had two close friends," Logan said. "One of them's turned up dead. That's not public knowledge. Two things I need your help on. First, I know I'd feel a hell of a lot better if the one who was still alive had someone keeping an eye on her. And second, I'm hoping that you or someone you know can anonymously inform the police about the one who's dead."

"The people who did this, are they the same people who are after Tooney and his granddaughter?" he asked.

"Yes."

"Give me the info. I'll take care of it."

Logan wrote everything down on a piece of paper, then gave Dev a quick description of Lara. "She can't know you're there."

"She won't."

"Thanks, Dev."

He gave Logan a nod, then left.

"Do you really think someone's going to try to kill Lara, too?" Logan's father asked.

Logan shook his head. "If they considered her a threat I think they would have gotten rid of her by now, but better not to take a chance, don't you think?"

For a moment, no one said a word, then Tooney looked up. "Find my granddaughter, Logan. Please, just…find her."

Logan hesitated, worried that he wasn't the right one to do this, that he'd make a mistake, that he'd fail once more.

Worried that he wouldn't get to her in time.

But he could see in Tooney's eyes that he was also the old man's only hope.

"Rise above, that's what we do, soldier," Carl had often said with a smile when faced with adversity. "Rise above."

Logan nodded, still holding Tooney's gaze, then said, "I will."

17

SO FAR Logan seemed to have been doing a lot of catch-up. What he really needed to do was get ahead of the game. To accomplish that, he needed to find someone who could help him, whether they wanted to or not.

As he saw it, he had three choices: Aaron the not-boyfriend, Ryan the neighbor, or Angie the roommate. Aaron and Ryan, because of their sudden absences, would take time to find, if Logan could locate them at all. Angie, on the other hand, was still around, or at least had been when he'd talked to her that morning. Hopefully, she wasn't gone, too.

Logan made a quick stop at the Home Depot in Playa Vista, then got to the girls' apartment by 7:30 p.m. With the exception of the sun having gone down, nothing else had changed—Ryan's apartment was still empty, and the curtains still pulled across the windows of Elyse and Angie's place. Logan rapped on the door, but, like before, heard nothing from inside.

Working security in trouble spots around the world meant knowing a variety of skills. The more you learned, the more likely you'd stay alive. As a trainer, it was Logan's job to teach his men some of these skills. Skills like how to pick a lock.

Wearing the thin rubber gloves he'd purchased at the hardware store, and using the other items he'd bought to serve as a makeshift lock-pick set, Logan set to work on Elyse's door, and had it open in less than thirty seconds.

He quickly slipped inside, then stood still, listening. Though the apartment was quiet, he was relieved to see it *wasn't* empty like Aaron's and Ryan's places. Of course, that didn't necessarily mean Angie was still around. The apartment had been Elyse's and her other two roommates' before Angie had moved in, so there would have been no reason to remove all the stuff.

The place was basically a mirror image of Ryan's apartment. In this case, the living room was to the right, and the dining room/kitchen to the left. Logan checked the kitchen first. There were several dishes in the sink, and a box of cereal sitting on the counter, but nothing that really told him if Angie had bolted or not. He headed into the back of the apartment.

There were two bedrooms at opposite ends of a short T-bone hallway, with a bathroom smack between them. Each bedroom was loosely divided into two separate areas, with beds, dressers, and, in three cases, small desks.

He found Elyse's room first. He knew this because of the framed picture on the desk under the window. In it, Elyse, Lara and Anthony were mugging for the camera somewhere along the beach.

There were several paintings on the wall next to her bed. The images were almost cartoonish. Illustrations, he guessed you'd call them. The common thread in each was a young girl who looked more than a little like the girl in the graduation picture Tooney had given him. In the paintings, she seemed to be playing the role of the observer, not quite part of whatever was going on, but always hovering nearby. The girl in the one that stood out most to Logan had wings far too large for her body, and was sitting in a barren tree watching some other kids go by. If the colors hadn't been so vibrant, and if there hadn't been a mischievous smile on her face, it would have been depressing, but it was far from that. When he looked at the bottom corner, he wasn't surprised to find it was signed *Elyse Myat.*

He moved to the other half of the room. There were a dozen photos pinned to the wall, but the girl who reoccurred in most of them was not Angie, so Logan assumed Elyse's room-mate had to be one of the other two girls.

He walked over to the second bedroom, and quickly determined that the bed nearest the door belonged to the last of the long-term roommates.

The other half of the room, Angie's half, was considerably less lived in. She had no desk, and what pictures she'd taped to her wall were limited to ones taken right there in the apartment. It was as if she had no life before moving in.

When Logan looked around the bed, he stopped and stared.

Sitting on the floor were a suitcase and a backpack. He checked inside each. They were stuffed with clothes and a few personal items. He zipped them up, then looked through the dresser he figured belonged to Angie. It was empty.

Clearing out, he thought, *but not cleared out.*

He thought for a moment, then walked back to Elyse's room, and found a clear spot on the floor next to the wall to sit.

An hour and twenty minutes passed. Several times during that stretch he wondered if Angie might have left town without her bags. It was always a possibility. But then a key entered the lock, and the door swung open, and someone stepped inside.

He sensed more than heard the person rushing through the apartment.

A light flicked on in the hallway spilling into Elyse's room. Quietly, Logan rose to his feet, ready to act if Angie or whoever it was decided to come his direction. Instead, the person entered the bathroom.

Logan repositioned himself so that he could see into the hallway, but wouldn't be noticed without effort. Soon the toilet flushed, then water ran in the sink. A few seconds after it shut off, the person stepped back into the hallway.

It was Angie, and she was obviously in a hurry as she all but sprinted into her bedroom.

Logan stepped lightly out of Elyse's room, and into the dark living room to wait.

It was only a few moments before he heard the suitcase bang against something. Once Angie reached the hallway, she stopped just long enough to flip off the light, then she entered the living room.

Logan remained motionless as she lugged her bags toward the front door. As soon as she passed his position, he moved silently in behind her, then reached out and grabbed a loop on her backpack, and gave it a tug.

"Going somewhere?" he asked.

She swallowed a scream as she whipped around, nearly losing her balance in the process. Logan held tight to the loop of her backpack, so when she turned, the bag had slipped from her shoulder and off her arm, until he was the only one holding it.

"Who are you? What do you want?" she asked.

"Just wondering where you were going," he said.

She took a hard look at him, then her eyes widened. "You're that guy from last night. Logan Hooper."

"Close enough." He glanced at her suitcase. "You seem to be in a hurry."

"I am." She tried to grab her backpack from him, but he swung it out of her reach. "Give it to me. It's mine."

"You and I need to have a talk."

"*I* need to get *out* of here. Give it back!"

"Talk first."

"I don't have time to talk with you."

"And why would that be?" he asked.

She looked at the backpack, then said, "Keep it." She picked up her suitcase and headed toward the door. But Logan got there first, and put a hand against it before she could pull it open.

"Please, let me go!"

"Once we talk, you can go anywhere you want."

"No! Please! If I stay here, I'm dead!"

For half a second, he was struck silent. Not by her words, but by the utter fear behind them.

"All right. Then we'll go somewhere else," he said.

"Fine," she said quickly. "Just, please, let's go."

He moved his hand, and let her open the door. Once they reached the ground level, she turned toward the back of the small complex, presumably heading for the tenant parking area.

"No," he said, then motioned in the direction of the street where his El Camino was waiting. "This way."

"Hell, no! You're crazy if you think I'm going to come back later to get my car. I'm taking it now."

They locked eyes for a moment. "All right," he said. "But you're crazy if you think I'm going to let you drive on your own. We'll go together, then you're going to have to drop *me* off close to here when we're done so I can get my car."

"Whatever. No problem."

Logan knew she had no intention on dropping him off anywhere near this area. In fact, he was sure she planned on getting into her car, and leaving before he had a chance to join her.

He let her lead them down a winding stone path to the back parking area. Most of the dozen or so spaces were full. Angie headed toward a blue Mini Cooper near the left end.

"I'm going to have to pull out first," she said. "The jerk in the slot next to me always parks too close."

As they got closer Logan could see that she was right, but he had no illusions she would actually stop to let him in. He was about to tell her they would both get in on the driver's side when a man stepped from the shadows, a gun in his hand.

"No one's going anywhere," the man said.

Angie reflexively brought the suitcase in front of her like a shield, but unless the clothes inside were made of Kevlar, her luggage wasn't going to do her much good.

The man walked steadily toward her, moving his gaze back and forth steadily between Angie and Logan. It was Tooney in the refrigerator at Coffee Time all over again. Logan knew instantly this man was only here for one purpose, to deliver the death Angie had been trying to avoid.

Logan had only one shot at this, and he knew it. He watched the man's eyes, and the moment they flicked from him back to Angie, Logan drew his arm back a few inches, then swung it forward, letting Angie's backpack fly from his hand on a low trajectory, straight at the man's knees.

Immediately, he followed.

The motion of the bag caught the gunman's attention. He turned, then twisted to the side to get out of the way. The bag missed him, but Logan didn't.

He slammed into the man's shoulder and pushed him face first into Angie's Mini. He wrenched the gun away, then landed two quick blows to the guy's kidneys. The man rolled onto his back, and threw a punch that grazed Logan's chin.

Logan didn't want to waste any more time, so he kneed him in the groin, and shoved him to the ground.

The man writhed in pain, and wasn't getting up any time soon.

When teaching self-defense techniques, Carl had always said, "Hit 'em fast, and hit 'em hard. Don't ever give them a chance."

Check. Check. And check.

Logan turned, intending to grab Angie and get the hell out there. But while her suitcase was sitting in the middle of the pavement, she was gone.

18

LOGAN SCOOPED up the man's gun, then headed straight for the street knowing there was little chance Angie had returned to her apartment. When he reached the sidewalk, he spotted her two buildings down, running away. Instead of chasing her on foot, he ran over to his El Camino and jumped in. By the time he pulled level with her, her pace had begun to slow.

As he rolled down his window, he yelled, "Get in!"

She looked over, but didn't stop.

"How far do you think you'll get like that? Just get in the car!"

A squeal of tires echoed down the street from somewhere behind them. Logan looked back. A car had just sped out of Angie's apartment complex driveway, and was now heading straight for them.

"Angie, now!" he yelled.

She didn't need any further prompting. Logan slowed but didn't stop as she raced around the back of the car, and opened the passenger door.

"Come on! Come on!" he yelled, his gaze firmly affixed on the rapidly approaching car in his mirror.

The moment her butt touched the seat, he hit the gas, but even as fast as they were accelerating, it wasn't enough. Seconds after Angie closed the door, they lurched forward with a loud, metallic crunch as the other car rammed into them.

Logan looked in the mirror again. One of the sedan's headlights had been knocked out in the collision, but he doubted the man sitting behind the wheel cared. The guy looked like all he wanted to do was finish the job he'd started, and throw Logan in as a bonus.

Logan glanced at Angie. "Hold on! We're going to make a quick turn."

If she acknowledged him, he didn't hear it.

He kept their speed up until the very last second, then backed off the gas, and turned the wheel. As he'd hoped, the guy behind them hadn't anticipated the move, and was forced to rapidly decelerate.

They ended up with about a half-block gap between them, which was a hell of a lot better than the half dozen feet they'd had before. Logan's initial strategy was to lose the other car in the maze of the less-populated, residential streets, but while the tactic had kept the sedan from gaining on them, they hadn't shaken him.

Ahead, Logan saw a busy, six-lane boulevard, and decided to try something different. His timing was perfect as he reached the intersection, and he was greeted with a space just large enough for the El Camino to make a right turn without stopping.

The sedan following them wasn't so lucky. It had to wait for several cars to pass before it could turn onto the road behind them.

At the next intersection, the countdown clock on the crosswalk sign was almost at zero. Logan weaved into the fast lane, pressed the accelerator to the floor again, and shot through the intersection as the traffic light went yellow.

He looked in the mirror, expecting to see that the sedan had been left behind. But instead of getting stuck at the light, the sedan pulled out into the oncoming lanes, and hit the intersection moments after the light turned red. Horns blared, and brakes screeched, but their pursuer didn't stop.

Logan swore under him breath, then scanned ahead. A half block up was a sign that read: 405 FREEWAY. Below the words were arrows, one for southbound traffic and one for north.

Logan kept out of either lane until the last second, then shot across the traffic and onto the 405 northbound on-ramp. The road dropped quickly toward the freeway. They got all the way to the bottom of the ramp before the now-familiar single-headlight car entered at the top.

The 405 freeway had always been one of the busiest in Los Angeles, and that evening was no exception. Though technically rush hour was over and everyone was going close to the speed limit, there were cars everywhere.

Logan moved from the slow lane to the next lane and then the next, dropping into gaps in the traffic the moment he spotted them. Soon they were approaching the junction with the I-10 freeway. Logan knew if he could get over to the transition without the guy tailing them realizing it, they could head east, putting their pursuer behind them for good. He eased the El Camino to the right, stopping just short of the transition lanes, then looked in his mirror to see if he could spot the other car.

"Watch out!" Angie screamed.

Logan's gaze quickly shifted from the mirror to the road. The cars ahead of them had suddenly slowed to a crawl. He hit the brakes, then whipped the El Camino into a hole that opened up in the lane to their right just a few seconds before they would have smacked into the car that had been in front of them.

He glanced at Angie. "You all right?"

The nod she gave him said, "Yes," but the look on her face said, "Hell, *no!*"

The transition lane they were now in was moving better than

the others. Apparently, whatever was causing the traffic jam was not on the 10 freeway.

Logan moved over to the far right lane so that they'd end up going east, then checked to see if they'd lost the other car.

For a second he stared into his mirror in disbelief.

Talk about persistent. The one-eyed car was driving on the shoulder between the right lane and the freeway sound wall, and would reach them before they got to the 10 freeway. Having no choice, Logan swung his car to the shoulder, too.

"What are you doing?" Angie asked.

He nodded toward the back window, and let her figure it out herself.

The drivers in the cars they were passing didn't look particularly happy that Logan had created his own lane. A couple of them honked, then one jerk pulled his car partially onto the shoulder in an attempt to block their way. His act of protest was ill-timed, though. The sound wall that had butted up against the edge of the shoulder ended a few seconds after he crossed over, and was replaced by a landscaped slope. Logan didn't even slow down as he veered the El Camino onto the hill, and went around the blocking car.

As the road curved to the right, the traffic began to speed up, and Logan slipped back into the regular lane. A few moments later they were on the 10.

Their pursuer was at least a dozen cars behind them now, but he was still there. Logan knew if he didn't do something drastic, the other car was going to stick to them until they ran out of gas.

He slowed, bringing the El Camino in line speed-wise with the surrounding traffic. A quick glance back confirmed that the sedan was now gaining on them. Logan then moved to the right, until he was one lane from the slow lane.

Angie looked at him, then out the back window, then back at him again. "What are you doing? He's going to catch us."

Logan kept his concentration on the road and said nothing.

"Hey! Mr. Hooper! You trying to get us killed?"

"Not planning on it," he replied.

"Then get a move on it. He's right back there!"

He could see her point at the sedan.

"Do it again," he said.

"Do what?"

"Point at him. Make him think we're worried."

"I *am* worried!"

"Fine, just make sure he sees that."

"Why?"

About half a mile ahead, Logan saw that the freeway curved to the left. It wasn't perfect, but it would have to do. He slowed some more, dropping below the average speed.

"Are you crazy?" Angie screamed. "He's just a couple cars back now!"

Logan moved into the slow lane.

"Dude! What the hell are you doing?" she asked.

"Where is he now?"

"He's right there! Coming up on your side! Ah, Christ. I should have kept running."

Logan looked into the side mirror, and could see the sedan tailgating the car in front of him, flashing his lights so that the driver would speed up or clear out of the way. Since the El Camino was to the right of the slower car, the man was forced to move to his left.

Now, with the lane ahead of him clear, the guy chasing them pulled up beside them, matching their speed. Logan waited until they were almost to the curve, then snapped the wheel quickly to the left and immediately back to the right, making it look for a moment like he was going to sideswipe the sedan.

Out of reflex, the other guy jerked his car away to keep from being hit. Logan figured he would do that. Survival instinct. But all that really mattered was whether Logan had planted the seed or not.

Do it, buddy. You know you want to.

They were a third of the way through the curve.

Any time now would be good.

Another few seconds passed. Then the sedan jerked toward them.

Immediately, Logan hit the brakes.

Beside him, Angie closed her eyes tight, bracing for impact. But she needn't have bothered. The back end of the sedan passed within inches of their front bumper, but shot by without the two cars touching.

As Logan had hoped, the other guy's momentum carried him all the way through the lane, over the shoulder and halfway onto the barren dirt beyond.

The moment the guy started to bring his sedan back onto the freeway, Logan sped up just enough to tap the front corner of his El Camino against the back corner of the sedan. As soon as they were touching, he jammed the pedal all the way down and turned the wheel to the left.

The push caused the sedan to swing out perpendicular to the freeway. Logan pulled around him and raced away, watching in his rearview mirror as the sedan spun over the shoulder and down a slope behind some office buildings.

He didn't know what happened to the car after that. The only thing that mattered to him was that the guy wouldn't be following them anymore.

19

TAKING THE first exit, Logan circled around and got back onto the freeway, heading west.

"Jesus. You're insane, aren't you?" Angie finally said once they were cruising down the freeway. She let out a half laugh, like she was just joking, but he knew she wasn't. "You're going to take me back to my car now, right?"

He didn't say anything.

When they reached the 405, he went north.

"Hey, it's the other way," she said.

He remained silent.

"I'm serious. I need to get my car and get out of here." When he still didn't respond, she said, "Are you even listening to me? Turn this damn thing around, and take me to my car!"

"I believe you promised to answer some questions."

She rolled her eyes. "Seriously? Fine. I'll answer your stupid questions. Just take me back to my car."

"Questions first."

She groaned, then leaned against the door like she was trying to get as far away from him as possible.

"Where's Elyse?" he asked.

"How the hell should I know? She was going to go visit her grandfather."

"Where's Elyse?"

"Seriously, dude, you really aren't listening to me."

"Where is Elyse?"

"Stop asking me that, Goddammit!"

"I'll stop when you give me a real answer."

"I gave you a real answer."

"You gave me a lie."

"The hell I did. I have no idea where she is."

"All right," he said. "Then let me rephrase. What happened to her?"

"I *don't* know." Though she tried to sell it, some of the conviction had left her voice.

Around them, the traffic began to slow just a little as they neared the crest of the Sepulveda Pass.

"I think you do know, but are too scared to tell me."

"Go to hell."

"Why was that guy after you?"

"What guy?"

Logan looked over, his face hard. She was still sitting as far away from him as possible, her head against the metal frame of the cab, trying to look innocent. In quick succession, he punched the accelerator, tapped on the brakes. The result was the satisfying *thunk* of her head hitting the car's frame.

"Ow! What the—"

"Why was that guy after you?" he asked again.

"You did that on purpose."

"We can drive all night, or you can start talking now."

She sulked in her corner.

"Okay, fine," he said. "What I can also do is take you to the police. Tell them you're involved in the disappearance of your roommate. That you probably also have something to do with the death of her friend Anthony."

"What?" she said, surprised.

"Didn't you know that?"

"I...I..."

Glancing over, he could see that, though she might not have actually known about it, she at least suspected something had happened to Anthony.

"They're going to want to know all about you and your buddies, Aaron and Ryan."

"Hey, they're not my friends."

Logan shrugged. "But you were working with them."

She said nothing, confirming he was right.

They passed the transition to the 101 and kept going north.

"What happened to Elyse?"

More silence. He was about to ask again when she finally spoke. "They took her."

"*Who* took her?"

"I don't know exactly. Aaron, I guess. A few others. I wasn't there."

"When did it happen?"

"Monday night. When she was with...Anthony."

That answered that. "Where were they taking her?"

"I have no idea."

He said nothing.

"Seriously," she said. "I don't know. I was just trying to make some extra money, that's all."

"You need to tell me what happened. Everything."

She moaned loudly, as if it would be too painful for her to speak. But then she said, "Look, I got myself into some trouble, all right?"

"What kind of trouble?"

She paused, then said, "I took some money. A lot. Ten grand. Well, a lot to me, anyway. I didn't think it was a lot to them. Thought I was being clever, taking a little here and there. But I needed the cash more than they did, you know?"

"More than who did?"

"The company I worked for. H. Wick Medical Supplies. I worked in accounts payable. Just a clerk, processing invoices. One day I came in and these lawyers were waiting for me in the conference room. They laid out copies of all the phony invoices I'd passed through. Said they were going to have me arrested."

"Did they?"

She shook her head. "I was fired on the spot, and I spent the next two weeks waiting at home for the police to show up. Only instead of the police, this other guy knocks on my door. Totally professional-looking, know what I mean? Expensive suit and nice shoes."

"Was he from your former employer?"

"No."

"The law firm?"

"He could have been, but he never said. He just gave me his name, Mr. Andrews, and that was it."

"What did he want?"

"He told me he knew what I'd done, and said that if my old company filed charges there was no chance I would avoid going to prison for at least a couple of years. Then he told me it was possible he might be able to take care of things, if I was interested." She paused. "I have a cousin who went to prison. He wasn't the same when he was released. It changed him. Hollowed him out. I was scared to death that would happen to me. So, why wouldn't I be interested?"

"And in exchange for this?"

She hesitated. "He wanted me to do something."

"Set Elyse up."

"No. No, not at all. I mean, I guess that's what he really wanted, but that's not how it was presented to me."

Logan waited.

"Mr. Andrews said all I had to do was move in with some girls in Westchester, and keep an eye on one of them while pretending to be a student."

"Elyse?"

"Yeah."

"Did he tell you why he wanted you to keep an eye on her?"

"Not exactly. He just implied that she might have been involved in something she shouldn't have been. You know, kind of like what I had been doing."

"What did you think this 'something' was?"

"Honestly, I didn't care. Mr. Andrews said he'd make sure the case against me was dropped, and told me he would even pay me a salary while I was doing the job for him. That sounded a hell of a lot better than going to jail."

"Doesn't sound like you think that now."

She looked out the window and didn't respond.

"So you've been watching her since January?" he asked to get her back on track.

"They…had to get one of the other girls to move out first," she finally said. "That took a few weeks. Then they made sure I was ready, and I answered the ad for a new roommate."

That was three months, plus the planning time before it, and more time getting Angie ready. This was no spur-of-the-moment action.

"So what did they have you do?"

"I was supposed to become friends with her, but we didn't exactly click, so…" She shrugged. "We hung out sometimes, but not very much. I just kind of kept tabs on when she was around and who she talked to."

"And who did you give the information to? Ryan?"

She laughed. "I didn't even know Ryan was part of it until last week. He moved in about a month after I did, when the people next door moved out. But, apparently, Mr. Andrews didn't think it was necessary to let me know who he was right away."

"So you reported to Mr. Andrews directly."

She shook her head. "No. Aaron."

"How?"

"He'd come over every once in a while. We pretended like he was an old friend of mine."

"And him hitting on Elyse and Joan? That was part of the plan, too?"

"I don't know. I just went with it."

Logan sat for a moment, shaking his head. "Once you were there, did you seriously think Elyse was involved in anything illegal? I mean, come on. You've got a brain, don't you? You must have realized something weird was going on."

"I tried not to think about it, okay?" she said defensively. "I just did what I was told so I could get my life back."

"At the expense of someone else's."

She said nothing for a moment, then, "Did they really kill Anthony?"

"Well, tell me this. Was Anthony the kind of person you'd think might take his own life?"

"Suicide? No way."

"Then, yeah. They killed him."

"But why would they do that?"

"I thought maybe you could tell me."

"I have no idea."

"None at all?"

"No."

"You did say he was with Elyse when they took her."

She thought for a moment. "Yeah. Maybe he tried to stop them. I don't know."

"Ryan and Aaron, were they like you? Doing jobs to get their names cleared?"

"We never talked about it, but I don't think so."

By then they had transitioned from the 405 to the northbound I-5. If they kept going they'd soon be out of L.A., on their way to Bakersfield. No longer worried she'd jump out, Logan exited the freeway, then reentered it going south, taking them back the way they'd come.

"Tell me about when she disappeared," he said.

"I already told you I wasn't there."

"But you knew about it."

"Only after it happened. Anthony picked her up, and they went out to dinner. An hour or so later, Ryan came over and told me she wouldn't be coming back, and I had to play dumb, act like she'd gone up to her grandfather's as planned."

"How long were you supposed to stay in the apartment?"

"Until the end of the month. I asked Ryan what I should do when the police started looking into where she'd gone. He said there would be no police. I was just supposed to tell anyone who asked that I'd heard her grandfather had gotten ill, and that she'd decided to stay up there a little while."

"Then why were your bags packed tonight? It's only been two days."

"Are you kidding me? I didn't sign up to be involved in a kidnapping. Besides, when I woke up this morning, Ryan's place was empty. That completely freaked me out, and I knew it was time for me to leave."

He was confused. "Then why didn't you take off right away?"

She laughed to herself and shook her head. "They owed me money. I thought maybe I could get it and pretend everything was fine, *then* leave."

Plausible, but it didn't quite add up. "But you were scared when you got back to your apartment. You even told me they were going to kill you."

She fell silent again. This time he was content to let her stay that way as long as she needed. Turned out, it lasted almost all the way back to the Sepulveda Pass.

"They have this place in Westchester, a house they rent, I guess," she finally said. "A few times Mr. Andrews would want to talk with me directly. That's where we'd meet. It was also where

I went to get my money every week. I had heard Ryan say he was supposed to meet Aaron and Mr. Andrews there this evening. So I waited until the end of the day, then went over. No one was around, so I waited in my car, out of sight. When I finally saw them arrive, I gave them ten minutes, then went back to the house. But before I got to the front door, I passed by one of the bedroom windows, and heard Aaron and Mr. Andrews talking inside. I stayed there long enough to learn they'd never intended for me to stay the rest of the month. That had just been a lie to keep me someplace easy to find." Logan could feel her gaze on him. "Mr. Andrews said someone would 'take care' of me tonight. *That's* why I was so scared."

"What's the address of the house?"

After she gave it to him, he pulled out his phone and called his father.

"I need Dev to get a few more guys," he said.

"More?" his dad asked. "Uh, okay. How soon?"

"Now. We'll be there in fifteen minutes."

"*We'll?*"

"Tell Dev I have a babysitting job for him," Logan said, then hung up.

"Wait," Angie said. "You're not taking me to my car?"

"You really think that's a smart idea? Someone else could be waiting there for you. I think it's better if I put you someplace where they can't find you."

Of course, that wasn't his only reason.

She didn't look particularly happy, but he didn't care.

20

THE ADDRESS Angie had given Logan was in a residential neighborhood, all single-family homes, no apartment buildings. He parked a block down, then donned the leather jacket he kept behind the seat, and slipped his newly acquired gun into the front pocket.

It was nearly 9 p.m., and the street had that settled-in-for-the-night feel. The house in question was one story with a front door near the middle, and an attached garage on the right. There were no lights on in the windows, and no cars parked in the driveway or at the nearby curb.

A front approach was out of the question. Logan would be in direct view of anyone on the street, and the last thing he needed was a nosy neighbor calling the cops.

He did a quick scan up and down the road, then ducked down the side yard next to the garage and quietly hopped the fence into the backyard. He paused for a moment, listening for any movement, but heard nothing. He then made his way along the back of the house until he reached a window.

Peering in, his stomach sank as déjà vu hammered away at his skull.

The room was empty.

He eased himself further along the wall, stopping just short of a sliding glass door. Leaning forward, he looked through it, bracing himself to see another completely empty room, but instead, found a sparsely furnished family room: a couple of old couches, a TV, and a dingy coffee table.

There was something else, too.

Halfway down the hallway on the far side of the room, light spilled out of a doorway.

He listened, but all was quiet. Maybe Aaron or Ryan or even this Mr. Andrews hadn't turned the light off when they left.

That thought had barely passed through his mind when he heard the very distinct sound of a toilet flushing.

Nothing happened for several seconds, then the light switched off, and a man moved into the hallway. He was tall and lanky, and though mostly in shadow, he reminded Logan very much of Elyse's neighbor, Ryan.

Logan pulled back out of sight as the guy started walking toward the family room. Five seconds later, a light came on.

Repositioning himself further out in the backyard, out of the halo of light, Logan looked through the glass door again.

It was Ryan, all right.

He plopped down on the couch and turned on the TV. For several minutes, he barely moved. Suddenly he jumped, then raised a phone to his ear a second later. The conversation was a short one. As soon as he was through, he leaned to his side and grabbed something. When he stood up, he had a large duffle bag in his hand. He strapped it over his shoulder, turned off the light, then disappeared off to the left.

Logan backtracked to the window of the empty bedroom he'd first seen. Light was now filtering in from the hallway beyond the room's open door. It stayed on for about ten more seconds, then switched off. This was followed almost immediately by the *thunk* of a heavy door shutting.

The heaviest doors in most homes were the ones that led to the outside. But Ryan wasn't at the front door or the back, and there wasn't any door along this part of the house that opened onto the yard. Then what had that—

The garage, Logan thought as he glanced to the left.

He ran to the fence, and climbed back over. As he landed, he heard two things: the roar of an engine, and the sound of an automatic opener pulling up the garage door.

He sprinted to the sidewalk, glancing over his shoulder as he did. The door was up just enough for him to see the taillights of a Lexus SUV.

Forty-five seconds later, Logan was in his El Camino, driving back by the house. The garage door was all the way open now, and the Lexus was nowhere in sight. He raced to the end of the block and looked both ways. Nothing.

Continuing through the neighborhood, he headed toward La Tijera Boulevard. It was the closest main road, and the most logical place Ryan would have gone. Logan's instinct turned out to be right. He spotted Ryan two streets shy of the main intersection.

Now that Logan had him in his sights, following Ryan was easy. Unlike Logan with the guy who'd been chasing him earlier, Ryan had no idea anyone was behind him.

They popped onto the 405 north, following the route Logan and Angie had taken earlier. But when they reached the 10, instead of going east, they went west toward the beach, getting off barely a mile later at Bundy Drive.

From there they went south, and very shortly the Santa Monica Airport came into view. Logan was hoping Ryan was just going to drive right by, but no such luck. On cue, the Lexus turned down Airport Avenue.

Logan stopped at the corner so Ryan wouldn't see his headlights following immediately after him, not at all liking what this might mean.

Santa Monica Airport was located right in the middle of the city, with a single runway long enough to accommodate most business jets. This made it a favorite of Hollywood celebrities who could fly in and avoid the mess at the larger, commercial airports, and be wherever they needed to be thirty minutes later. In other words, a person could go almost anywhere from there with a lot less hassle.

Logan waited until Ryan neared the first of the hangars before turning down the road.

Off to his right, he could see a small aircraft coming in for a landing, but overall the airport itself seemed pretty quiet. Checking his watch, he saw that it was a quarter after nine, and was willing to bet the airport had a curfew that probably went into effect in the next couple of hours. He looked at Ryan's vehicle.

"So are you flying somewhere?" he said out loud. "Or are you here for some other reason?"

Brake lights flashed ahead, then Ryan's SUV turned into a parking lot. Logan immediately did the same, finding a smaller lot tucked between two buildings.

As he got out, he pulled on his jacket and felt the knock of his pistol against his hip. For half a second he wondered if he should leave it. Just sneaking around an airport could easily get him into trouble, but doing so with a gun? That would be serious jail time. But it was a choice between a potentially bad outcome versus a potentially life-ending one if he couldn't defend himself. The gun stayed in his pocket.

Back on the road, he kept to the shadows as much as possible, hoping they would be enough to conceal his presence. He'd only gone a short distance when he saw Ryan step into the street and cross over to the airport side, walking up to a small building directly across from the lot where he'd parked. As he reached the door, someone inside opened it and he walked through.

The moment it closed Logan darted across the street and

headed west along a tall fence that separated him from an open area where several small planes were parked. He stopped at the first building he came to. Next to a faded blue door was a sign that read:

LITTLE ALICE'S AVIATION
FLIGHT SCHOOL AND
AIRCRAFT MAINTENANCE

Logan looked through the window. The streetlights provided enough illumination for him to make out a counter, a couple of desks, and a seating area. Beyond the desks, a door opened onto a darkened room. Just as he hoped, no one was there.

He made sure there were no cars coming, then pulled out the modified lock-pick set he'd used at Elyse's place, and set to work on the door of Little Alice's Aviation.

It took him longer than the apartment had. This door had two deadbolts, and a lock in the knob. He had finished both deadbolts, and was just starting on the last lock, when a car started coming down the hill toward the airport.

He focused on the lock, keenly aware that the headlights were drawing nearer and nearer.

"Come on," he whispered, his teeth clenched, urging the lock to cooperate. When the car arrived, he needed to either be inside or walking away.

He took a deep breath, moved the pick again, then felt the lock finally release.

Rushing inside, he shut the door, then looked through the open vertical blinds at the street.

As the car drove by, he could see two men inside. The driver he didn't know, but the passenger looked very much like the same man who'd been chasing him and Angie. Apparently he survived his crash.

Logan moved one of the blinds just enough so that he could watch them pull into the same parking lot Ryan had used. It seemed a pretty safe assumption they'd walk over to the same building, too, so instead of watching, Logan headed through the office into the darkened room in back.

He flicked on his flashlight, and took a quick look around. The room was set up as a classroom. There were a dozen chairs with attached desks all facing a dry-erase board on the far wall. There was also a door to the left that could only have led outside.

Night air greeted Logan as he opened it. Beyond was a concrete sidewalk, then a wide paved area, and finally what he could only describe as a carport for planes. All the spaces were filled with small, prop-driven aircraft.

He scanned the entire area to make sure no one was around, then stepped outside. The building Ryan had gone into would be on the other side of the sheltered planes. Logan walked over to it, and made his way to the far end. When he got there, he could see the runway directly in front of him, maybe fifty yards away, just beyond an access road and a strip of grass.

He rounded the side of the shelter, then stopped at the rear corner and peeked around. Back toward Airport Avenue was the building Ryan had entered.

There was a lot of activity going on down there, all centered around a sleek-looking private jet parked nearby. Logan could see lights on inside its cabin and was pretty sure there was someone in the cockpit moving around. The door at the back of the building was open, and light was shinning from inside it as well.

Unfortunately, everything was too far away for him to make out any details. He needed to get closer.

On the other side of the jet, directly across from his position, was an open area where nearly two dozen small planes were parked. It would provide a much closer, unobstructed view of the jet and the back of the building. The problem was getting there without drawing attention.

He glanced around. There was a wide spot in the access road, about a hundred feet away, where half a dozen planes were parked. If he could get there, and work his way along the aircraft until he could cross over to the other lot, that might work. And if at any point someone saw him, there were enough planes around that he could act like one of them was his.

He crossed over to the grass strip, and turned down it. When he reached the aircraft, he paused, looking back toward the jet. So far no one was rushing in his direction, or trying to see what he was doing.

He continued on until he was directly across from the open parking area where he ultimately wanted to be. This was going to be the tricky part. While he hoped he wouldn't be noticed, he was going to be in plain view for at least ten seconds. The best he could do was to make it look like he had zero interest in whatever was going on at the jet. When it appeared that no one was looking in his direction, he crossed the access road at a diagonal *away* from the jet.

Once he reached the safety of the first plane, he looked back.

"Dammit," he said under his breath.

He hadn't been as clever as he'd thought. Two men were standing on the tarmac, facing in his direction. One of them was pointing at the road where he'd just crossed.

He watched as they talked for a moment, then the one who had pointed started walking back toward the building, while the other began heading toward Logan.

That was an even bigger problem than it could have been. If the guy found him, there'd be no way he could play off the lie that he was just checking his plane.

Logan had met this guy before, in the refrigerator at the back of the Coffee Time Café.

21

USING THE planes to mask his movements, Logan scuttled back to the next row, then started trying the door of each aircraft that he passed.

Locked.

Locked.

Locked.

Locked.

Big-city people. No trust.

By the time he arrived at the fifth plane, Tooney's assailant had reached the parking area. Logan tried the next door, and was already in the process of moving on when he realized the handle had actually turned.

Easing the door open, he crawled inside. The plane creaked as it took on his weight. He just hoped it wasn't loud enough to be heard from more than a few feet away. He closed the door, then scrunched down in the space between the front and back seats. A blanket would have been nice, or something else to cover himself with, but there was nothing.

All he could do now was wait and listen.

At first he could only hear the man's footsteps, but then a

familiar rattling sound joined them, and Logan instantly knew the guy was trying the doors of the planes.

Logan glanced over to see if there was a way to lock his cabin door from inside, but if there was, he couldn't spot it from his current position, and couldn't risk twisting around to take a closer look.

He slipped the gun out of his pocket and pointed it at the door, hoping he wouldn't have to use it. The steps and the rattling grew nearer. Logan had no idea exactly where the man was, but he couldn't have been more than a few planes away.

Suddenly an outburst of music cut through the night, stopping after a few seconds, mid-note.

"Yeah?" a voice said, the same voice Logan had heard in Tooney's café. "No. Nothing. Are you *positive* you saw someone?...It was probably just a maintenance guy or something....Yeah, okay. Be right there."

Logan assumed the man had hung up, but he held his position because he hadn't heard him walk away.

One minute passed, then two. Then—

A foot scraped on the tarmac, then another, and another. Soon the scrapes became footsteps that grew fainter and fainter until Logan could no longer hear them.

He resisted the urge to check for another minute. When he finally did look out the cockpit window, the man was all the way back at the jet.

Logan returned the gun to his pocket, and exited the plane. As quickly as he could, he made his way over to a dark area near the fence, then moved along it until he reached a small storage shed that was about as close as he dared get to the jet.

The first thing he did was to write down the tail number and a general description of the aircraft in his notebook. It was a sizable plane that was probably about as large as the airport could handle. Logan had no doubt it could easily fly from one coast to the other with fuel to spare.

From his vantage point, he could see the open cabin door, and a short staircase that led down from the plane to the tarmac. Outside the building, four men huddled together. Ryan was one of them, as was the guy who'd just been searching for Logan. One of the other two was younger, like Ryan, which made Logan think he might be the recently-moved-out Aaron Hughes. The final guy was black, and probably in his early thirties. Logan had never seen him before, but wondered if he might have been the black guy Joan and Maria had mentioned.

After about five minutes, Ryan and the guy Logan decided to anoint as Aaron went inside the building. The other two talked for a few more seconds, then headed over to the jet. One of the guys called inside, then a man wearing a simple uniform appeared in the doorway. From the way he was dressed, Logan thought he was probably the pilot.

The three men talked for several moments, then one of the men on the ground pulled out a phone and made a call. The conversation went on for no more than thirty seconds, then he hung up and said something to the other two.

The pilot nodded, seemingly satisfied, and disappeared back into the plane. A few moments later, the jet's engines fired up. This seemed to be the cue the guys in the building had been waiting for, because soon Ryan, Aaron, and the man who'd chased Logan and Angie on the freeway came outside and joined the others.

Standing together at the foot of the stairs, the men seemed antsy, none of them saying very much. Then Ryan suddenly glanced over his shoulder toward the access road. A second later, the others did the same.

Logan followed their gaze, and immediately spotted a dark Chevy Suburban approaching from the east. Once it turned off the access road, it circled the plane, then pulled around the wing to get as close to the aircraft as possible. The two front doors opened, and two men stepped out. The driver had a similar look and feel to the other men waiting with Ryan and Aaron. The passenger, on the other hand, was older. Maybe mid-forties, and dressed in a well-tailored, dark suit.

Mr. Andrews?

There were no hugs or handshakes, just a tight gathering as the group listened to the man in the suit. When he was through, he pointed at the SUV.

Almost immediately, the Suburban's back passenger doors flew open, and a man got out from each side. The one who'd been sitting behind the driver leaned back in like he'd forgotten his bag or something, but what he pulled out wasn't a bag. It was a small, young, Asian woman.

The distance made definitive identification difficult, especially since Logan had only seen a picture of Elyse and had never met her in person. But he had little doubt that the woman was indeed Tooney's granddaughter.

She appeared to be drugged as the man half-walked, half-carried her toward the plane.

Just a couple of hundred feet separated Logan from the girl he had promised to find, the girl he had promised to bring back to her grandfather. But there was absolutely nothing he could do about it. If he tried, the only result he could see was one that ended with both the girl and himself dead.

Feeling completely helpless, he watched as the man loaded her onto the plane. As soon as she was on board, Aaron, Ryan and the three who had been waiting with them followed the suited man up the steps.

The guy who'd been driving and the other one from the backseat got back into the Suburban and pulled it over to the side, out of the way.

Logan assumed they were just parking it, and would be joining the others, but then the plane's entry door was pulled up and slammed shut. Almost immediately the jet began to taxi away.

Wherever the plane was headed, it was going, and there was

nothing Logan could do about it.

At that moment, it would have been so easy to slip into despair. Given the bad turns his life had taken, it would have been understandable. But it was because of those turns, and the chance to do something to chip away at them, even if just a little, that he resisted the temptation, and concentrated on what he had to do next—find out where that plane was headed. And the sooner he did that, the better.

As the jet headed toward the runway, Logan pulled out his phone and called Ruth's cell. Once it started ringing, he stepped out from behind the shed, and began walking in plain sight toward the building the others had been using.

It took five rings for her to answer. "Who is this?"

"It's Logan."

"Oh, Christ. Harper, didn't I tell you not to use this phone?" She paused. "Oh, God. It's after one a.m. What do you want?"

"I'm sorry. I didn't have a choice. I need you to check on a plane for me."

"A *what?*"

"An airplane. A jet. One of those executive types."

He was halfway to the building now, gesturing broadly with his hands like he was reacting to what was being said on the phone. But his movement had nothing to do with Ruth. They were meant to draw the attention of the men in the Suburban.

"Look, I am *not* your personal information house, okay? Call someone else."

The gestures worked. The vehicle started rolling forward on a course to cut Logan off.

"Ruth, I know that. But there *is* no one else. And I really need your help."

She was silent for a moment. "Dammit. You're going to make a habit of this, aren't you?"

"I'm trying not to."

"You're obviously not trying hard enough. Hold on."

As he waited, the Suburban pulled to a stop ten feet from the building, then both front doors opened, and the two men who'd stayed behind got out.

"All right," she said. "I'm ready."

He gave her the plane's identification number. "I really need to know who owns it, and where it's supposed to be headed."

"How soon?"

"Now would be good."

"Seriously?"

"I'm...I'm sorry."

She was quiet for a moment, then said, "I'll call you back as soon as I can."

The line went dead. Logan, though, kept the phone pressed to his ear, and nodded like he was listening.

As soon as he was within earshot of the men waiting for him, he said, "Yeah, they're all secure. Just doing a final check of the east buildings....No, should be there in ten minutes....Okay. See you then." He touched the screen, pretending to hang up. As he neared the Suburban, he smiled. "Evening, gentlemen. I assume you guys have a pass to be out here."

The two men eyed him suspiciously, then exchanged a look. "Sure. Of course we do," the older-looking one said.

"Can I take a look at it, please?" Logan stopped in front of them, the smile still on his face.

The older one looked at his colleague. "Get it."

The other man walked back to the Suburban, and pulled a paper pass off the dash. When he returned, he handed it over. Logan gave it a careful look.

"Which one of you is Mr. Williams?" he asked.

"I am," the guy who'd been doing the talking said.

"So you would be Mr. Dean?" Logan said to the other one. "Uh-huh."

Logan looked at his watch. "Your pass expires in just a couple of minutes. You should probably be on your way."

"You work for the airport?" Mr. Williams asked.

"Night security."

Mr. Dean's eyes narrowed. "Then where's your uniform?"

"I'm not a rent-a-cop. I own the security company, so I can wear whatever I damn well please."

In the distance, Logan could hear the jet's engine revving up and getting ready for take-off.

"Were you here for that plane?" he asked.

"I don't think that's any of your business," Mr. Williams said.

"Well, if you weren't here for that plane, then what are you here for?"

Before either of them could answer, the jet began roaring down the runway, making it impossible to hear anything. Both men turned their heads to look.

Don't ever give them a chance.

Mr. Williams was standing in the unfortunate position closest to Logan, so he was the first to go down. An open palm uppercut under the chin did the trick, sending a surprise shock to his brain that instantly shut his system down. His partner didn't notice until it was too late, and quickly joined his friend on the asphalt.

Logan made sure they were both out, then searched them.

They were both carrying pistols, Smith & Wessons. And though they did have driver's licenses in the names of Williams and Dean, they also had ones in the names of Hoover and Jenson. So it wasn't a leap to assume their real names were none of the above.

Logan checked the door of the building. It was locked, but only by a single deadbolt. He picked it quickly, then hauled the two men inside. With some duct tape he found in one of the cabinets, he secured their wrists and ankles, then splashed water from a cooler in Williams's face. It took three cups before Williams finally sputtered and opened his eyes.

"What the hell?" Williams said, as he realized he was

restrained. He looked around, then caught sight of Logan. "Let me go, you son of a bitch! You're messing with the wrong person, man."

"Mr. Williams, where are your friends headed?"

"What friends?"

"The ones you gave the girl to. The ones on the jet?"

He shrugged. "Sorry. Don't know."

Logan smiled, then kicked him hard in the ribs. "You're already in this for kidnapping. Quite possibly human trafficking, too. You sure you don't want to cooperate?"

"You ain't no cop. You can't charge me with anything."

"That's true. But you know what that means? I don't have to follow any of their rules. Where are they going?"

"Go to hell."

Logan kicked him again.

"Ah! Come on. Stop it!"

"You tell me what I want to know, and I will. Until then…" Another kick.

"Who the hell do you think you are?"

"I'm the guy standing over you with my foot in your ribs, and your guns in *my* pocket. Good enough? Maybe we should see how hard that head of yours is."

Logan adjusted his stance so that it appeared as if he were going to kick the guy in the temple.

"Dude, lay off, all right? I don't know where they went. They just hired us for the job here, you know? A little muscle, a little driving, some babysitting."

"Who hired you?"

When it didn't look like the guy was going to answer, Logan tapped his ear with the toe of his shoe.

"Okay, okay," Williams said. "The guy's name is Andrews. That's all I know."

"The suit who was in the car with you?"

"Yeah."

"Who does he work for?"

"I'm telling you, I don't know anything more."

"And I'm telling you, I don't believe you."

"It's the truth, man!" he pleaded.

"You never met anyone else in charge?"

"No."

"Just this Andrews guy?"

"Yeah. Yeah. Just him. How many times do you want to hear it?"

Logan wasn't sure whether to believe him or not, but he knew he didn't have the time to waste trying to get the info out of him.

Once again he got a hold of Dev through his father, and arranged for some more of the Marine's vet buddies to pick up these two and hold them somewhere until Logan decided what they should do with them.

"You got quite an operation going," Dev said once Logan had explained everything.

"It's not a problem, is it?"

"Hell, no. It's great to be doing real work again."

22

RUTH CALLED Logan back as he was pulling into the motel parking lot just before midnight.

"Please don't tell me the plane's stolen, too," he said.

"Now that *would* be interesting, wouldn't it? No, not stolen," she said. "Chartered."

"From who?"

"A place called Midwin-Robb Express. The plane was chartered by a company called Kajiwara Research, specifically by a man named Robert Andrews."

"What do you know about Kajiwara?"

Sarcasm dripped from her voice as she said, "Wow. I *so* did not expect you to ask that question. Luckily, I accidentally looked them up while I was at it. Well, tried anyway."

"Tried?"

"Kajiwara's a shell company, incorporated in the Cayman Islands. Runs through a half dozen other corporations that I've been able to find so far."

"Where does it end?"

"*That* I don't know."

Logan hesitated, then said, "Can you keep looking?"

"You are definitely getting me fired."

"That is definitely not my intention. I promise." He paused. "What about the flight plan?"

"The one on file has them going to Tokyo."

Logan was afraid of that. Not Tokyo specifically, but just somewhere out of the country. There was a very real possibility that Tokyo was not even their destination, and had just been used to explain their initial flight path.

"I really need to know where the plane ends up. If it *is* Tokyo, fine, but if not, I need that location. Can you…keep tabs on it?"

"Logan, please."

"Ruth, can you?"

She hesitated. "I don't know, maybe."

"That's all I can ask," he said.

"Goodnight, Logan. Don't wake me up again."

She clicked off.

It had been a long day, packed with a hell of lot more than Logan had bargained for. But as much as he would have loved to just lie down and fall asleep when he walked back into his room, he couldn't. Time was the enemy. With each passing second, Elyse was moving farther and farther away.

He found a phone book in the nightstand drawer. Midwin-Robb Express was listed under Airplanes, Charter. He called the number and, as he'd hoped, a live voice at an answering service picked up. A charter jet company in Los Angeles, where entertainment industry big shots kept ever-changing schedules, had to be available 24/7 if they wanted to stay in business.

"I need a plane," he said. "I have a client who needs to leave for New York first thing in the morning."

"May I have your name, please?"

"Sure. James Cole."

"All right, Mr. Cole. If you give me your number, I'll have someone call you back in just a few moments."

True to her word, his phone rang three minutes later.

"Is this Mr. Cole?" the woman on the other end asked.

"Yes, it is."

"Hi, my name's Debbie Midwin. From Midwin-Robb Express? You called about a charter?"

Logan was impressed. She sounded like it was the middle of the day, not midnight.

"Yes, I did. I'm hoping you can help me out of a bind. My client has an event he needs to attend in New York tomorrow afternoon, but he's here in L.A. right now. How soon do you think you could get him there?"

"We have a plane at the Van Nuys Airport that can take off at six a.m., and get him there a little before two p.m. eastern time."

"He was hoping he could fly out of Santa Monica."

"Well, we do have a plane there that's also available tomorrow, but the airport's closed until seven a.m."

"So, two p.m. in New York, then?"

"Yes, sir. Around that."

"That would work."

"That's great. Would you like to book it?"

He paused for effect. "Well, here's the problem. My client is...*particular*. Before I can book anything, I'll need to see the plane first."

"Of course," she said, without missing a beat. She'd obviously heard this tune before. "When would you like to look at it?"

"Can we do it in, say, fifty minutes?"

"One a.m.?"

"Yeah."

"No problem," she said. She gave him the address. "Can I ask who your client is?"

"I'm sorry, but I can't tell you that right now. If everything's cool, and we book the charter, of course you'll know then." He paused, then in a faux whisper added, "But I can say he probably won't be bringing along the Oscar he just won."

He thought he heard a smile in her voice as she said goodbye and hung up.

Logan took a cool shower in hopes it would revitalize him. It wasn't the perfect solution, but it helped.

He had just pulled on his pants and was grabbing a clean shirt out of his bag when someone knocked on his door.

He wasn't surprised to find his dad standing outside. Harp immediately pushed past him. "I saw your car. How long have you been back?"

"Not long," Logan said. He waited at the door for a few seconds in case any of his dad's friends were with him, but apparently he'd come alone. Logan shut it, and pulled on his shirt.

"Well? What happened?" his father asked. "Dev got all 'can't talk right now' as soon as he got off the phone with you, then disappeared."

"Elyse is alive."

"What?" His father's eyes grew about as wide as Logan had ever seen them.

"I saw her."

"You saw her? And she's alive?" His dad's voice stuck in his throat. Logan could tell he'd been assuming the worst, but hadn't voiced it for his friend's sake. "Where is she? We should go get her." He started for the door.

"It's not that easy," Logan said, stopping him.

"Why not? If you know where she is, we just need to—"

"Dad, she's on a plane."

"A plane?" his father said, as if the word was foreign to him. "An airplane?"

"Yes."

"Where's she going?"

"The flight plan says Tokyo."

"Tokyo?" His dad sank onto one of the beds and sat there

for a moment, staring at the floor, before he turned his gaze back to his son. "Why did you let her get on?"

"She didn't get aboard by herself. Someone put her there."

"And you just let this happen? You should have grabbed her."

"It wasn't exactly an option at the time, okay?" Logan paused, trying very hard not to let his own frustration show. "At least we know she's still alive. And, for the moment, we also know exactly where she is."

"You mean in a *plane*, above the *ocean*?"

"Yes," Logan said, ignoring his father's tone.

Harp looked defeated, like he'd let down Tooney, and there was nothing he could do to make it right.

Logan sat down beside him. "You wanted me to find her and bring her back. Dad, that's still what I'm going to do."

"Do you think you really can?"

The answer that came immediately to mind was, "I don't know," but instead he said, "I'm not going to stop until I do."

Neither of them spoke for a few seconds.

Finally, Logan said, "Wherever she's gone, Dad, I'm going to have to follow her."

"Well, that's not a problem," his father replied, grabbing onto the thread of hope Logan had given him. "I told you we'd cover all costs."

"I'll need cash. A few grand at least, and that's not counting the plane ticket."

"The boys and I will go to the bank tomorrow."

"You should probably do it first thing," Logan said. "I'll need to leave as soon as I can."

"For Tokyo?" his dad asked.

"That, I don't know yet."

Harp gave his son a smile, then said, "Thanks, Logan. I'm glad you're here, and I know you'll do the best you can."

I hope so.

23

THE ADDRESS Debbie Midwin had given Logan was to the same building in which he'd questioned Mr. Williams and Mr. Dean. But that wasn't a surprise.

He parked in the lot directly across from it this time, and knocked on the door.

A few moments later, a smiling woman of about forty-five opened it. She was short, maybe five-three at best, and dressed in jeans and a green sweater. By her demeanor, it could have just as easily been 1:00 p.m. as 1:00 a.m.

"Mr. Cole?" she asked.

Logan nodded, smiling. "You must be Ms. Midwin."

"Just call me Debbie. Come in, come in."

As soon as he was inside, she shut the door.

"I want to thank you for meeting with me this late," he said. "I know it's a huge inconvenience."

She shook her head dismissively. "Not at all. You'd be surprised at how many late nights we put in here."

As she led him from the reception area into the back room, he heard something moving around. "Is someone else here?"

She smiled. "Just Roger. Roger, come here." A few seconds

later, a golden retriever ran up and nuzzled Debbie's hand.

When he saw Logan, he ambled over. "Hey, Roger. How you doing?"

The dog sniffed his fingers, then gave them an experimental lick. After that, they were fast friends.

Debbie pointed at the door to the airfield. "The plane's in a hangar nearby. We just need to—"

"I was thinking we could discuss business first," Logan said. "If you don't mind."

She turned back. "Of course. Whatever you'd like."

She motioned to a desk in the middle of the room. After they were both seated, Logan let her give him what he assumed was her normal sales pitch.

Finishing up, she said, "As you can imagine, we deal with a lot of people looking for discretion. For that reason, we never discuss our client list with anyone. In our case, less publicity means better business."

"I certainly can appreciate that. Tell me, do you fly just domestically? Or...?"

She looked momentarily confused. "Didn't you say you wanted to go to New York?"

"Yes. On this trip. I was thinking more long term."

"Oh, sure." She smiled. "We'll fly anywhere our clients need to go, except war zones and that kind of thing, of course." She let out a little laugh. "We're all about customer service, but we're not fighter pilots."

"I wouldn't expect you to be." He paused for a second. "My client might need to fly to Japan later in the month. Is that doable for you?"

"As a matter of fact, we have an aircraft making that very trip as we speak."

"Oh, that's good to know," he said, fake-surprised, then chuckled. "So you have a client going to Japan, huh?"

"Well, through Japan, anyway."

He let the subject drop, and asked if she could run up an estimate of what the New York trip would cost his client.

"No problem," she said, then pulled a keyboard out from under her computer terminal.

When people typed passwords into their computers, they generally checked to make sure whoever was with them wasn't looking. But when they did the actual typing, they would focus either on the keyboard or the screen. Logan was petting the dog's head when Debbie did her check, but as soon as she looked away, he moved his gaze just enough so he could see which keys she tapped to unlock her computer: roger1207. He figured the numbers must be the dog's birthday.

Once the estimate was printed out and in Logan's possession, she said, "Shall we see the plane now?"

"Absolutely."

The dog led the way, running ahead, stopping until they caught up, then running ahead again. They were almost to the hangar when Logan shot his hand into his pants pocket and pulled out his phone.

"Sorry," he said to Debbie. "This should only take a second." He pretended to hit a button, then moved the phone to his ear. As he spoke, Roger loped over, and nuzzled his hand. "Hello?....Yeah, I'm here now....What? But I thought....Are you sure that's what Tom wants?....Okay. Okay. No problem." He hung up his fake call, grimacing.

Debbie took a step toward him. "Everything okay?"

Logan ran his hand over Roger's head, then said, "Well, no, actually. I'm *so* embarrassed. My client's changed his mind, and decided not to go. I feel horrible for having made you come out at this time of night, but it looks like we won't need a plane in the morning after all." He closed his eyes for a second. "It's not the first time he's done this, so I guess I should have expected it. I'm really sorry."

"No, no. Don't worry about it," she said. "It happens more

often than you'd guess. At least you know about us now. I could still show you the plane, if you'd like."

"I've taken up too much of your time already. But I guarantee you when the Japan trip comes up, you'll be at the top of my call list. I owe you that much."

"We'd definitely appreciate the business."

He let her show him out, gave the dog a final pat, then apologized again as she locked the front door behind them. Not surprisingly, she was parked in the same lot Logan was.

Logan got into his El Camino, started it up, then pulled out his phone and pretended to be talking again. He didn't know if he was getting good at it or not, but he did seem to be doing a lot of talking to dead air that night. As Debbie drove by, he gave them a wave, then slipped the phone back in his pocket once they were out of sight.

Three minutes later, he was sitting at Debbie's desk, typing in roger1207. In no time, he found the file for the charter flight Elyse was on. Interestingly enough, the client—Mr. Robert Andrews—had stated that he and his associates were escorting the sick daughter of a businessman home. Only home wasn't Tokyo. That was merely a fuel stop.

Home was Bangkok, Thailand.

The country right next door to Burma.

24

THE FIRST flight Logan could fly out on was at 12:55 p.m. on Cathay Pacific. There'd be a plane change in Hong Kong, and by the time he reached Bangkok, it would be nearly midnight the following day. In the best of circumstances, he would be at least fourteen hours behind the people who had Elyse, but he thought it prudent to assume the difference would be closer to sixteen.

Would that be too late? As much as he tried not to think that way, the thought did keep creeping in.

His father was true to his word. He and his friends came to Logan's motel room before he left and gave him an envelope containing five thousand dollars in cash.

"If you need more," his dad told him, "just let me know. I expect you to check in every day, too."

"Don't," Logan said. "I'm not going to stop whatever I might be doing just to let you know what's going on."

"I didn't mean that, but—"

"Dad, please. If I can, I'll call. If I can't, I won't."

Harp was going to say something else, but Barney put a hand on his shoulder. "Do what you need to do, Logan."

Logan nodded his thanks.

"And just in case," Barney said, handing him a small bottle. "Sleeping pills for your flight."

On the way out, Logan stopped by Tooney's room. Elyse's grandfather was sitting on the bed, his packed bag on the floor near the door. As soon as Logan left for the airport, he and the others were all heading back to Cambria.

"Are you doing okay?" Logan asked, sitting down beside him.

"I'm happy she's still alive, but...am still worried."

"I'll...I'll bring her back."

Tooney looked at Logan and tried to smile. "I know you will."

Logan patted him on the arm, then stood up. "I gotta go."

"Thank you, Logan," he whispered. "Thank you."

Logan didn't know what to say, so he simply nodded and left.

Outside, Dev was waiting next to the El Camino, ready to drive Logan to the airport, then take his car back up the coast.

"Thanks for all the help," Logan said once they were on the road.

Dev shrugged like it was no big deal. "I assume you just want us to hold on to everyone?"

Logan hesitated. "Eventually we're going to want to turn them over to the police, but I don't want to do that yet. Let's see if I can learn anything that can help us out first."

"Okay."

"That is, unless your people do mind."

"They don't mind."

They fell silent for several blocks.

"Dev, I need to ask you for a little more help," Logan said. "I'm hoping someone you know might have contacts in Bangkok who can assist me. Probably someone who—"

He stopped as Dev pulled a piece of paper out of his shirt pocket, and handed it to him.

"What's this?"

"What you just asked for," Dev said. "A phone number. When you get there, call it."

"A friend of yours?"

"A friend of a friend."

Logan hoped he'd say more, but in typical Dev fashion, that was it.

"So you were expecting me to ask for help," he said.

"If you didn't, I would have given it to you anyway. Tooney's a good guy. Find his granddaughter, Logan. And if you can, make the ones who took her pay."

Logan wasn't sure how long after his plane had taken off that he fell asleep, but he knew they hadn't reached cruising altitude yet. Barney's pills really worked. By the time Logan woke, he'd been out for seven hours. Which was nice until he realized he still had about another seven to go before the plane was due to land in Hong Kong.

He filled some of the time by working on his laptop. In the morning before he'd left the motel, he'd received an email from Ruth containing Forbus's latest information on Burma. Not having time to look at it then, he'd saved it to his hard drive. He'd also found some stuff online about Elyse's mother, Sein, and saved those to the computer, too. Now that he had nothing else to do, he was able to go through most everything.

Ruth's Burma info didn't really add much to what he already knew. Decades of repression, peppered with occasional bouts of protest that were always put down. The latest had been in the fall of 2007 after the government had raised fuel prices, putting further strain on a population that had very little money in the first place. This time the Buddhist monks in the city of Rangoon had gotten involved, leading the protest until government thugs had put a stop to that. Logan could understand why Sein had such a passion for trying to free the people of her birth country.

When he'd looked her up online, there had been hundreds of links. Human rights websites, Burma-centric websites, news articles, interviews. There were also several dozen videos of talks she had given, and a couple of television interviews. He hadn't downloaded everything, but those he did, he watched.

He was surprised that she didn't look much different than the girl he remembered from twenty years before, and was impressed by her intelligent, matter-of-fact delivery. He'd expected more emotion, more rhetoric, but her calm, confident demeanor was so much more effective than any ranting would have been.

She talked about the crimes the Myanmar generals had committed, the deaths they had been responsible for, and the stranglehold they had on Burmese lives. Then she talked about her mother, how Thiri had gone to support Aung San Suu Kyi in hopes of making Burma a place her children could come back to without fear.

"Though they took her life, they did not take what her life was about. Her dream is still alive in me, like it should be in you. When tyranny and oppression are imposed on one person, they are imposed on us all. We must not stop until our brothers and sisters enjoy the same freedoms as we do."

It was all pretty heavy stuff. Logan was almost glad when his battery ran out of power.

After a few hours' layover in Hong Kong and a second flight—this one only two and a half hours long—he finally landed in Bangkok.

It didn't take long to clear immigration and customs, and soon he was in a taxi on the way to a hotel his dad had booked for him online.

Logan had been to the country once before, in the summer between the Army and college. It was long enough ago, though, that he didn't recognize most of what he saw on the drive.

The Angel City Hotel was a little boutique place, five stories high with a dozen rooms on each floor. While the building itself might have been old, the interior décor and the front façade were all new. Logan's room was surprisingly large with tiled floors, a king-size bed, and a bathroom he could have set up a cot in, all for less than the price of a room at a discount motel back home.

He took a shower and changed his clothes. Though it was around 12:30 a.m., his body clock was telling him it was only 10:30 in the morning. His stomach was also sending him the message that it wanted to eat *now*.

When he'd arrived, there'd been a lot of activity on the street, despite the late hour. Dozens of food vendors were set up along the sidewalks, while several of the shops were still open. As he went back outside, his intention was to pop over to the 7-11 he'd seen across the road, and pick up whatever he could find to munch on, but the aromas coming from some of the nearby food carts drew him over.

A lot of the people he used to work with were skittish about eating food from street vendors, especially in developing countries, but Logan never was. Perhaps if he'd ever had a really bad reaction, he might have thought differently, but he hadn't. So he picked out a couple of skewers of pork, a fried rice patty, and a bowl of vegetables and noodles. He then sat at one of the temporary tables that had been set up near the carts.

As he knew it would be, the food was delicious. It was also dirt cheap. If he kept eating like this, the WAMO boys were going to get most of their money back.

When he finished, he did a quick calculation in his head. Though it was the earliest hour of morning here, it was still afternoon in D.C.

"Logan, you've got to stop calling," Ruth said in a strained whisper when she answered his call.

"I know, but at least I'm using your cell."

"I told you not to call me on it either!"

"Sorry. Were you able to keep track of the plane?"

She remained silent for several seconds, then said, "After Tokyo, it went to Taipei, then Bangkok."

Though he knew from the records at the Midwin-Robb office that the plane had been scheduled to come to the Thai capital, it was nice to hear it independently confirmed. "Do you know what time it arrived?"

"Around noon, local time."

Noon? He wasn't sixteen hours behind. He was only a bit more than twelve. It wasn't particularly great news—twelve hours was still half a day—but it was better than he'd hoped.

"Great. Thanks, Ruth. And thanks for the Burma info, too."

"You can thank me by never calling me again."

She didn't give him the chance to respond before disconnecting the call.

As he stood up from the table, he pulled out the piece of paper Dev had given him. The polite thing to do would be to wait until morning to call, but he didn't have time to be polite.

He dialed the number. Unfortunately, the only thing that answered was a beep. There wasn't even any greeting or instructions. He left his name and number, hoping he was actually being recorded, then hung up.

Okay. So, now what? The best answer he could come up with was sleep. He might not get a chance later, so he knew he should grab it while he could.

Back in his room, he took one of Barney's pills, and stretched out on the bed, staring at the ceiling. As he started to slip under, the image of the man carrying Elyse into the plane played across his mind. He tried calling to her, but she didn't even look up. Then the scene at the plane gave way to Elyse in a cap and gown, then those were replaced by a simple dress and wings growing from her back. Then even the wings faded away, and the girl was no longer Elyse. It was *her.* She was standing near the tan wall, tears flowing down her cheeks. As she began moving away from him, he yelled out. But it only made her run faster, and faster, and—

Logan's phone vibrated on the nightstand. With some effort, he pushed open his eyes, and picked it up.

"Hello?"

"Logan Harper?"

"Yes."

"You called me."

What? Called who?

Then, through the haze of the pills he'd taken, he remembered the number from Dev. He'd been expecting a man to call him back, but the voice belonged to a woman.

"Yes. Yes, I did. I'm sorry, but I don't know your name." He paused, waiting, but apparently she wasn't ready to share that information with him yet, so he went on. "I got your number from a friend in California. He said you might be able to help me."

"I'm familiar with your situation, Mr. Harper."

He sat up, his senses coming back to him. "You are?"

She remained quiet.

"Then you know a girl's life is in danger," he said. "It's been a long time since I've been in Thailand. I don't have any contacts, and I don't speak the language. I'm looking for someone to point me in the right direction. I was hoping that maybe you—"

"Be downstairs in ten minutes," she told him, cutting him off. "You'll be picked up."

The line went dead before he could say anything else.

25

LOGAN WAS out in front of the Angel City Hotel seven minutes later. His mind was still cloudy with sleep, but moving around was helping a little.

He scanned the road in both directions. The number of people on the sidewalks had thinned, and many of the vendors had left. Off to the right, he saw a pair of headlights turn onto the street. He edged closer to the curb, anticipating that it was his ride. As it neared, he could see it was a taxi, but it raced past the hotel without the driver even glancing in his direction.

In the distance he heard thunder, and looked to the sky. It was cloudy, but at the moment there was no rain. He wondered if he should go inside, and see if they had a spare umbrella at the reception desk, but just then a motorcycle taxi, like one of the hundreds he'd noticed on the drive from the airport, pulled to the curb. Like most of the other drivers he'd seen, this one was a younger man wearing an orange vest.

"Harper?" the driver said, catching Logan off guard.

"Yes."

The kid nodded at the empty space on the seat behind him. It certainly wasn't the ride Logan had been expecting, but if that's what the mysterious voice had sent for him, so be it.

He climbed on, then grabbed each side of the seat to maintain his balance as they took off, helmetless, down the street.

The way his driver weaved through traffic, Logan half wondered if the kid had a death wish or something. He lost count of how many times they came close to hitting or being hit by another vehicle, but, scientifically, he would categorize it as *a lot.*

The wild ride went on for nearly twenty minutes before they finally stopped at the side of the road. The street they were on was wide but quiet, making Logan think that Bangkok was finally starting to wind down. The buildings that lined either side were packed right up against each other. Most of the lower floors were occupied by businesses, none of which seemed to be open during the middle of the night. The upper floors—most of the buildings were at least five stories high—looked more like apartments. A few had lights on, but the majority were dark.

The driver pointed at a door directly across the sidewalk. There were no markings on it or nearby to indicate what might be inside.

The moment Logan hopped off the bike, the driver drove off, leaving him standing alone on the sidewalk. He walked up to the door not knowing if he should knock or just go in. He decided to just open it. If it turned out he should have knocked, he could apologize after.

Instead of leading into a room, though, the door opened onto an empty staircase that went up one level and ended at another closed door. The incline was steep and the treads were narrow, so he watched his step as he made his way to the top.

He tried opening this one, too, but it was locked, so he was forced to knock.

There was a delay of several seconds, then the door opened into a small, dimly lit room. As soon as he stepped inside, the door closed behind him. He looked back. A short, thin Asian man wearing a crooked smile stood facing him.

"Please," the man said, his voice strained like his throat had been injured. He pointed at the opposite side of the room.

Logan turned back around, and realized the wall the man was motioning to was actually just a dark drape.

"Please," he repeated.

Logan walked over and pulled the drape back. Beyond was a large, loft-style room. It was considerably brighter than the entry room had been, mainly due to dozens of candles scattered throughout the space. The room had that over-the-top decorated feel: orange end tables, fur-covered cubes, a sculpture made of old computer parts, bar stools in hot pink, and paintings on the walls that were the definition of abstract.

There were also ten people. Men mainly, but also a few women, and all Asian. They'd all been talking when Logan first stepped in, but quickly stopped and were now staring at him.

"Please," the thin man said behind him, urging Logan on.

Once they crossed the room, the man showed Logan to a chair near where the others were sitting.

"Mr. Harper," he said, introducing Logan.

"Hi."

"Hello."

"*Sawadee, ka.*"

"Welcome."

Logan nodded and smiled grimly in return, but kept his mouth shut, waiting for the person who'd called him to identify herself. But no one spoke up.

For nearly two minutes, they all sat in silence. Then Logan heard a faint noise behind him, followed by the sound of footsteps on the tiled floor. Before he could turn to look, the same voice he'd heard on the phone called out, "You must be Mr. Harper."

Entering the room through a doorway in the far corner were two men and a woman. One of the men was wearing a gray suit, white shirt, and dark tie. The other was in a pair of jeans, black button shirt, and cowboy boots. Where the first had short hair and was clean-shaven, the second had hair that fell almost to his shoulders and was sporting a goatee. The suited guy reminded Logan of an accountant, while the other one he would have pegged as a musician straight in from a club.

But the woman was even more surprising, and it had nothing to do with her impressive height or striking blonde hair, or the electric blue dress she wore. Unlike everyone else present except for Logan, she was Caucasian.

Logan stood as she swept across the room.

"You look exactly like your picture," she said. "A few years older, perhaps, but you've aged well."

He was suddenly wary. "What picture?"

She looked at one of the men sitting nearby, then rattled off something in what Logan assumed was Thai.

The man immediately grabbed a piece of paper off an orange end table, and handed it to her. She examined it for a moment, then turned it so Logan could see. "This one."

He tensed. The picture was his Forbus employee photo. In this case, it was part of the newspaper article that had raised questions about his conduct in Carl's death and other matters concerning Forbus. Two days after the article came out, his status had switched from suspended with pay to terminated.

"Where did you get that?" he asked, trying to keep his voice even.

She gave him a pitiful, are-you-serious look. "The Internet, of course. Oh, don't worry. I don't care if you were guilty or not. I just wanted to have a way to identify you when you arrived."

"I wasn't guilty."

"I said I don't care. Dev Martin vouched for you, and that's all that matters to me."

"You talked to Dev?"

"Of course, this morning. He gave me the details about why you're here. Thought it might assist me in figuring out what kind of help I could provide."

"This morning? You mean before the jet arrived?"

"The private plane? Yes…" she said, drawing the last word out.

"Were you able to follow them from the airport? Do you know where they are?"

She smiled. "Why don't you sit down?"

"Please. We don't have time to waste."

"We *do* have time to sit."

One of the people who had been sitting on a fur cube near Logan moved so that the woman could take it. Reluctantly, Logan sat back down, too.

"All right. We're sitting," he said.

"First, no one asked us to go to the airport to follow them," she told him.

He felt the sinking sensation of lost opportunity.

"Second, even if they had, there wouldn't have been enough time to get there before they were gone."

This revelation didn't help much. If *he'd* been thinking correctly before he left Los Angeles, he would have had Dev call her right away. As it was, Logan hadn't even asked him to call at all. Doing so had apparently been Dev's own idea. Logan owed that man a beer or three when he got back.

"So there's no way to know where they went," he said, feeling like he was back at square one.

"I didn't say that."

He looked at her. "Are you saying you *do* know?"

"I didn't say that, either."

He could feel frustration bubbling just below his skin, but he took a breath and reined it in. He couldn't afford to lose focus now. "You haven't told me your name."

"That's true," she said. She was silent for a moment, then laughed. "You can call me Christina. They all do." She swept her hand out, taking in the others.

"Can I ask where you're from?" Logan said. Her accent was a mix—a little American with a hint of British, and a few pronunciations that sounded almost Australian.

"Sorry," she said, shaking her head, but giving no further explanation. "Now, about those who arrived on this jet. I may not know where they went, but that doesn't mean I can't find out."

"Please," Logan said. "That would be a huge help." He took the silence that followed for hesitation, so he added, "I don't have unlimited resources, but I can pay you if that would make a difference."

Her mouth twisted in an ugly sneer. "I wouldn't do this for money." She looked past him at the others. "Everyone out."

Without a word, they all rose and started for the door. Everyone, that was, except the two men who'd come in the room with her.

Once the four of them were alone, Christina said, "Any help I give you is because of an old friend I owe a debt to that I can never repay. He's the one who gave Dev my number. He's the one who asked me to help you if I felt I could."

"Please, thank him for me when you speak to him again."

She gazed at Logan, then said with a nod, "I'll do that." She paused. "I haven't been entirely inactive since I talked to Dev this morning." She motioned at the nervous-looking, suited man behind her. "Mr. Prem has...*contacts* in the government. More specifically, within Immigration and Customs." She looked back. "Mr. Prem? Can you tell our new friend what you reported to me earlier?"

Mr. Prem cleared his throat as he stepped forward. When he spoke his accent was thick, but understandable. "Van waiting at private hangar when plane arrive. Seven men get off plane. All *farang*."

Christina held up a hand, stopping him, then looked at Logan. "Are you familiar with this term? *Farang*?"

He shook his head.

"It's the word Thais use for foreigner," she explained, then she nodded at Mr. Prem to continue.

"Six men white. One man black."

If you didn't count the flight crew, or any other airline employee who might have been on board, that worked out to the same seven men Logan had seen get on. "Was there a girl?"

Mr. Prem hesitated, then nodded. "Yes. One girl. Asian. Young woman. One man carry her out in arms, like she asleep."

Unless the girl was a decoy for some reason, Elyse was here.

"At 12:23, van leave airport." He took a step back, indicating he was finished.

Logan wasn't, though. "What about Immigration? They just let them through with an unconscious girl?"

Mr. Prem looked nervously at Christina. She gave him a nod, so he stepped forward again. "Girl have Thai passport. Men with her say she got ill on plane."

"And the officials believed that?"

"Why wouldn't they?" Christina asked. "There was nothing suspicious. There are plenty of rich businessmen in Thailand who hire *farang* to keep tabs on their children traveling aboard. One of them arrives home sick? It's probably something Immigration sees at least once a month. And you need to remember, Mr. Harper, this is Thailand, not the States. Government officials are keenly aware of where the money is in this country, and the only attention they want to bring to themselves is that they've been very helpful."

"What about tracking down the van?" Logan asked. "Is that something you can do?"

She didn't answer, but instead looked like she was contemplating how she wanted to respond.

Finally, Logan shook his head and said, "I don't understand why you seem reluctant to help me."

"I want to help you. I'm just not sure whether I should or

not."

"Why is that even a question? Dev must have made it clear what was going on. The girl they have, she's being used as a pawn by the Burmese government to keep her mother from speaking out against them. She's just a kid. A college student. She didn't do anything wrong."

"Do you have actual proof that the Myanmar government's responsible for taking her?" she asked.

The expression on the face of the man in the black shirt soured for a moment, then returned to neutral.

"I don't," Logan admitted. "But her grandfather is convinced that's what happened, and the fact that she was brought here, within a hundred miles of the border, is enough to convince me he's probably right. What's going to happen to her if they take her over there?"

Again, he sensed something in the longer-haired man. A tension. But if Christina noticed, she made no mention of it.

"Don't get me wrong," she said. "I'm not a fan of the generals. They're oppressors and killers, we all know that. But things are delicate over here. A wrong move could affect many other things that are also important."

Logan stood up. "I've obviously come to the wrong place. Thank you for your time."

He turned for the door, but Christina reached out and touched his hand. "Mr. Harper, please. Sit back down."

He hesitated for a moment, then did as she asked.

She leaned toward him. "I've been lucky to have had a certain amount of success here. But to do that, I've had to create a reliable information network that stretches beyond the borders of Thailand. I have people in Cambodia, Vietnam, Laos, Malaysia, Indonesia, China, and Myanmar...*Burma*. I have been told there is no chance the generals in Myanmar, no matter how crazy they are, would have sent people to the United States to kidnap anyone."

"I don't know what to say," Logan told her, shaking his head. "I don't have the proof, but, honestly, I don't care if it's them or not. I just want to get the girl back. I promised her grandfather, and I'm not going to let him down. So, please, I'm asking you for your help."

He locked eyes with her, daring her to tell him no.

After several seconds, she frowned, and stood up. "The truth is, Mr. Harper, I can't help you."

His shoulders sagged. He was about to ask her why she bothered bringing him here, when she motioned to the man in the black shirt.

"But I think my friend Daeng here can."

26

"WE'LL LEAVE you two alone," Christina said, then motioned for Mr. Prem to follow her back to the door they entered through.

As soon as they were gone, Daeng held out his hand. "Don't expect me to call you Mr. Harper."

Logan was surprised. He had assumed Daeng was Thai, but the man's accent was pure American. They shook hands. "You can call me Logan."

Daeng must have sensed the confusion in Logan's voice, because he smiled and said, "Hollywood High, class of '99."

"You're not from Thailand?"

"I am. But that's not what you're asking, is it? I was born here, but went to live with an aunt in Thai Town in Los Angeles when I was just a kid. I'm Thai on my dad's side. My mom?" He held Logan's gaze for a moment. "She was Burmese."

Logan realized that explained Daeng's reactions earlier while Christina had been talking about Burma. Hopefully, it would make Daeng more motivated to lend a hand. "So can *you* help me track down the van?"

Daeng smiled. "And here I thought you were going to give

me a challenge."

As they stepped onto the sidewalk in front of Christina's place, a car that had been parked down the street drove over and stopped at the curb. The driver jumped out, and opened the back door. He had the same tough look as Daeng, only with much shorter hair.

Daeng let Logan enter first, then he slid in after him. Before the driver had even climbed back behind the wheel, Daeng was unbuttoning his shirt. "She likes us to dress up when we talk business. I refuse to wear a suit, but I figure I can at least wear one of these."

As Daeng pulled off his shirt, Logan noticed that his upper body was covered in colorful tattoos—a tiger on his shoulder, a serpent wrapped around one arm, and, taking up much of his back, the Buddha.

The driver handed back a T-shirt, and Daeng pulled it on. On the front was a picture of Einstein sticking out his tongue.

"So where are we going?" Logan asked as they sped down the street.

"I don't really have as much use for Mr. Prem as Christina does, but sometimes he's helpful. He did get us the van's license number after all. Thought maybe we'd pay the owner a visit."

"You know where he lives?"

"I will soon enough."

Logan allowed himself to relax a little. He wasn't at a dead end. This was exactly the kind of help he needed.

The streets were now much easier to get around than when Logan had taken his little suicide ride through the city on the back of the motorcycle. In fact, Daeng's driver seldom had to slow at all, except at lights. Logan was even getting used to the feel of riding on the opposite side of the road from the one back home. Thailand, like several Asian nations, drove British style.

They were on the road for a little more than five minutes when Daeng received a call. When he finished, he said, "The van's owner lives way out on *Sukhumvit*. It's going to take us a little while to get there, so if you want to nap, this would be a good time."

Any lingering effects Logan had been feeling from the sleeping pill had been completely negated by the evening's events. He was wide awake. "I'm fine."

Daeng shrugged. "Your call."

Logan stared out the window, watching the city go by. It appeared most people had finally packed it in for the night, but every once in a while he'd see a couple of street vendors still set up along a sidewalk, surrounded by customers enjoying a late-night meal.

After a little while, he glanced at Daeng. "You, uh, work for Christina?"

Daeng grunted a laugh. "No. Sometimes our paths cross, that's all."

"What is it she does?"

"A little bit of everything, I think. She's been here forever. Knows everyone, knows what buttons to push and which asses to kiss." Daeng smiled. "How old do you think she is?"

"I don't know. Forty-seven, forty-eight. Something like that."

"Sixty-one."

"You're *kidding*." Not that Logan thought sixty-one was particularly old anymore, but she hadn't looked even close to that.

"Not kidding. I think she has a plastic surgeon on retainer, but don't quote me on that. She's been here since the war."

"The Vietnam War?" Logan asked, surprised again.

Daeng nodded.

"She couldn't have been much out of high school," Logan said.

"The way I heard it, that would be about right."

"What, exactly, did you hear?"

Daeng hesitated for a moment, then said, "Apparently she had a brother in the Army who'd gone MIA. She came here because it was the closest she could get to the war. She used to hang out in places where soldiers took R&R, trying to find someone who might have heard something about her brother. She even paid a few of them to try and find him. One guy did it for free. He was the one who found him. But by that point her brother was only dog tags and bones. After that, instead of going back to the States, she just stayed."

"I wonder why she stayed."

Daeng shrugged. "I heard this story from someone else. Christina never talks about her past, at least not to me. Maybe none of it's true."

A little further on, the driver slowed, then said something to Daeng. They talked back and forth for several seconds, then the driver moved into the right lane and made a U-turn at the next break. Keeping his speed low, he moved all the way over to the left.

Daeng said something, pointed ahead, then said to Logan, "It's just down that *soi*."

At first Logan wasn't sure what he meant, then the car turned on a small road—a *soi*, he guessed—and drove half a block down before stopping at the curb.

Daeng looked past him out the window. "That's it." He nodded at the building across the street.

All three of them got out and crossed over to it.

The apartment they were looking for was on the third floor. Logan was surprised when they got there to find three men waiting in the hallway outside the apartment's door. There were several hushed greetings, and he quickly realized these men were with Daeng.

One of them rushed ahead, and instead of knocking on the door, he just opened it.

Daeng went in first with Logan right behind. They passed through a small entryway and into a living room. On a couch was a short, doughy man who couldn't have been more than forty.

He was dressed in a white T-shirt and a pair of boxer shorts. He looked nervous.

There were two more of Daeng's men in the room. One was standing near the couch, while the other was in a doorway that led to the rest of the apartment.

Daeng spoke in Thai, and the man in the doorway answered. Seemingly satisfied, Daeng led Logan over to where the pudgy man was sitting.

"You speak English?" he asked the man.

"*Nitnoy*," the man said nervously. "A little."

"Okay, then we'll talk in English."

The man eyed Logan for a moment, then looked back at Daeng. "Please no hurt me. Me, my family, we do nothing."

"No one's planning on hurting you." The guy looked like he didn't understand, so Daeng spoke in Thai, translating what he'd already said, Logan assumed. The man responded in kind, but Daeng shook his head. "English, remember?"

Logan leaned over to Daeng and whispered, "His family's here?"

"Wife and son in back."

Suddenly Logan didn't feel so comfortable about the situation.

"You have a van you rent?" Daeng asked the man.

"Have two van."

"Okay, two then. You drive one of them?"

"Yes."

"And the other?"

"My wife brother."

"Which one of you picked up the group at the airport today?"

"We both at airport today."

"I'm talking about the people who came in on the small plane. With the girl who was sick."

The man looked even more nervous now.

"Was that you?" Daeng asked.

"Ye…yes. Was me."

"Good. I want to know where you took them."

"I…I…"

"Is there a problem? You had to take them somewhere, didn't you? Where was it?"

The man's gaze shot back and forth between Daeng and Logan, then he began speaking rapidly in Thai. At the end he seemed to be repeating himself, pleading.

"What's he saying?" Logan asked.

"He says the people he gave the ride to made him promise to say nothing about them or where they went. They said if they found out he did, they would kill him and his family."

"Yes, yes!" the owner said. "Please. Cannot say. Please understand. Have family."

Logan could see that Daeng was about to start in again, so he quickly said, "Let me."

He crouched down in front of the owner of the van, lowering himself so that they were eye to eye. "No one wants to hurt you or your family, okay?"

The man just stared at him, his eyes full of terror.

"The sick girl who was with the people you picked up, they kidnapped her." Logan could instantly see the man didn't understand. "Took her. Against her will." There was still incomprehension in the man's eyes.

Logan looked back at Daeng, who then said something very quickly in Thai.

The man's eyes widened as he realized what Logan had meant.

"I need to find her. I need to bring her home to *her* family. You understand?"

The man nodded.

"We need to know where you took them. You have to tell us."

The man began shaking his head violently. "No. No. My family. Cannot."

"But the girl has a family, too."

The man closed his eyes and continued to shake his head.

Logan stood back up. He'd thought for sure he'd been getting through to him. "There's got to be some way to get him to tell us," he said to Daeng.

Daeng turned so that his back was to the man. "We could rough up his wife and kid."

"Absolutely not!" Logan said. That was one road he would never go down.

"I was actually kidding. This guy's done nothing but get hired by the people you're looking for. I don't hurt the innocent."

Logan relaxed a little. "Sorry."

"My fault, not yours," he said. "I have an idea that might work, though."

Daeng turned back, then began speaking to the man in Thai. Logan could see some of the man's tension fade. The van owner asked a few questions. Daeng answered two of them, then looked at Logan after the third.

"I've offered to put them someplace where I can guarantee their safety until this is over. He's open to that, but…"

"Yes?"

"The vans are his only means of income. If he's not working, he's not making any money."

Logan nodded. Here was a problem he could solve. "I can cover the rental fees."

"I thought you might be able to." Daeng turned back to the man and relayed the information.

For the first time the guy smiled and began to look like he was no longer worried he was about to die. He spoke with Daeng for another minute, then got up and went into the back room.

"Come on," Daeng said, then headed for the front door.

"He told you where they are?"

"He told me where he took them."

"Great."

Daeng hesitated, then said, "Maybe."

27

LOGAN AND Daeng spent another twenty minutes traveling through town before they got out of the car again. They
were under what appeared to be a long concrete bridge, in an
area populated with more apartment buildings.

"Skytrain," Daeng said, following Logan's gaze up at the
bridge. "Public train. Runs above the city."

There didn't seem to be any trains operating at the moment.

Logan came around one of its support pillars, and was surprised to see a wide, dark river off to their left.

Daeng started walking toward it. "This way."

There was a gentle breeze coming off the water, making the
warm, humid night almost pleasant. Daeng stopped on a sidewalk near the river's edge. Beyond it was a wide cement area, with
a pair of ramps that sloped down to an empty dock.

"The van owner said this is where he dropped them off,"
Daeng said.

"Where, exactly, are we?"

"Sathorn Pier."

"So from here, where would they have gone?" Logan asked.

"Anywhere along the Chao Phraya."

The Chao Phraya, that was a name Logan remembered from his previous trip. It was the royal river that split the city in two.

"So they could be anywhere."

"Sure, but the choice is odd. Why even use the river? The van owner said they didn't take one of the public ferries, or even hire a boat once they got here. He said there was a boat already waiting for them." Daeng paused, then said, "The only thing I can think of is that they *needed* to use the river."

That thought had crossed Logan's mind, too. It was either that, or they had used the river to cover their tracks in case they were worried about being followed. But it seemed to Logan that moving from car to boat and boat to car again with such a large group that included one incapacitated girl would have attracted unwanted attention, doing the exact opposite of helping them disappear.

"Okay, so what would they have needed it for?" he asked.

"Maybe a hotel?" Daeng suggested. "There are a few along the waterfront."

Logan shook his head. A group like that, checking into a big hotel? Same unwanted-attention problem.

"They could have been meeting someone at another pier," Daeng offered.

"Possibly. But then, why not just drive there?"

Daeng looked down the waterfront. "There are also a lot of private residences along the river, apartment buildings, shacks. Nothing that's particularly fancy, but some do have docks, and a few are actually built over the river, so depending on the type of boat they were in, they could have gone right underneath."

Logan thought about it for a moment, then nodded. "That makes more sense to me."

"Don't get too excited," Daeng told him. "There's miles of riverfront here, and thousands of places for people to live in. It might take us weeks to figure out which one they're using, and chances are they're going to be gone by morning."

Logan grimaced. Daeng was right, of course. "What would you do in their situation?"

"I wouldn't be in their situation," Daeng said. "I don't kidnap people."

"Hypothetically. You'd be concerned about security, right?"

"Sure."

"Would you be concerned enough to have guards posted around the clock?"

Daeng considered it for a second, then nodded. "I would."

"Yeah," Logan said. "So would I."

"Okay, so they're being careful. How does that help us?"

"If it was the middle of the day right now, or even the evening, I'd say it wouldn't help us at all. But it's three a.m. The river's quiet. The streets are mostly empty. If we were ever going to notice someplace being guarded, wouldn't this be the best time?"

"You want to go out on the river? Right now?"

"Tell me that I'm wrong."

Daeng paused, then said, "No. You're not wrong. It's a good idea. The noise from a boat motor might stir them up, too. Make them easier to spot. Still, there's a very good chance we won't find them."

"I know, but we definitely won't find them if we just stand here."

Daeng nodded his head in agreement.

"I think our only problem is finding a boat at this hour," Logan said, frowning.

"In that, my friend, you're mistaken."

Daeng led them down to the dock, then drew in a deep breath and let out an ear-piercing whistle.

At first, there didn't seem to be any reaction, then some voices drifted over the water from off to their left—two people, it sounded like, talking to each other. Suddenly a motor started up, and a few seconds later, a Thai longboat emerged out of the darkness.

The boat looked just like its name implied—long and narrow. Over a dozen people could fit on board, but no more than two side by side. Like the longboats Logan remembered from his first trip to Thailand, its motor was a big monster of a thing that hovered above the rear of the vessel. On the water side, a pole ran out from the motor to a propeller mounted at the end. On the boat side, the pilot used a shorter pole to steer the craft by moving the whole engine in whichever direction he wanted to go.

The boat's pilot was all skin and bones, and hadn't bothered straightening his hair after Daeng's whistle had woken him up. But he was smiling as he pulled up to the dock, and seemed genuinely pleased to have customers as he gestured for them to get in.

Daeng instructed his man who'd driven the car to stay on shore, then he and Logan stepped onto the boat.

"Two choices," Daeng said, as he took the plank seat behind Logan. "Up river or down."

"This is your city. What do you think?"

"Up."

"Then we go up."

Daeng related the instructions to the pilot, and they motored out onto the river.

Though the Chao Phraya was quiet, it wasn't silent. There were a few boats moving up and down it. Most were smaller crafts with people fishing off the sides. But there was one group of three gigantic black barges moving down the center of the waterway toward the ocean, their progress guided by a small but powerful tugboat. Logan could also see black patches moving along the surface at a steady pace. They looked to him like clumps of vegetation, but were too far away for him to know for sure.

Their pilot followed the curve of the shoreline, keeping

them no more than a hundred feet from land. Daeng had been right. The riverfront was packed with structures that came right up to, and sometimes over, the water. The buildings were mainly apartments, some of them with what amounted to metal stacks hanging off the backs.

If Bangkok had been in the U.S., developers would have long ago bought up all the property, torn down what was there, and turned it into high-priced real estate with shops and restaurants and five-star hotels. Logan could see a little of that happening here. There were a few hotels that boasted their own piers, and looked like they'd set you back plenty of Thai *baht* for a night's stay. But these he could count on one hand. Mostly, it was basic apartment living. Nothing fancy at all.

As they trolled along, Logan and Daeng watched the shore, focusing not so much on the buildings themselves as on any out-of-place movements.

"How far up do you think they could have gone?" Logan asked.

"Technically, they could have gone miles."

"I assume there are multiple piers?"

"Dozens."

Logan frowned. "Then wouldn't it make sense that they'd choose a pier closer to their destination?"

"To me, it would."

"So, if that were the case, they've got to be pretty close."

"*If* that's what they did."

"Yeah, if," Logan said. "But we have to narrow things down. We can't cover everything before it starts getting busy again. So that's as good a target as any."

Daeng pointed further up the river. "There are a couple of piers over there, harder to get to from the land side. So let's say they could have gone as far as four piers away. After that, if it were me, I would have started somewhere else."

"Let's make it five just to be safe," Logan said, "then we'll swing around and hit the other side."

As Daeng let the pilot know the plan, a thought came to Logan.

He looked at Daeng, and nodded toward the pilot. "Do you think Sathorn Pier's his home base? I mean, he was sleeping there."

"Probably."

"You think maybe he was around when the others got onto their boat?"

Daeng looked at him, surprised. "That's an excellent question." He talked with the pilot for nearly a minute, then said, "He wasn't there, but he says his friend told him about a group of *farang* that had rented a boat ahead of time, and left the pier early yesterday afternoon. He says they headed this way."

"Does he know where they went?"

Daeng shook his head.

"At least we know we're going in the right direction," Logan said.

"If he's talking about the same group."

Logan was silent for a moment. "We're playing with a lot of ifs here."

"I wasn't going to point that out."

They talked very little over the next several minutes. Twice they saw people sitting at the back of buildings, smoking cigarettes, but neither instance appeared suspicious.

Daeng pointed at a spot about a couple of hundred yards ahead. "That's the fourth pier."

Logan tried not to think about it, but it was clear his plan wasn't working. Chances were they'd already passed the place. And if he couldn't find them, how was he ever going to—

"Do you hear that?" Daeng asked.

Logan listened. It took him a moment, but then he heard it. The sound was at almost the same pitch as their engine, but its rhythm was just slightly off.

"Another boat?" he asked.

Daeng nodded.

They scanned the river ahead.

"There," Logan said a half minute later.

About fifty yards ahead, and very tight to the shore, was the dim shape of a longboat. He watched it for a moment, then decided it was probably just another local out for some early morning fishing.

"I think he's headed downriver," Daeng said.

Logan returned to his search, wondering if they should just turn around and head back to the car.

Several seconds passed, then Daeng said, "Logan?"

He was staring at the other longboat. It was almost directly in line with them now, moving in the opposite direction, closer to shore. The building it was passing was all lit up, spilling its light onto the boat's two occupants—a pilot and a solo passenger in the middle. And not just any passenger, either. A lanky and young farang passenger.

Ryan.

Logan turned away so he wouldn't be spotted. "That's one of them," he whispered.

There was a moment of silence, then Daeng said, "Apparently so." He shouted something at their pilot, and their speed suddenly picked up.

"Why did you—" Logan stopped himself.

The other boat had also picked up speed, and had turned toward them.

"Hold on!" Daeng yelled.

Their pilot took a sudden turn to the left toward the center of the river. Warm water sprayed over the side, hitting Logan in the shoulder and face, but he barely noticed. He was focused on the dark shape of the other boat as it continued to follow them.

Their pilot shouted something, then Daeng yelled back. Whatever Logan's new friend had said, the look on the pilot's face went from looking pissed off to subservient in a flash.

Without warning, their boat swerved to the right then back to the left. Logan grabbed both sides so he wouldn't fall out as they tilted through the turns. Glancing at the water, he could see they'd just gone around a wide patch of vegetation, this one a tangle of vines and leaves that actually seemed to be alive, not just a flotilla of castoff branches rotting on the water.

The other boat had either a better engine than theirs or a better pilot, because it was definitely closing in.

"We need to go faster!" Logan yelled over the sound of the motor.

Daeng shook his head. "The pilot said that's all it's got."

Just then something hit the boat about four feet in front of Logan, creating a small hole in the sidewall.

He pointed at the damage. "Daeng! They're shooting at us!"

Daeng leaned sideways so he could look around Logan and see what he was talking about. But before he could say anything, his hand flew up and grabbed the side of his head. At the same instant, Logan heard something rip through the air a foot to his left.

Daeng doubled over, his face wincing in pain as he pressed his fingers against his head.

Logan looked back at their pilot, and pointed to the right. "That way! Now!"

He didn't know if the guy understood his words, but the pilot got the gist of Logan's motion. He shoved the steering pole around, sending up a rooster tail of water as the boat whipped through the turn.

"Back and forth," Logan said, pointing in one direction, then the other. Up to that point, they'd been too much of a stationary target. They had to keep changing directions.

He leaned down next to Daeng, not waiting to see if the pilot did as he instructed. He could hear Daeng breathing heavily.

"Where did it hit you?"

He was trying to see the wound, but Daeng had twisted his head so the injury was facing down, out of Logan's view.

The pilot suddenly screamed out.

Looking back, Logan saw that the man had scrunched down behind the bulk of the engine, one hand hanging onto the steering pole. Though he looked frightened, he didn't appear to be hurt. Before Logan turned away, the pilot screamed again as a bullet smacked into the engine, sending a couple of sparks into the air.

Logan looked back at Daeng. "How bad is it?"

Daeng took a deep breath, then lifted his head. "I'm fine!"

"Let me see."

Daeng turned, and moved his hand. The side of his head was covered in blood, making it impossible to see where the wound was.

Glancing around, Logan spotted a bottle of water back near the pilot.

"Throw me that," he said, pointing at it.

The pilot didn't move.

"Throw it to me!" This time he emphasized his words by jabbing his finger at the bottle.

Reluctantly, the pilot picked it up and tossed it over.

"Don't keep us going in one line," Logan said, pantomiming again to remind him.

He then cracked open the bottle and poured it over the side of Daeng's head. Once the blood was cleared away, he could see that a bullet had torn through the upper part of Daeng's ear, creating a flap that extended from the back of the helix almost all the way to the front. If it had taken another quarter inch with it, the whole top of the ear would have been gone.

"It's not pretty," Logan told him. "You're going to need to get it stitched up when we get back, but you're going to be fine." He pulled off his shirt and placed it over the wound. "Press this against it."

Daeng didn't look like he really wanted to, but he did it just the same.

Logan glanced up and saw that they were now on the opposite side of the river from where they'd started, but still heading north. He scanned ahead, hoping for a wharf or canal or anything that they might be able to use to their advantage. He was just starting to turn back when a large, shadowy form moving steadily down the center of the river caught his eye.

"What's that?" he asked.

Daeng looked over. "A barge, I think." There was controlled pain in his tone.

Logan watched for another second. Yes, a barge, just like the ones he'd seen earlier. And if there was one barge, then there was probably at least one more tethered behind it.

Logan could see the tug now, too. It had a few dim lights on and looked tiny in comparison.

"Tell the pilot to head over there," Logan said. "We can use it as cover."

Daeng yelled back the instructions, but instead of the boat turning, the engine started to rev down. Daeng yelled again, but the man's response was short, and though Logan couldn't understand the words, he was pretty sure he knew what the guy meant: "Go to hell!"

Their pilot then put a foot on the edge of the boat, and jumped into the water.

28

AS THEIR pilot started to swim away, Logan looked back and saw Ryan's boat closing fast.

He started to scramble back toward the engine to get it going again, but Daeng moved first. The motor suddenly roared back to life, and they shot away from the shore.

"Do you know what you're doing?" Logan yelled.

"I sure as hell hope so."

They were headed straight for the barge now, with the other boat a lot closer to them than Logan preferred.

"Can't you go any faster?"

By the look Daeng gave him, Logan was pretty sure they were going as fast as they could.

A searchlight on the tugboat flicked on, illuminating the water in front of them. Daeng whipped the boat to the left, running alongside the barge and staying out of reach of the spot. But Ryan's boat turned a few seconds too late, and the light caught them. Several people yelled across the water, and a horn on the tug blasted twice, but within seconds the other longboat was back in the dark, too.

As they raced past the first barge, Logan could now see that it wasn't a convoy of two but of three, each looking like a large football field on a raised, black pedestal, gliding through the water. Just before they reached the halfway point of the second one, Daeng shouted, "Hang on. I'm going to try something."

Logan was already hanging on, so he tightened his grip and hoped whatever Daeng was going to do would work.

Less than five seconds later, Daeng cut the engine way back, and swung the boat around so that it looked like they were going to ram right into the side of the barge. But suddenly the bulky vessel in front of them was replaced by the gap between it and the third barge. Daeng gunned the engine, shooting them through the quickly closing space and onto the other side.

Logan looked back. The other boat hadn't been able to turn in time. They were going to have to go all the way around the third barge.

Daeng turned their boat so that they were traveling in the same direction as the barges, only faster. On their right, the gap they'd shot through was coming up again. Logan nearly lost his balance as Daeng whipped them back through to the other side.

"A little warning would have been nice!" he shouted.

"Sorry!" Daeng replied.

As they emerged, they could see the tail end of Ryan's boat disappearing around the back of the third barge. Daeng turned them south, then matched their speed to the convoy.

For several minutes, they continued on in this way, their presence masked by the massive barge at their side. Logan constantly scanned in both directions, ready to shout out if the other boat reappeared. Finally, Daeng lifted the propeller out of the water, and they slowed until they were simply moving with the current.

Beside them, the dark hulks moved by, until the third barge passed and they were alone in the river again. Daeng dipped the propeller back in the water, and aimed them across the wake toward the other side. Then, just as they were clearing the first of the swells, the sound of another engine cut through the night.

Ryan's boat.

"You've got to be kidding me!" Logan yelled.

Apparently, Ryan and his pilot had been doing the same thing Logan and Daeng had, only on the other side of the barge. Now they were headed straight at them.

The pilot of the other boat yelled across the short distance between them.

"He wants us to stop," Daeng said.

"Don't!"

Daeng kept them moving forward as fast as possible, the front of the boat flying out of the water, then bouncing hard against the river with each swell.

As the other pilot yelled at them again, Logan saw something directly in front of their boat. "Watch out!"

But his warning came too late. By the time Daeng started to turn, they had already traveled into one of the floating islands of vegetation. Logan heard the propeller chew on some of the vines, then catch and stop cold, killing the engine at once.

The other boat slowed as it approached, then stopped beside them, just outside the vine trap. Logan kept his back to them, hoping they could somehow get out of this without Ryan getting a look at him. Because if that happened, and Ryan reported back that Logan was here, the people who had Elyse might decide it was time to cut their losses and make her disappear forever.

"You speak English?" Ryan asked.

"Little," Daeng said, falling easily into a Thai accent.

"What about your friend there?"

"No speak."

"What were you looking for?"

"Looking for? *Mai khao jai.* Don't understand."

There was a pause, then Ryan asked, "What were you doing?"

"Doing? Fishing. On boat."

"I don't see any fishing equipment."

"Fall out when you chase us."

"Right. Sure. What were you doing?"

"I tell you already," Daeng said.

"You there in the middle. What were you doing out here?"

Logan didn't move.

"Hey, I bet you *do* speak English. Tell me what you were doing! You were looking for something, weren't you? I could tell."

Logan continued to act like he couldn't hear him.

"Move us in closer," Ryan said to his pilot.

The motor on the other boat throttled up for a moment. A few seconds later, there was a bump, and the boat Logan was in rocked back and forth.

"Why were you out here?" Ryan said, his voice only a few feet away. "Hey. I'm talking to you. Turn around."

Logan continued to stare out at the water.

"Tell him to turn around," Ryan said.

The pilot spoke in Thai, relaying the command to Logan.

Slowly, Logan rose, his back still to Ryan.

"Turn around," Ryan commanded.

When he didn't move right away, Ryan grabbed Logan's shoulder, then pulled at him. Logan resisted for a moment, then finally turned.

A second passed before recognition flashed across Ryan's eyes. "What the hell? *You?*"

"I thought we agreed you wouldn't do anything stupid again," Logan said, then slugged him in the gut.

He'd hoped the blow would send Ryan over the side of his boat, but Ryan caught himself, then swung his gun around, its barrel making a quick arc that would end with its muzzle pointed at Logan's chest. Before that could happen, though, Logan leaped at him.

There was no way for Ryan to stop their combined momentum this time. He went into the river, and Logan went with him.

They plunged several feet beneath the dark, muddy surface, their arms intertwined. Logan tried to push Ryan away, but Ryan fought back, using his gun as a club. He landed one blow, but on his second try it slipped from his hand, and fell toward the riverbed.

His lungs screaming for air, Logan pushed away from Ryan, then broke the surface, gasping. A second later, Ryan came up, too.

He took a few rapid breaths, then said, "How the hell did you find us?"

"Where's Elyse, Ryan?" Logan asked.

"Nowhere you'll find her."

"Where is she?"

Ryan started to laugh, but it quickly died in his throat as Logan began swimming toward him. He immediately started moving away, but he was a mediocre swimmer at best and no match for Logan. He seemed to sense this, because just before Logan got to him, he stopped.

Pulling up just short of Ryan's reach, Logan began treading water. "You're coming with us. I don't want to hurt you, but if I have to, I will."

The arrogant laugh was back. "You don't get it. I already reported in that I was pursuing a suspicious boat. The others are out looking for me now. They'll probably be here before we even get out of the water."

"Which way did you tell them we were going?" Logan asked. "North?"

Ryan said nothing.

"Take a look around. You see those lights right over there?" Logan pointed at the east shore. "That's right about where you originally spotted us. We're already past that point now. This current's moving pretty quickly, too. In a few minutes we won't be able to even see them anymore. And your friends? They'll just keep going in the other direction."

Ryan tried to keep his face blank, but he was doing a bad job of it.

"We're going to swim back to the boats, and you're going to come with us," Logan said.

Ryan looked at him for a moment, then gave a reluctant nod.

As they neared the boats, Logan saw that Daeng had moved into the one with the working motor.

"Where's the pilot?" Logan called out, not seeing the guy who'd been with Ryan.

"Swam off right after you two fell in."

Suddenly concerned, Logan said, "Which way did he go? We've got to get him before he gets to shore. If he tells them about us…"

"Don't worry," Daeng said. "He won't. He'll be concerned they'd blame him for you getting away. I guarantee you he'll lie low until they're gone."

This didn't completely relax Logan. "I hope you're right."

"I am."

As Ryan neared the boat, Logan said, "Get in."

"You should let me go," Ryan told him. "I promise, I won't say anything to anyone."

"Get in the boat."

"Come on. What are you going to do, huh? Beat me up? No matter what, I'm not going to tell you anything."

Logan swam in closer. "Get. In. The. Boat."

Ryan glanced down at the water, resigned. As he turned and reached out, Logan thought he was going to grab the hull and pull himself in, but instead he put his hand on the side and pushed himself under.

Logan immediately dove after him, then blindly reached out, grasping at the area where he thought Ryan might be. His fingers brushed against a pant leg, but it quickly slipped away. He swam beneath the hull, and reached out again. This time he got a hold of Ryan's foot for half a second before it kicked out, making him lose his grip.

The breath he'd taken before going under had been a quick one, and as he passed under the bottom of the boat, he could feel his air running out. He found the hull with his hand, then followed it up until his head broke the surface between the two longboats.

As he breathed, he looked for Ryan, but there was no sign of him.

"Did I miss him? Did he come up?" he yelled at Daeng.

"I haven't seen him."

Logan had to find him. Unlike the pilot, Ryan would definitely go back to the others. He expelled all his air, then took as deep a breath as he could, and went back under.

He knew Ryan had to have come up for air somewhere. There must have been a break in the vines, or perhaps there was space on the other side of the boat that Daeng and Logan had been on. That was something he could check.

He passed under the hull of the second boat, then felt his way back toward the surface, but he was blocked before he could get there by a solid wall of vines. No way Ryan could have come up there.

Just as Logan was about to move his hand off of the vines, he felt several unnatural tugs. He tried to get a fix on which direction they had come from, then pushed back down, and propelled himself under the floating island.

He used one arm to power his swim, and the other to search for Ryan. For the first few seconds, the only things he touched were stray vines dangling down below the mass. Then the back of his hand knocked against something definitely not vine-like. As he turned his wrist to get a better angle on it, it pulled away, but not before he got the impression he'd come in contact with a leg.

His lungs weren't burning yet, but he was quite a ways under the vines, so he needed to make sure he saved enough time to swim back to open water. He decided to allow himself fifteen more seconds, then reached out again to see if Ryan was still nearby.

Once more he found a leg, but instead of kicking him off again, Ryan let him grab hold this time. He then pulled his leg up in a tuck, bringing Logan to him. Logan was about to let go, worried that Ryan was just drawing him in so he could kick him in the head, but then Ryan grabbed desperately at his wrist, and seemed to be urging Logan to pull him.

Logan did, but was only able to move him a foot before Ryan stopped with a jerk. He tried again, but the result was the same.

Heat slowly began building at the bottom of Logan's lungs. Ignoring it, he swam in closer, and felt along Ryan's torso and up to his shoulders. That's when he discovered what was wrong.

Ryan's arm was entangled in the vines.

Logan ran his hands rapidly across them, attempting to find a way to free him.

Suddenly Ryan began thrashing. Logan began working faster, pulling at the vines, and ripping them from underneath.

Ryan jerked. Once. Twice. Then he stopped moving completely.

Logan kept at it even as his lungs began screaming to stop what he was doing and get to the surface.

He yanked on a clump of vines, then suddenly Ryan's arm fell free.

Quickly he grabbed Ryan around the shoulders, then he swam out from under the vegetation, and up to the river's surface. As soon as his head broke through the water, he sucked in as much air as he could.

"Daeng!" he yelled. "Over here."

He couldn't see the boat, but he knew it had to be nearby.

"Daeng!"

He propped Ryan's head on his shoulder, painfully aware he wasn't breathing. Not far away he heard the longboat's motor kick in. As soon as Daeng pulled beside him, they got Ryan onto the boat, and Logan flopped in after him.

Logan had learned CPR in the Army, and had unfortunately been in the position to use it more than once. Starting in on Ryan, he was hopeful, because of the kid's age and physical condition, that he could bring him back. But after nearly ten minutes, he realized it was no use.

Ryan was dead.

Daeng waited a few seconds, then said, "Let's put him back in the water."

"The water? Why?" Logan asked.

"You're after the girl, not him. If someone sees you with the body and the police find out, they're going to ask questions. You'll be detained. Can you afford that?"

No, Logan thought. It was just like with Anthony. He would have to let someone else deal with it.

Carefully, they rolled the body over the side, and dumped Ryan into the Chao Phraya. Logan heard Daeng whispering under his breath, then realized that he was praying. He thought maybe he should do the same, too, but no prayer came to mind.

When he looked at the river again, Ryan was gone.

29

THOUGH LOGAN and Daeng had narrowed down the part of the riverfront where Elyse was most likely being held, they still had no idea of her exact location. They decided their best bet was to encircle the area with watchers—two crews in longboats "fishing" on the river, and ten other men scattered in an arc on the land side. Daeng thought he could drum up maybe four to six additional men who could roam the area, and try to pick up leads from the people who lived in the neighborhood.

As much as Logan didn't want to, the thing he needed to do was get a few hours of sleep. Daeng promised to call the instant anything happened, then dropped him off in front of his hotel.

Though it was the phone that woke Logan four hours later, it wasn't Daeng on the other end. It was Ruth.

"Where exactly are you?"

"Huh?" Logan said, still half asleep. "What are you talking about?"

"You left the country, didn't you?"

"Is that a problem?" Before she could reply, he said, "Wait. Just give me a second." He pulled himself out of bed, and carried the phone into the bathroom where he splashed some water on his face. Once he felt his brain starting to work again, he put the phone back to his ear. "What's going on, Ruth?"

"I had an…unexpected conversation this afternoon." It was still Friday evening in New York.

"Unexpected?"

"Forty-five minutes ago, Jon Jordan came into my office." Jordan was the C.O.O. of Forbus Systems International. He was the prick who'd been behind turning Logan into a scapegoat, though Logan could never prove that. "He wants to know why I was interested in Bracher Schwartz and Associates."

Logan tried to place the name, but it was unfamiliar. "Who are they?"

"Bracher Schwartz is a New York law firm. The same firm that was involved with setting up the shell companies that included Kajiwara Research. Remember them? Your friends who chartered that jet?"

She had his attention now. "This law firm, they're real? Not a shell?"

"Very real, and, apparently, very well connected. One of the senior partners plays golf with Mr. Jordan."

"Well, that's…interesting. Do you think the shell companies lead back to Forbus?"

"If they did, I certainly wouldn't be calling you," she said. "But I did touch a nerve, that's for sure. Mr. Jordan was also curious why I was looking at our Burma files."

"You have a problem, Ruth. Someone's spying on you."

She huffed out a derisive breath. "They spy on all of us here. That's the nature of our business, remember?"

"Tell me more about this Bracher Schwartz place."

"Harper, I'm calling you to tell you I can't help you anymore."

He paused. "Look, I know I've put you in a bad spot, but I didn't mean to do that. Ruth…a young woman's life is in danger."

"What are you talking about?"

He hesitated again, then said, "She's been abducted."

"Abducted?"

"Yes."

"What about the authorities?"

"If they get involved, this girl won't see twenty-one."

"Are you just feeding me a line?"

"No. I'm not. You know I'd never do that."

"Dammit." She took a few seconds, then said, "Okay, here's the deal. This law firm handles a lot of international business. They have offices not just in New York, but in D.C., London, Geneva, and Singapore, too. They're deal makers."

"Do they do any business with the Burmese government?"

"Given your earlier request, I actually thought about that. But as far as I can tell, nothing. Burma's kind of a touchy area. It's actually illegal for U.S. firms to do business there. Well, technically, the Executive Order states that companies are not allowed to do business with the top people in the government or their families, but if you want to do business there, that's who you have to deal with."

Logan knew that didn't mean there weren't ways to work around it. "Did you happen to check if they actually had a Robert Andrews on staff?"

"I did, and they don't. But…"

"But what?"

A pause, then "Hold on, I'm going to text you a photo." He could hear her moving her phone around for several seconds. "There, sent. You should get it in a moment."

"What's the picture of?" he asked.

"I just want you to look at it first. It might be nothing."

Before he could ask anything more, his phone buzzed. He accessed the text, then touched the photo so it would fill his display. It was a group shot—two older men in front, a couple of younger guys to the side, and three others in the background.

They were on some steps leading down from a building.

He switched the phone to speaker so he could talk and view the picture at the same time. "Okay. So, what am I looking at?"

"The picture's from the *New York Times*. It's outside the Federal Courthouse in New York City. The two older gentlemen are Samuel Schwartz and Charles Bracher. The two others with them aren't important. I want you to look at the three in the back, specifically the guy on the right. You should be able to enlarge it enough."

He centered the person in question, increased the size of the photo, then stared at it for a moment. "That's him."

"Robert Andrews?"

"Yes. I'm sure of it."

"I was afraid of that."

"Who is he?"

Silence, then, "His real name is Scott Bell."

"He works for Bracher Schwartz?"

"Technically, he runs his own security firm. Of course, it *is* located in the same building as Bracher Schwartz's home office." She was quiet for a moment. "I went out on a limb, Logan. I talked to one of our people in New York. He says Bell handles all the firm's dirty work."

"Ruth, you didn't have to take that chance."

"It doesn't matter. It's already done."

"Do you trust this person enough that he won't tell anyone you talked to him?"

"He's a decent guy. He won't say anything."

"So which client is Bell doing work for now?"

"That, I don't know. But my friend did tell me who some of their clients are."

"Who?"

She let out a not-quite-tension-free laugh. "You have any openings at your garage? I might need a job after this."

"We'd be happy to have you."

She paused, then said, "One of their big clients is a Silicon Valley tech firm called Okomoto Systems. They specialize in mobile devices and applications. Then, of course, there's Laredyne Industries. You've heard of them."

He had. They were a defense contractor like Forbus. "What about their connection to Burma?"

"I didn't really look into them, but I doubt it. Again, it *would* be illegal."

"True, but how many times has Forbus gotten into gray areas overseas?" Logan asked.

"I'm sure I don't know what you're talking about."

He smirked. "What about other clients?"

"LRB Oil, H. Wick, a medical supply company out of Indianapolis, a regional fast food chain. That's about all I got at this point."

H. Wick? He'd heard that name recently. But why would a medical supply company be involved in—

Angie.

The company she had stolen the money from. Hadn't she said it was H. Wick Medical Supply? The company may very well not have been part of what was going on, but at the very least their attorneys—Bracher Schwartz—would have been aware of Angie's embezzlement. She would easily have become an asset they could exploit.

"Thank you, Ruth. You've done more than I could have ever hoped."

"You know, you never actually told me where you are."

"You sure you want to know?"

She paused. "Please tell me you're not in Burma."

"I'm *not* in Burma."

There was another pause. "You're in Thailand, aren't you? That plane."

"Yes."

"Be careful, okay? And...and I hope you find the girl."

"Me, too," he said, but by then she'd already hung up.

After he showered and got dressed, he looked at Bell's picture again.

A law-firm fixer with a penchant for kidnapping, and, if Logan was right, murder. What kind of game was he playing? And was this actually for the law firm, or was he acting for someone else entirely? The generals in Myanmar, perhaps? As ludicrous as that idea had been at one point, Logan felt it was a very real possibility now.

He called Daeng. "Sorry to wake you," he said as soon as Daeng picked up.

"You didn't. I just got off the phone with one of my men by the river."

"And?"

"Go downstairs. Someone will pick you up in a few minutes."

Knowing he needed to stay flexible, Logan brought his backpack with him as he headed out of the hotel. At the curb, he found the same motorcycle driver who'd taken him to Christina's the night before.

This time the ride only lasted fifteen minutes before the driver pulled to the curb a couple of blocks shy of the river, in an area where there seemed to be few other *farang* around.

Daeng was standing in the doorway of a pharmacy a few feet away, talking on his phone. There was a bandage on his injured ear, but otherwise he looked the same as he had the night before, save for the T-shirt. Einstein was out, and Bender, the robot from *Futurama*, was in.

As Logan walked over, Daeng nodded a hello, then held up a finger indicating he wouldn't be long.

When he hung up, Logan asked "What's going on?"

"We figured out what building they were in."

"*Were?*"

"That's the bad news," Daeng said. "Either they were already gone by the time my men were in place, or they snuck out this morning and we missed them."

Disappointed was not nearly a strong enough word for what Logan suddenly felt. "Is that possible?"

"Anything is possible," Daeng said. "But I chose my men carefully. It would have been very unusual for them to have missed anything. But there *is* good news. They're not *all* gone."

"What?"

"The girl and most of the others, they're not there anymore. But two *farang* men were still inside when we found the building."

"Did you detain them?"

Daeng shook his head. "Not yet. They're still there. Apparently, they're cleaning up."

Of course, Logan thought. Making sure there were no traces that they'd been there. Just like back in L.A.

"Do you want me to have my men move in?" Daeng asked.

Logan said nothing for a moment, thinking. If Daeng's people grabbed them now, who knew how long it might take to get them to divulge where Elyse was.

"No," he said. "We'll let them finish what they're doing, then follow them. In the meantime, get me as close as you can. I want to see exactly who was left behind."

30

LOGAN AND Daeng spent five and a half hours in an empty apartment across an intersection from the building Elyse had been held in.

More than once, Logan asked if it was possible that the men who were supposedly still there might have snuck out some other way. Each time, Daeng had dutifully checked, but the report would always come back that the men were still inside.

"I'm not sure I've actually told you thanks yet," Logan said after Daeng checked for him one more time. "Without you and your men, I don't know what I would have done."

Daeng shrugged. "You would have found her. You would have just done it a different way. You're more resourceful than you look."

"Thanks, I think."

"You're welcome."

"I'm serious, though," Logan said after a few seconds. "You've done a lot more than you needed to."

"I've done exactly what I needed to."

Logan looked at him. Daeng's eyes were focused through the window on the other building, but after a moment, he glanced over. "What?"

"That's just kind of an odd statement."

"Is it? Aren't you doing the same?"

The question surprised Logan. He was doing what he felt he had to do, but was it *exactly* what he had to do? Only if he were able to bring Elyse home alive. Otherwise, what he was currently doing would turn out not to be enough. Again.

Daeng seemed to sense Logan's discomfort. He smiled, then said, "How's the weather in L.A.?"

Logan looked out the window. "Nice when I left. Seventies."

"I miss that. Most of the time it doesn't even get down to seventy during the night here."

"How long were you in Los Angeles?"

Daeng was silent for a moment. "Almost ten years."

"You must have been young when you got there."

"Eight and a half."

Logan felt like he probably asked more than he should have, so he said nothing. But apparently he was wrong.

After a brief pause, Daeng said, "My mom had died three months before, and my dad...well, let's just say he wasn't cut out for raising a kid on his own. So he sent me off to live with his sister in the States."

On the street below, Logan watched a pickup truck drive by, mattresses stacked high in the back.

"I was fortunate, though," Daeng went on. "My aunt had loved my mom, so she made it a point for me to learn all I could about my Burmese background. My father would have never done that. My mother's people, *my* people...they haven't had it easy. The things the generals over there have done..." He gestured in what Logan assumed was the direction of Burma. "No one should do those things." He paused, then glanced over. "Would you believe I used to be a monk?"

"I thought I heard somewhere that all Thai men spend a few months being a monk."

Daeng waved a dismissive hand in the air. "I'm not talking about a temporary monk. I spent three years in that life. The temple I lived in was in a town several hours north of here. It was peaceful. At the time, I thought I would never do anything else. But in 2007, things changed. That fall, there were protests in Burma."

"I've read about them," Logan said.

"I felt moved by this, and thought that the time had finally come for my mother's people to free themselves. When I heard that the Burmese monks in Rangoon had taken up on the side of the people, and were actually leading the protests, I knew I couldn't just stay here in Thailand and do nothing. Against the wishes of my temple, I snuck across the border and made my way to Rangoon. I wanted to do what I could."

Like Tooney's wife.

"For two days I wore my robes and marched in the protests with my brother monks, and my mother's countrymen. There was an excitement in the air, a feeling that maybe we could actually change things this time. I stayed at a temple with over two hundred other monks right in the city, but since I had come late, and was the outsider, I was given floor space with three others in a room that was normally used as a classroom. The next day, all two hundred monks were going to go to a rally. It was to be the biggest yet. Only in the middle of the night, the secret police came." Daeng paused. "The first thing I heard was screaming from the hall where most of the monks were staying. Somehow the four of us in the classroom had been overlooked. I wanted to rush out and try to help, but the others held me back. They knew what would happen if I went out there. Many monks were hauled away that night and never seen again. If I'd opened that door, I would have been one of them.

"Instead, my friends led me out a back window and away from the temple. We found a family that gave us clothes so that we could change out of our robes, and hats so that we could try to cover our bald heads. Those three monks stayed with me all the way to the border. But they didn't cross with me. They wanted to make sure I got out, so I could let people know what had happened." He stopped again, his eyes watching the street, but Logan wasn't really sure which city he was actually seeing. "They went back to Rangoon to continue the fight. Two of them disappeared the next day. The other was crippled.

"When I came back here, I never put my robes on again. It wasn't some kind of protest or fear that the Myanmar secret police would find me. I was back in Thailand. There was nothing they could do to me. What made me quit was that moment in the temple in Rangoon while my brothers were screaming in pain, and the temple was filled with chaos. I wanted to rush out…yes, to help them, but I also wanted to hurt those who were hurting my fellow monks. I felt rage, and hatred, and it didn't go away when I returned. I knew I couldn't be a monk anymore.

"What I could do, though, was find other ways to help. Make some money on the black market here, send some much needed supplies there. Help smuggle out videos so the rest of the world could see what's happening over the border, and make sure the lines of communication were never severed. Of course, no matter how much I do, it's not enough."

He turned and looked at Logan. "This Elyse, she might be American, but she's also Burmese. We have to look out for one another, you know." After nearly a minute of silence he said, "What about you? Why are you doing this?"

Once more, Logan was caught off guard. Why was he doing this? First and foremost for Elyse, because she was in no position to help herself. And for Tooney, of course. And even for his father.

But he was also doing it for Carl.

And, ultimately, for the girl in the street.

"I'm helping a friend," he said, and left it at that.

Just after noon, Daeng's cell phone rang. He smiled as he talked and nodded at Logan.

"They're finishing up," he said when he was through.

They positioned themselves so that they had a clear view of the door they expected the men would use as an exit. Five minutes later, it opened, and the two men walked out, each carrying a large duffle bag.

"Recognize either of them?" Daeng asked.

"Both." The first was the guy who'd carried Elyse onto the airplane in Santa Monica. The second was the guy Logan assumed was Aaron Hughes.

"So we've got the right guys?"

"Definitely."

Logan and Daeng watched as the men flagged down a taxi, then hopped in. A few seconds after it took off again, a motorcycle taxi with one of Daeng's men on it followed. And three minutes after that, Logan and Daeng were doing the same in Daeng's car. They drove around for a half hour, then the driver, who'd been keeping in constant contact with the guy on the motorcycle, turned his head and spoke with Daeng.

"The cab pulled over, but only one of the men got out," Daeng translated. "I have people following both now, but which one do you want us to stick with?"

"The younger guy," Logan said, thinking of Aaron.

Daeng had a quick exchange with the driver, then said, "He's the one still in the taxi."

"Then we follow the taxi."

Logan checked his watch. It was just after 4:30. Who knew where Elyse was now? His only hope was that Aaron or the other guy would lead them to her.

A couple of minutes later, Aaron's taxi made a second stop.

"He's taken the duffle bags out, and entered a construction site," Daeng told Logan, relaying the information from the driver.

"Can you get us close enough so we can see?" Logan asked.

The driver took them to within a block of the structure. It was a ratty, unfinished building that looked like construction had stopped soon after they'd poured the concrete for each of the seven floors, and long before any interior work or walls on the outside had begun. Moss and dirt covered the pillars, while wild grass and bushes had been left to flourish across the lot. Logan got the impression that several people were making the place their not-so-temporary home.

Daeng took the phone from the driver so he could talk with his man on the scene. "He's gone all the way through the building to the open area in back," he said to Logan as he listened.

Logan looked ahead, straining to see, but that portion of the lot was out of sight.

"He's talking to someone...a squatter, it sounds like...my guy can't get close enough to hear the conversation...okay, the *farang* is handing over the duffle bags...the squatter's carrying them to...I guess there's a fire pit back there...he's putting the bags in the fire...the *farang's* watching...the bags are fully in flames now...okay, hold on, hold on...they're walking back toward the street and...the *farang* is handing him some money..."

Talk about thorough, Logan thought. Aaron and his friends were apparently not willing to just toss whatever they'd cleaned up into the trash. They wanted it burned. That was too bad. It would have been nice to see what was inside those bags.

"...he's heading back to the taxi now," Daeng finished.

Logan looked down the street. A few seconds later, Aaron came out from the building and climbed into his cab. The pursuit then continued as before.

The third stop was at a building that couldn't have been more different than the one Aaron had just visited. It was a modern-looking, glass business tower, twenty stories high. One of Daeng's men was able to get into the lobby just as the elevator doors closed on the car Aaron was in. The man watched the indicator. It stopped on the fourteenth floor, then headed back down.

"Send him up," Logan said, after Daeng asked him what he wanted to do.

According to the man, there were several different suites on the fourteenth floor: an import-export business, an accounting firm, and a few offices that were only marked with names of people.

"Make sure he doesn't give himself away," Logan warned.

Daeng shook his head. "He won't."

Suddenly he pressed the phone tightly against his ear, listening hard.

"I think the *farang* just came out of one of the offices. My man can't talk."

There was a tense several minutes when they didn't know what was happening, then Daeng said, "They're in the main lobby, heading out. He says another man came out of the office, too. A *farang* also. They both got on the elevator, and my man joined them."

"You're kidding," Logan said, concerned.

"It's okay. Standing in the hallway like he was, he'd have been more noticeable if he hadn't gotten on."

That may have been true, but it still had Logan worried.

"He says they didn't talk on the way down, but did give each other a little nod as they got out at the bottom. Also says our guy is now carrying a large envelope."

An envelope? Logan was very interested to see what was inside of that.

Daeng was silent for a moment, then said, "The two *farang* are outside now. The young guy is heading back to his taxi, but the other one is walking down the street. What do you want to do?"

"Your guy in the building, is he the only one other than us

following the cab?"

"No. There are three others."

Logan raised an eyebrow, impressed. "Then have him follow this new guy, and see where he goes. The rest of us will stay with the cab."

Suddenly they had quite an operation going. Along with the group following Aaron's taxi, there was a man tagging after the guy who'd gotten out of the cab before Aaron had burned the duffle bags, and now there was this new guy, too.

Logan's phone began to vibrate in his pocket. He frowned as he read the name on the display screen: DAD. Things were a little too crazy at the moment to deal with his father, so Logan sent the call to voicemail.

Half a minute later, his phone rang again.

"Dad, not now," he said, realizing the only way to get rid of him was to talk to him.

"Logan, is that you? I think we got disconnected before."

"No, I sent you to voicemail on purpose. I'm a little busy here."

"We haven't even heard from you. We didn't know if you made it or not."

"I made it, okay? I'll call you later."

"Have you found her?"

"That's what I'm working on *right now*."

"Oh. Oh, okay. So you're busy?"

"Dad, please. I'll call you later. I promise, okay?"

His father said nothing for a moment. "Tooney wants to know what you really think the chances are of finding Elyse and bringing her home."

Logan took a breath. "Better than I would have hoped. Now, I really gotta go."

"Wait, there's something else you need to know."

"What?"

"Elyse's mother is on her way to Thailand."

Logan paused. "Sein?"

"She finally called Tooney back. Yelled at him for not telling her what was going, then said she was going to go take care of it herself."

"How did she find out?"

"We don't know."

"Great. Just…great."

"I'm sorry."

"It's okay, Dad. Nothing you could do. I've really got to go now."

"Okay. I love you."

"I love you, too."

Daeng was staring at Logan as he hung up. "What was that all about?"

"A complication we don't need."

"What complication?"

Before Logan could answer, Daeng suddenly pulled the phone away from his ear and looked at the screen. He then pushed a button, said something, then listened for several seconds. Finally, he looked over. "It's the man I have following the guy from the meeting with Aaron."

"What's going on?"

"Apparently, he entered another office tower. My man followed him up to the eighteenth floor, only when he got out of the elevator, he was on one of those floors where a single company uses the whole space. There was a reception area and a waiting room, but the guy he was following was gone. My man immediately came back down."

"Did he get the name of the company?"

"Let me check." Daeng talked into his phone again. The back and forth went on longer than Logan would have thought necessary. Daeng then said, "Sorry. His English isn't so good, but he knows the alphabet, so I made him spell it for me. He had to find the directory downstairs first. The place is called Lyon

Exploratory Research. Mean anything to you?"

Logan shook his head. "Never heard of it." He pulled out his notebook, and jotted down the name so he wouldn't forget.

"The cab's pulling over again," Daeng announced. "They're at…oh, crap." He leaned forward and said something quickly to the driver.

Suddenly they were accelerating down the street, no longer trying to blend in with the traffic. They came around a corner onto a wider road, then stopped in front of a large building with hundreds of people milling around.

"Where are we?" Logan asked.

Daeng already had his door open and was starting to climb out. "Hualamphong train station," he said. "Come on!"

Logan jumped out and ran after Daeng through the crowd.

"I told my guy to follow the *farang* inside." Daeng lifted his phone back to his ear, and had a quick conversation with his man. Without warning, he came to a sudden stop, grabbing Logan's arm so he'd do the same. "He's just inside. Seems to be waiting for something."

He led Logan over to a spot against the outside wall.

"Maybe this is just another quick stop," Logan suggested.

Daeng shook his head. "His cab's gone."

"So where's he going then?"

"Trains go all over the country. He could even go all the way to Singapore if he wanted. Or he could head over to the MRT, the subway, and take it to somewhere else in the city."

Daeng's phone vibrated once. The conversation that followed only lasted a few seconds before he lowered his cell again.

"That was about the *farang* who got dropped off earlier. He said the guy just pulled up in front of the train station."

"*This* train station?"

"Yes."

That explained who Aaron was waiting for, Logan thought.

Daeng nodded toward the street. The man who had been on

clean-up duty with Aaron was walking toward the station entrance. Logan was pretty sure the guy had no idea who he was. Still, he turned away as the man neared just in case.

Daeng was on his phone again, this time with the man inside the building. "As soon as the two *farang* found each other, they were joined by a third."

"A third?"

"Yeah. A black guy. He handed them train tickets, and now they're all heading to the platforms."

Logan took a step away from the building. "They're leaving?"

"It looks like it."

They shared a quick look, then ran for the station entrance.

Once through the doors, they found themselves in a large, central hall, its roof rising above them in a gentle arc that stretched the length of the space. In the middle was a tiled area crowded with people, and on one side there were a couple hundred plastic, orange-colored seats all facing the same way. Along the edges of the hall were small shops selling food and magazines and whatever else travelers might need.

"This way," Daeng said.

They quickly worked their way through the crowd to the glass doors at the left end of the hall, where they were met by Daeng's man. Through the doors, Logan could see the platforms, several of which had trains waiting next to them.

The two men talked quickly, then Daeng said to Logan, "You see them?" He pointed out the window. "Over there, just about to get on that train."

"I see them," Logan said.

"Then come on. We need to hurry."

Instead of leading Logan through the door, Daeng headed straight for the ticket counter in the other direction.

"My bag," Logan said, suddenly remembering that it was sitting in the back of the car.

Daeng said something to his man, who then ran off while Daeng and Logan continued to the counter. The line was a dozen people deep, but Daeng pleaded their case and got them to the front. As soon as it was their turn, he told the clerk what they wanted.

There was a quick conversation, then Daeng asked Logan, "You have sixteen hundred *baht*?"

Logan pulled a couple of one thousand *baht* bills out of his pocket, and Daeng exchanged them for two tickets and change.

"We've got to run," Daeng said, glancing up at a station clock. It was almost ten after six. "The train leaves in two minutes."

As they neared the glass doors, the man who'd been driving them around town rushed up, carrying Logan's backpack.

"Thanks," Logan said, grabbing it as they passed each other.

"*Mai bpen rai*," the man said.

As they reached the platform, Logan asked Daeng, "You want to tell me where we're going?"

"Chiang Mai."

Though it had been a while since Logan had been in Thailand, he knew that Chiang Mai was in the northeastern part of the country, hundreds of miles from Bangkok.

"How long's that going to take?" he asked.

"All night."

31

LOGAN AND Daeng made it on the train before it started to roll, but just barely. They were still looking for their seats when they felt a lurch as the engine began to pull them out of the station.

"There," Daeng said, nodding toward two empty bench seats at the end of the cabin.

He took the one facing forward while Logan took the other.

"No first-class tickets left," he said. "You'll have to put up with second."

"What's the difference?"

"First class gets their own cabins."

Their car was set up like a series of tableless diner booths running down each side. The booths were open to the aisle in the center, but had walls separating the ones on the same side. Padded gray plastic cushions covered the seats, and were comfortable enough for the ride ahead. And while four people could easily fit in each booth, Logan noticed that they were never occupied by more than two.

A pair of elderly Thai women were sitting across from them, sharing some food and laughing while they talked. When one of the women saw Logan looking over, she held a piece of fruit toward him.

He smiled, but shook him head. "No, thanks."

She held it there for a second longer, then shrugged and pulled it back.

"*Mai, khrap*," Daeng said, looking at Logan. "*Khob khun, khrap*. It means no, thank you."

Logan tried it out a few times until Daeng said he had it close enough. The two ladies nodded encouragingly when he finally got it, one of them even clapping a couple of times.

"I didn't see the others when we walked through," Logan said in a low voice once the women had returned to their conversation.

"Neither did I," Daeng said.

"We're sure they didn't get off before the train left?"

"My guy would have called us if they had. The real question is, are they going to where the girl is?"

That had been a worry running through Logan's mind since the moment he realized the others were getting on a train. "I hope so."

They sat there silently for a few moments.

"How many stops are we going to make?" Logan asked.

"Maybe a dozen. Don't know for sure."

That was more than Logan had hoped for. The others could get off at any time during the night. "First thing we need to do is figure out where they are so we can keep tabs on them."

"That should be easy enough," Daeng said. "How many of them know what you look like?"

"None of the ones on the train, actually. The two who've seen me before aren't here."

"Still, maybe I should be the one who looks around," Daeng said. "Your *farang* face will stick out, and could give us problems later if they spot you somewhere else. Me, I'm just another Thai."

Logan didn't completely buy the argument, but it made enough sense that he said, "Go ahead. I'll wait here."

As Daeng headed out, Logan slouched down on his bench, antsy. For the last couple of hours his adrenaline had been running at full tilt while they followed Aaron through the city. Top that off with the rush to get on the train, and he was having a hard time getting into relax mode.

He looked out the window. They were still in Bangkok, rolling by areas he was pretty sure most tourists didn't visit. At one point they seemed to pass through what looked like a little village built between the tracks and the city a hundred feet away. There were huts and stores all crammed together and built from scrap, and around them families ate and children played.

He heard the car door nearest him slide open, and sounds from outside momentarily rushed in before it closed again. Between the door and their booth was an area with a sink and a small room with a toilet. So it was a few seconds before the man who had come through the door appeared. He was wearing a uniform, and as soon as he reached Logan's booth, he said something in Thai.

Logan hesitated a moment, then retrieved his ticket and held it out, assuming that's what the man wanted. The guy's smile told him he was right. As the conductor was marking Logan's ticket, the train door opened again. Once more there was the delay, then a man squeezed around the back of the conductor. Logan caught a glimpse of his profile, and immediately turned to the window. It was the Caucasian guy who'd been with Aaron.

A hand touched Logan's shoulder. He hesitated, then turned, bracing himself in case they'd somehow been able to ID him. But it was only the conductor trying to give him back his ticket.

"Sorry," Logan said, taking it from him. "Thank you. *Khob khun....khrap*."

"*Khob khun, khrap*," the conductor said, then turned to the women in the opposite booth.

Cautiously, Logan leaned into the aisle and looked toward the far end of the car where the other man had been heading. The guy was just opening the door to move on to the next car. As he did, he nearly ran into Daeng. There was a moment of awkwardness as they moved around each other, then Daeng bowed his head a few inches, and the door shut between them.

"He came from the front of the train," Logan said once Daeng had rejoined him.

"Yeah, I figured. I didn't see any of them in the cars back there. It's all second class like us, so I'm guessing they're probably up in a first-class cabin."

"Where do you think he was going?"

Daeng shook his head. "Nothing back there but more cars like this. Probably just stretching his legs."

As soon as Daeng left to check the cars in front, Logan decided to make sure the man who'd walked through didn't get a chance for another look at him when he came back.

He went over to the sink just opposite the door to the toilet, and hovered there, keeping an eye on the door at the other end of the car. Logan's plan was to simply step into the room with the toilet the moment he saw him. Unfortunately, a few seconds before the man returned, one of Logan's new Thai friends from across the aisle decided to use the facilities.

Now he was caught in a situation where if he returned to his seat he'd draw attention to himself, and if he stayed where he was, it would be easy for the man to take a good look at him. It could be it wouldn't matter, but, if possible, he preferred to remain anonymous for the moment. So the best chance he had to do that was to head into the next car, and hope that the toilet there was unoccupied.

He slipped out the door into a short, noisy passageway, then opened another door and stepped into the next car. Immediately he could see that this one was different than the one in which he and Daeng were assigned. The walkway took a short jog to the left, and ran along the side of the train for a little bit before passing a kitchen area, then opening into a simple dining room.

Several of the tables were occupied, and two waitresses seemed to be sharing the duty of serving the customers. There was a snack counter, too, separating the kitchen from the dining area.

What he wasn't seeing was a bathroom.

He quickly headed across the dining area to the door on the other side. Passing through it, he was once more in the no man's land between cars, only this particular passage had been set up so that people could move to the sides, out of the way, and smoke next to open windows.

He knew the further he continued down the train, the more chances he was taking that he'd be spotted. So he decided this was going to have to do. He moved over to one of the windows, his back now to the train's doors.

The sun had set in the last ten minutes, and the space was not well lit, so the shadows were also his friend as he leaned into the window to sell the illusion he was smoking, then waited. He expected the door behind him to open within half a minute, but it didn't. In fact it was almost three before someone passed through, and it was a woman, not the guy he was hiding from.

He held his position, wondering where the hell the man had gone. After another minute, the door opened again. Someone stepped through, then Logan heard something scrape against the second door a couple of times.

"Dammit," a voice said.

Logan resisted the urge to turn.

"Hey, can you give me a hand?"

Logan still didn't move.

"Buddy, you speak English? I could use some help."

Logan turned, but tried to stay as much in the darkness as possible. Sure enough, it was the guy he'd been trying to avoid. "Sorry," he said. "Daydreaming."

"No problem. Can you open this door for me? My hands are kind of full. Got through the other one, but now I seem kind of stuck."

He was holding several bottles of beer and some packages of food, which explained why he'd been delayed.

"Sure," Logan said.

He squeezed by the man and opened the door.

"Thanks. Appreciate it."

As the guy disappeared inside, Logan knew he probably should just turn around and head back to his seat, but an opportunity had just been presented to him that he couldn't pass up.

Since a person could only go two directions on a train, if someone was walking down the aisle behind them, there'd be very little reason for them to think they were being followed.

Logan let the man have a good five-second lead, then he entered the car.

This, too, was unlike the second-class car. But it wasn't another dining car. This one was first class. The aisle ran along the windows on the left, and on the right were white doors to the private cabins.

As the man neared each cabin door, Logan tensed in anticipation, but the man made it all the way to the end without stopping. There he paused, then looked back and saw Logan.

"You coming this way too?" he called out.

"Yeah, I am."

"Get the door for me again?"

"Of course."

As they passed into the next cabin, the man said, "Thanks, man. I feel like I should tip you. Want a beer?"

"No, thanks. You keep them." Logan paused. It was too late to worry about the guy remembering his face, so he added, "Unless you're actually going to drink all of them yourself."

The guy laughed. "Not that I couldn't, but I'm sharing these."

Suddenly they were friends, and Logan was no longer walking twenty feet behind him, but only three.

"At least those will help pass the time," Logan said.

"That's what I'm hoping."

Logan almost asked how far the man was traveling. The question was on his lips, an innocent inquiry from a fellow passenger. But he hesitated, then decided it was one step too far.

They were halfway through the car when the door ahead of them opened, and Daeng came through. He nearly missed a step when he saw Logan walking toward him right behind Aaron's friend. Logan could see that Daeng was trying to figure out if he needed to do something or not, so he raised a hand a few inches, indicating that everything was okay.

As they got nearer, Daeng moved against the window so they could pass. Once the man had gone by, Daeng gave Logan a look that very clearly asked what the hell he was doing. Unfortunately, there was no easy way for Logan to reply.

As before, Logan helped with the doors as they moved out of one car and into the next. This time, though, the man stopped three cabins down.

"Thanks, again," he said, as he moved out of the way so Logan could keep going.

"No worries. Enjoy the beer."

Walking slowly away, he heard the door slide open.

Someone inside said, "Took you long enough."

The man's reply was lost as the door closed again.

Quickly, Logan turned and headed back the way he'd come.

He found Daeng in their booth back in second class. As he sat down, Daeng raised an eyebrow and said, "I see they didn't kill you."

One side of Logan's mouth moved up in a smirk. "So, tell me, were *you* able to figure out which cabin they were in? Because I was."

32

EVERY TIME the train stopped at a station, either Logan or Daeng would step out onto the platform, and keep an eye on the first-class cars to make sure the others didn't leave. At around nine, they grabbed something to eat in the restaurant car, and dined to the singing of a group of three Irish backpackers who'd had a few too many Chang Beers.

When they returned to their car, their booth was no longer a booth. The porter had transformed not only theirs, but all the other booths into upper and lower sleeping berths. Each was only wide enough for one person. That explained why there were only two people per booth. Some people had apparently already checked out for the night as baby blue curtains were pulled across the aisle side of several of the berths.

"You take the top one," Daeng said.

"Since I paid for the tickets, you take the top one," Logan told him. The lower berth had a wider bed.

"And here I thought I was doing you a favor. Maybe I should charge you for my services."

Daeng got the lower.

Since the train would be making stops throughout the night,

they agreed to split the time into two-hour shifts so that one of them would always be awake. Logan had first shift, and took a train-length walk every thirty minutes to keep his focus.

It was odd how quiet everything had become. With the exception of his new Irish friends, it seemed like the whole train was asleep. Even the porters and the people who'd been working in the now-closed restaurant were nowhere to be found.

The three from Ireland—Barry, Brian, and Saoirse, pronounced *Searsha*—were camped out on one of the lower berths.

"Kicked out of the dining car when it closed," Brian told Logan. "You can walk through, but you can't sit there any longer. Who closes a dining car at ten?"

Every time Logan passed, they'd offer him a beer, and try to coax him into sitting so they could talk about the places they'd visited, and the ones they were still planning on seeing. The beer he passed on, but a couple of times he stayed for a few minutes to pass the time.

The only cars he avoided were the front two first-class ones, the closest of which being Aaron and the others' cabin. No sense in pressing his luck.

When the train stopped at a station, he always made sure he was at least two cars deep in second class, so that when he stepped onto the platform—not much more than concrete slabs in front of most of the station buildings—he would be less noticeable if the others stepped out, too.

When midnight came, he switched with Daeng, and tried to get a little sleep.

It only felt like seconds, though, before Daeng was shaking his shoulder, and they switched places again.

At the sink, Logan splashed water on his face, then started his walk.

The Irish backpackers had apparently decided enough was enough, because the curtain was pulled over the berth they'd been sitting in, and the area was quiet. Logan half wondered if they'd knocked out on their own, or if it had been "suggested" by some of their neighbors that they might want to curtail the conversation and get some shut-eye.

Whatever the case, he was left alone.

He decided to use the time thinking over everything again, retracing his steps, rerunning conversations, and trying to make sure he hadn't missed something that might be important.

As he was remembering Elyse's apartment, he started thinking about the paintings on her wall, the same girl in each image always on the edge of the action. In some, she seemed to just be watching, while in others it was like she wanted to join in but was waiting. Then there was the winged girl in the tree, alone but smiling like she had a secret. Even so, there was an innocence about her, a life on the verge of being lived.

It was only natural that he then started thinking about Carl and Afghanistan and the day everything changed.

The heat of summer hadn't taken hold of Afghanistan yet, which was fine by Logan. Unlike Carl, he wasn't a fan of the heat. They'd flown over to meet with a group of their men who'd been sent in to serve at a checkpoint just outside of Kabul.

Easy stuff, really. They just had to run a few assessments, and make sure the men were up to speed on everything required of them.

It had been going well. Very well, in fact. The guys were in good spirits, and their physical condition exceeded expectations. Unless something unexpected happened, Logan and Carl would be home by the weekend.

Ironically, both things came true.

It was Carl's idea, but it could have just as easily been Logan's.

For the first time in years, Carl had a serious girlfriend. Her name was Brenda, and they'd been going out for nearly four months. Every time he and Logan traveled somewhere he made sure to pick her up something interesting.

On this trip, he'd heard from some security guys who'd been in the country for a while about some tablecloths that were supposed to be big hits with the wives back home.

Tablecloths, of all things. Logan still couldn't believe that.

That day they finished early, freeing up most of their afternoon. So Carl had talked their Afghani guide into taking them and a few other Forbus guys to the shop where these cloths were sold.

Technically, they weren't supposed to be in that part of town. But they *were* there, and, because they never went anywhere in country without their weapons, they were armed, too.

Logan could have stopped the trip from happening. He even suggested to Carl that maybe they should wait until they could get an official escort.

"Relax," Carl had said. "It's not that big of a deal. You'll buy one for Trish, too. She'll love it."

Logan knew even then he should have stood his ground and insisted, but Carl had been acting kind of distracted for the previous couple of weeks, and it was nice to see him excited about something again. So Logan simply said, "Okay," making everything that happened afterward his fault, at least from his point of view.

The ambush caught them two streets away from the store. The gunfire seemed to come out of nowhere. One second they were driving, and the next their guide was dead, and their vehicle had crashed into a wall.

Then there was the little girl in the street.

Logan found out later she was only four. Where she had come from, he never knew. But suddenly she was there, running in the wrong direction, *toward* the flying bullets. Most of the guys had gotten out of the other side of the vehicle and were returning fire. That meant Logan and Carl were the only ones who saw her.

Carl reacted first, but only because he spotted her first. Logan was running right behind him.

They were halfway to the girl, when the bullet caught Carl in the chest, spinning him to the ground. The shooter was on the roof of a building across the street. Logan immediately brought up his gun and got off two quick shots before the guy could train his rifle on him. The gunman staggered toward the edge of the roof, then fell into street, dead.

"You're going to be okay," Logan said, as he grabbed Carl's shoulders and pulled him out of the line of fire.

As soon as Logan was kneeling beside him, Carl whispered. "The girl. Where's the girl?"

Logan looked around. He spotted her walking along the tan wall, tears streaming down her face, but still moving toward the firefight.

He looked at his brother-in-law. Carl was bleeding badly. If he was going to live, Logan needed to stay with him and do what he could.

Carl must have seen the agony in Logan's eyes. "Get the girl," he whispered.

But Logan hesitated, not ready to desert his best friend.

Carl coughed, then said a little louder, "Get the girl."

He was right, of course. Logan stood up. "I'll…I'll be right back."

He raced down the road to the wall, expecting a bullet to pierce his skin at every step. As he neared her, she saw him, then started to run away, moving into the street.

"No!" he yelled.

He sprinted after her, and scooped her up.

Chaos surrounded them as he ran with her in his arms back toward Carl and the safety at the end of the road.

He had no idea when it happened. In the over two years since, he'd gone over it in his mind, step by step, but he still couldn't figure it out. The only things he knew for sure were that when he picked her up, everything had been okay, but when he reached the end of the street, a bullet had already cut its path through her abdomen.

Three Afghani women came running out of one of the homes, screaming at him and crying. They took the girl from him, leaving behind only the blood that covered Logan's hand and clothes. He had no idea how long he stared after them before he remembered Carl.

"Did you get her?" Carl said, his voice barely audible.

Logan wiped the blood off his hand, then took Carl's and held it tight. "Yes. I got her."

Carl smiled, "Good," then a moment later, the last of his life slipped away.

When they got back to the base, Logan learned that the girl died on the way to the hospital.

If he hadn't stopped to help Carl and kept running, he was sure the girl would still be alive. If he had left the first time Carl had told him to get her, he was also sure she'd still be alive. And if he had just stayed with Carl, and done what he could, it was very possible his brother-in-law would still be alive.

But instead, they were both dead, killed by just a few seconds of inaction. His inaction.

It was news for weeks. SECURITY FIRM DEBACLE IN KABUL: 5 CIVILIANS DEAD and OFF DUTY RENT-A-SOLDIERS KILL INNOCENT BYSTANDERS. Those were just two of the headlines, many were even worse.

Trish didn't wait for weeks, though. Two days after he'd returned with Carl's body, when he admitted his own perceived guilt in his best friend's death, she walked out. "I can't look at you anymore," she had said. "You even admit you might have been able to save him, but you didn't. Every time I see you, I see him. I see his dead face. You took him from me. You took my brother."

Faced with a PR disaster, Forbus went hunting for a scapegoat. Logan was the obvious choice. They made it sound like it was his idea to go on this trip. They made it sound like Carl was the one who protested. To sweeten the pot, they even floated the rumor that Logan was responsible for some abnormalities in the books. Jon Jordan himself gave him the choice: leave on his own or be publicly dragged through the courts.

Logan didn't put up a fight. He didn't correct any of the misperceptions.

He just left.

33

AT AROUND 2:30 a.m., the train began to slow as it approached the next station. Logan was on the first-class side of the dining car, so he hustled to the back of the train, and waited by one of the doors until they pulled to a complete stop.

As before, he stepped down onto the concrete pad. This time he did a few stretching exercises to get his blood flowing. Even then, his mind was still a little foggy, so he almost didn't realize that someone had stepped off the same first-class car where the others' cabin was.

The lights on the platform left something to be desired, but the passenger did him the favor of moving down the train into the halo cast by a lamp on the outside of the station.

It was Aaron.

Logan's first thought was that the others were getting ready to leave.

He moved back to the door, ready to jump on and grab Daeng. But none of Aaron's companions appeared.

"Okay, so what are *you* doing up?" Logan said under his breath.

Aaron pulled something out of his pocket and raised it to his ear. A phone, Logan realized. Unfortunately, he was too far away to hear what Aaron was staying, so he pulled himself back onto the train, then rapidly made his way to the smokers' area passageway just beyond the dining car. There, he leaned against the open window and listened.

There was nothing at first, not even footsteps. For a second, he thought that maybe Aaron had already finished and gone back inside. Then Logan heard a foot kick at the concrete almost directly below him. Involuntarily, he pulled back a few inches.

"Yeah, yeah…okay," Aaron said. "No problems at all…yeah, I'm sure…okay, okay…we'll see you in a few hours, then."

Logan heard the muffled tone of the call being disconnected. There was some movement, then a scratching sound followed by the intake of a breath. A second later, he caught the whiff of cigarette smoke.

Aaron took a few steps, then stopped. Logan could hear him blow out a stream of smoke. Suddenly, he was enveloped in its cloud, and had to choke off a cough.

"Who's up there?" Aaron asked, surprised.

Dammit.

Logan ducked into the dining car, intending to rush back to his bed and get behind his privacy curtain in case Aaron came looking for him. But he only made it halfway across the empty dining car before the train started rolling again. He tottered to his right, grabbed the nearest table to keep from falling down, then started on his way again. He was just moving around the snack counter into the narrow passageway when he heard the door behind him open.

"Hey, you!" Aaron yelled.

There was no way he would get into his berth now. That left him two choices: keep going until he reached the end of the train, or stay in the dining car where there was no one but the two of them. Either way he sensed there would be a confrontation in his future. And while he liked his odds no matter where it happened, it would be best, he thought, if they weren't surrounded by sleeping passengers.

Having walked the train a dozen times already, he knew there was a little nook at the backside of the kitchen near the exit to the next car.

He raced down the passageway, took the sharp left that marked the end of the kitchen, then tucked himself into the nook.

Five seconds later, Aaron blew past him, then stopped at the car door without opening it. It was easy to imagine what was going through his head. *I didn't hear it open.*

That's right, Logan thought. *You didn't.*

Aaron's youth was his downfall. Once he realized he'd been tricked, he whipped around so he could figure out where Logan had hidden. What he didn't expect was that Logan had silently slipped out of the nook, and was standing two feet behind him.

"What the hell?" Aaron shouted, jerking back.

"Aaron Hughes?" Logan asked.

Aaron's eyes widened, confirming what Logan had already assumed.

"Hello, Aaron," Logan said. "Nice to finally meet you. I'm Logan Harper."

Aaron stared at him, confused. "Harper? Harper. You're…you're that guy." Though he had never seen Logan before, he'd obviously heard his name from Ryan or Angie back in Los Angeles.

"I'm that guy," Logan confirmed, then hit him in the jaw.

Aaron stumbled backwards into the wall, and fell to one knee. He wasn't out, but he was definitely shaken up.

Logan grabbed his arm and pulled him back to his feet.

Aaron took a swing, but Logan easily moved out of the way and grabbed Aaron's wrist, using its momentum to guide the kid's fist into the wall. There was a satisfying crunch.

Aaron yelped out in pain, then tried to swing at Logan with

his other hand. Logan decided it was time to do him a favor. He twisted Aaron around, then put his arm around the kid's throat and cut off his air just long enough for Aaron to slip into unconsciousness.

It really wasn't a fair fight from the beginning. Logan had had years of military training and experience, plus the element of surprise. Aaron had maybe a year or two as a cocky bastard in high school, and little else.

It was Aaron's own fault it had even happened, though. Logan hadn't wanted to fight him in the first place. Aaron didn't *have* to chase him after he'd heard Logan cough. He could have let it go, and assumed Logan was just someone out getting a little fresh air in the middle of the night. It would have sure made a hell of a lot more sense from his point of view than finding the guy who'd been snooping around looking for Elyse back in L.A.

Logan dragged him down the passageway, and laid him on the floor behind the snack counter. It was only a temporary solution, but it was out of sight in case anyone else came by on a late night stroll.

He then went and woke Daeng.

"My turn already?" Daeng said as he opened his eyes.

"I need your help."

"Now?"

"Yeah. Now would be good."

Logan led him back to Aaron. The kid was still lying on the floor, not having moved an inch.

"Is he dead?"

"No."

Daeng glanced at Logan. "This isn't exactly keeping a low profile."

"I thought we could use this to our advantage."

"This should be interesting."

"The train's got to stop again in the next hour or so, right?"

Logan said. "I was thinking that might be a good time for Aaron to get off, and forget to get back on. Do you know anyone in this part of the country?"

"I know people in all parts of the country."

Logan had hoped as much. "Someone who could meet us in the middle of the night, and take possession of our friend here?"

Daeng looked at Aaron for a moment. "That could be arranged."

"Excellent." Between Daeng and Dev, Logan was creating a network of people stashers. Whatever it took, he guessed.

"His friends are going to come looking for him," Daeng said.

Logan shook his head. "Not until morning."

"You can't count on that."

"They were drinking, so I gotta think they're going to be out for a while."

"What about him?" Daeng asked. "He wasn't sleeping."

"True," Logan conceded. "We should put him someplace out of sight until we hand him off. One of the bathrooms would work. And while we're waiting I'll see if he's up for a chat."

Daeng let out a quick, low laugh. "I wouldn't mind having a man like you working with me. Maybe we should talk when we're done with this."

Logan moved around, and got his hands under Aaron's shoulders. "Help me carry him."

34

LOGAN TIED Aaron to the toilet with some twine they found behind the snack counter, then closed himself in the bathroom with him. Daeng was still working on finding someone to meet up with them while also standing guard in the passageway in case any of Aaron's buddies showed up.

Once Logan was satisfied the kid wouldn't be able to break his bonds, he slapped him across the face a couple of times. Finally, Aaron groaned, his head lulled back, and his eyes opened.

When he saw Logan, he tensed. "You have no idea who you're messing with. Let me go. Now!"

"You know, Mr. Williams…or was it Mr. Dean? Anyway, one of them said something similar to me when I had them tied up in Santa Monica. And yet, I'm still here."

There was a flicker of surprise in Aaron's eyes.

"And if I remember correctly," Logan went on, "your friend Ryan said I should have let him go, too, not long before he died in front of me last night."

Aaron couldn't let that one go. "What are you talking about?"

Logan shrugged. "He decided not to cooperate."

"You're lying."

"Really? Did he show up back at your place on the river after his shift was over? You know the one I mean. That space you sanitized with one of your friends before heading for the train."

Aaron stared at him.

"You left in a cab, dropped your friend off, then took two duffle bags to a deserted building and had them burned. Come on, you remember this, right?"

Aaron was gaping now.

"Then that meeting you had in a fourteenth-floor office? And the guy you met with, you know where he went after?"

"Stop," Aaron said, his voice a whisper. "They're going to kill me."

"Actually, I'm not going to give them that satisfaction," Logan told him.

Aaron stared at him. "What do you mean?"

"I mean you might die, but it won't be at their hands. It's the age-old choice, Aaron. Answer my questions truthfully and you live. Don't, and I throw you off the train." Before the kid could respond, Logan added, "You may not believe Ryan's dead right now, but you'll certainly believe it the second you're flying through the air before your head smacks into the ground." He paused. "Where's the girl?"

"I don't know what you're—"

"Don't be stupid, Aaron. Where is she?"

Aaron seemed to be assessing his options, so Logan gave him a moment, knowing if he were halfway smart, he'd realize he only had one. Finally, he said, "Chiang Mai. Or should be by now."

"How did they get her there?"

"Drove. By van."

That made sense. If they were going to transport her that far, it was the only means they could use that would avoid unnecessary questions. The cleanup crew could just take the overnight train to join them.

"Why Chiang Mai?"

Aaron's mouth twisted like he was trying to keep his lips from parting. With effort, he said, "It's where the handover is supposed to happen."

Logan's skin grew cold. "What handover?"

"I don't know the answer to that. I swear. Mr. Andrews is in charge. I'm just one of the team."

Just one of the team. The words made Logan want to belt Aaron as hard as he could, to hell with whether Aaron would be able to talk again or not. And to hell with whatever damage it would do to Logan's hand. Aaron was distancing himself from responsibility, and that was something Logan could never stand. But he held it in, pushing his anger down to where he could save it for later, if needed.

"What time is this supposed to happen?" he asked.

"Sometime tomorrow…uh…I mean, later today. I don't know the exact time. We're getting picked up at the station, and then we're supposed to go help get things ready."

"Where?"

Aaron shook his head. "Only Mr. Andrews knows."

"Where?" Logan repeated, his hand clenching into a fist.

"I don't know! *I swear to God!*"

As annoyed as Logan felt, he was pretty sure Aaron was telling the truth. "At the meeting on your way to the train station, what did the man give you?"

"Give me?"

"Don't even try to lie. We were watching, remember?"

"An envelope," Aaron said quickly. "He gave me an envelope."

"What was inside it?"

"I have no idea."

"You didn't look?"

"Why should I? It's not for me."

"Who's it for, then?"

"Mr. Andrews. I'm supposed to give it to him when I see him."

"Where is it now?"

"In…in my cabin."

"Where exactly?"

"The front pocket of my backpack."

Logan made him describe the backpack, then go over everything again just in case he could catch him in a lie or shake something new loose. But Aaron's answers remained the same. A few minutes later, there was a knock on the door.

"It's me," Daeng said.

Logan opened it a crack.

"We're nearing the station."

"You got someone to meet him?" Logan asked.

"All set."

"How long until we get there?"

"Five minutes."

Logan shut the door, and turned back to Aaron. "Sorry," he said.

"Sorry about what?"

A moment later, Aaron was unconscious again.

35

THE OFFLOADING of Aaron went smoothly. Afterwards, Logan and Daeng got a few hours of sleep, then woke early, and were sitting in the dining car just a little past 6 a.m.

Daeng ordered a bowl of noodles, while Logan went with only coffee.

"So you still want to try it," Daeng said, once Logan had gone back over the plan they sketched out after they'd gotten rid of Aaron.

Logan nodded. "It could be important."

"It could also cause problems."

"I'm trusting that you'll be able to keep that from happening."

Daeng grunted, but said nothing else.

For the next half hour, Logan did little more than stare out the window at the tropical jungle that covered the hills around them. The train was moving slowly now, the upward climb a challenge for the engine.

As he was contemplating getting another cup of coffee, Daeng said softly, "Here they come."

Logan casually raised his empty cup to his lips, pretending to take a final drink, while Daeng focused on what little was left in his bowl of noodles. From the corner of his eye, Logan could see two people walking past their table, then suddenly stopping.

"You're the guy who helped me last night, aren't you?" a voice asked.

Logan looked over. The man who spoke was the guy Logan had helped by playing doorman. Standing next to him was the other member of their group.

"Hey," Logan said, smiling. "Beer guy, right?"

"Yeah," the man replied, no humor in his voice. "We're looking for a friend of ours. Wondering if you might have seen him."

Logan kept the smile on his face, staying in friendly-tourist mode. "How much did you guys have to drink?"

"He's in his early twenties," the man said, ignoring the comment. "About my height. Short brown hair. White guy."

Logan paused like he was thinking. "There've been a few people like that in here this morning, but most headed toward the back of the train when they left. Was he traveling back there?"

"No."

"Hmmm." Logan shrugged. "Sorry. I guess not."

"What about your friend?" the other guy asked, looking at Daeng.

"Oh, uh, I'm not even sure he speaks English." To Daeng, Logan said, "Do you understand?"

Daeng glanced up from his bowl. "No speak good," he said, his accent thick.

"You see another white guy like me? Younger?" Logan asked.

"*Farang* everywhere on train. Many. Many."

Logan turned back to the men. "I don't think he's going to be much help. Your friend's probably at the end of the train, hanging out with the backpackers."

"Thanks," the guy said.

"No problem."

As soon as they passed the snack counter and disappeared down the passageway, Logan was up and heading toward the front of the train. Daeng, per their plan, stayed right where he was.

Logan moved quickly through first class until he reached the door to Aaron's cabin. There was no lock, so it slid open easily when he pushed on the handle. The curtain was already drawn across the window in the door, so he was able to work without being watched.

There were only two berths in the room. That surprised him. Counting Aaron, there were three of them. Logan located all the luggage, but there was no backpack. He was sure Aaron hadn't lied to him about that. So where was it?

He quickly went through each bag anyway, but the envelope wasn't in any of them.

Standing up, he frowned. Two beds, three people, with beds barely big enough for even one.

They must have another cabin. There was no other explanation.

He was about to head back into the hallway when he realized there was a door in the sidewall. If he'd noticed it earlier, his mind must have written it off as the entrance to an en suite bathroom. But now, he realized, that didn't make any sense at all. There was a toilet and sink at the end of every car. Having one in a cabin would take up too much space.

He tried the door. It was unlocked so he stepped through, and found himself in the neighboring cabin. Here only one berth had been used. And the bag on the floor was a black backpack, exactly like the one Aaron had described.

As Logan took a step toward it, he heard the front door to the other room start to open. Quickly, he shut the adjoining door, then went to the backpack and zipped open the front pocket. The large, rectangular envelope was right inside.

Grab it and go! A voice in his mind told him.

But he knew that might be a mistake. What was in this envelope might not be that important, yet could cause problems if it went missing.

He shot a quick glance at the door, then unclasped the flap and slipped the contents halfway out.

In the other cabin, he could hear someone moving around, but no voices.

The envelope held two packets of papers, each stapled in the top corner. The language the documents were written in used a whole different alphabet than English. And though he'd only been in Thailand a short time, he'd seen enough Thai script to know this document wasn't written in Thai, either. He looked at the second packet. It was hard to tell for sure, but he got the feeling that it was a duplicate of the first.

Making a split-second decision, he sealed one of the packets back in the envelope, and returned it to the backpack. The other he kept. He then headed for the door that opened to the public passageway.

He paused, listening. Whoever was in the other room was still there. As carefully as he could, he slid the main door open and stepped out.

Two minutes later, he walked back into the dining car. Daeng was talking to the man Logan had helped the night before, but the other guy wasn't around. Without looking, Logan rolled the document into a tube, concealing the words written on it, and walked up.

"Find your friend?" he asked.

The man turned quickly, then relaxed when he saw Logan. "Not yet."

"Have you talked to the porters? They could probably help."

"Thanks," he said, in a way that told Logan they'd already done that. The man looked at Daeng. "Thank you, too, for trying to help."

"I keep eyes open, okay," Daeng said. "If see, I tell."

"Thanks."

The man headed toward first class. As soon as Logan was sure he'd left the car, he said, "I thought you were going to try to keep *both* of them away."

"I'm sorry. The other one shot right past me. I take it he didn't see you."

Logan shook his head.

Daeng looked at the paper in his hand. "You took it?"

"There were two. I think they're the same thing, but I have no idea what they say."

He unrolled it, and handed it to Daeng.

After glancing at the first page, Daeng said, "This is in Burmese."

"Can you read it?"

"Not quickly, but yes." Daeng scanned it for a moment. "It's some kind of contract. A lease, I think."

"You mean like for a building?"

Daeng read some more, then shook his head. "Like for oil rights."

36

THE TRAIN pulled into Chiang Mai at 9:40 a.m. Daeng got off ahead of the crowd and headed straight into the station, while Logan let several passengers exit before he stepped onto the long platform.

With the population of Chiang Mai nowhere near the ten million that lived in Bangkok, it was no surprise that its train station was much smaller than the one in the nation's capital. Logan guessed the red-roofed main building would probably fit entirely within the central hall of Hualamphong. But compared to the stations they'd stopped at throughout the night, Chiang Mai's was huge.

Logan slowly made his way down the covered platform, all the while keeping an eye on the crowd leaving the train. So far, he had yet to see Aaron's two friends.

At the end of the platform, he passed through one of several large, arched openings into the main building. Just inside, he found a tourist information booth, and let the girl who was manning it try to talk him into staying at one of the local hotels.

She was in the middle of her pitch when Aaron's two friends passed by on their way through the station toward the parking area out front.

"Thank you," Logan said to the girl, cutting her off. "I'll think about it."

He fell in behind the men. As they neared the front entrance, Logan spotted Daeng standing to one side, his phone to his ear. The men walked within a couple feet of him, not giving Daeng a glance.

Logan paused under the cover of the station, and watched them walk out to the curb and look around. Within seconds, a car drove up and stopped directly in front of them.

I know you, Logan thought as the driver climbed out.

It was Tooney's attacker.

The two men from the train placed their bags in the trunk, then all three got into the car.

Just after the vehicle pulled away, Logan walked quickly out of the station, and put his hand up to call over a taxi.

"No," Daeng said, coming up behind him and grabbing him arm.

He guided Logan over to a sedan parked in a nearby spot, then told him to get in.

There was a young guy already behind the wheel. His head was clean-shaven, and he was wearing a T-shirt and jeans. Daeng spoke rapidly to him, then the kid dropped the car into gear and they took off. Their driver turned out to be more than up to the task of following the other car. He was able to keep them within sight without ever getting too close.

After a while they came to the outskirts of the city. There were still buildings and businesses and homes around, but they were spread out, and the businesses seemed to be more focused on manufacturing and similar services than on retail.

Ahead, the other car's brake lights flashed suddenly, then the vehicle took a left off the road. It stopped momentarily in front of a gate built into the opening of a cinder-block wall, then the gate lifted, and it drove inside.

"Keep going past," Logan said.

A couple of hundred feet on, they made a U-turn, then stopped on the shoulder in front of a roadside restaurant. They watched for several minutes to see if the car reappeared, but it didn't.

"At the far front corner," Daeng said. "You see him?"

Logan looked. Just visible above the top of the wall was the head of a man. He seemed to be watching the road.

"Yeah," he said.

"We should go into the restaurant. He may have spotted us when we turned, and he'll be more curious if we don't get out."

The place wasn't much more than a glorified food cart with a permanent roof over the eating area. They took a table near the front so they could keep an eye across the street, then, for appearance's sake, Daeng ordered them some food.

"What do you think?" he asked Logan.

"Aaron said the handover was going to happen today."

"You think that's where it's supposed to take place?"

Logan looked over at the wall. It encircled a large property with a couple of commercial-type buildings in the center. "Figure the guys from the train must have reported that Aaron was missing before we even got to Chiang Mai. If I were in charge, I would want to talk to them in person as soon as possible. What I wouldn't want, though, is have them brought someplace where I had another meeting set up. So either the handoff's happening right now somewhere else and these guys are just sitting there waiting, or it's happening later and they're having their debrief right now." He looked at Daeng. "I'm going to assume it's the latter."

"If that's the case," Daeng said, "there's a pretty good chance the girl is—"

"—right over there," Logan finished for him, his eyes firmly fixed on the cinder-block wall. "Which means I need to get inside."

"Do I need to point out again that it's guarded?"

"I know. But so far they've shown a lack of interest in using local help. If they've only got the people they came with, then they'll be spread pretty thin guarding that place."

"We don't know that for sure."

"Again, true." Logan paused for a second. "At the very least, we know that they have someone up front." He put a napkin in the middle of the table. "This is the walled-in property. And this is us." He set a soup spoon in their approximate position relative to the napkin. Using his finger, he traced a route across the table-top. "If I'm careful, I should be able to work my way around and come at them from here." He tapped the back corner of the napkin. "To your point about not knowing for sure, I'll have staged goals. One, assess their security. And two, depending on the results of number one, enter the property, and see what I can find out. What I need you to do is create a diversion up front." He put another spoon where the front gate would be. "Doable?"

"In my sleep," Daeng said, but then frowned. "But I'm not completely comfortable with this."

Logan sat back. "All right. What do you suggest?"

"That I come with you."

"What about the diversion?"

"Don't worry," he said. "It'll be handled."

37

WITHIN THIRTY minutes, Logan and Daeng were on the move.

Their driver stayed at the restaurant to act as spotter in case anyone left the compound. If they did, his job was to follow them and report back.

Logan had no idea who was going to be doing the actual diversion. Daeng dealt with them on the phone, checking in every few minutes as he and Logan worked their way through the neighborhood, and around to the back corner of the target lot.

When they got there, they found enough junk lying around to create a step that would make getting over the wall a little bit easier.

"Let me know when you're ready," Daeng said. His diversion team was standing by on the other end of the line.

Staying in a crouch so that his head would remain below the top of the wall, Logan climbed up on the step. "I'm ready."

"Okay," Daeng said into the phone.

Nothing happened. Logan gave it a few seconds, then looked back at Daeng. "Anytime now."

"Patience," Daeng said.

There was another minute of nothing, then just before Logan was going to ask if something was wrong, he heard a loud voice coming from the direction of the front gate. It was soon joined by others. None of them sounded angry, though. In fact, their tones were just the opposite. Logan thought he even heard laughter.

This time when he looked at Daeng, he raised an eyebrow.

Daeng smiled. "Diversion, Burmese style."

"Burmese?"

"Refugees. They sneak out of the camps to find work here in Chiang Mai. When I'm able, I send whatever I can their way. So they're happy to help."

Logan raised his head above the wall just high enough so he could peek over. Standing just beyond the gate was a crowd of maybe a dozen people. They were smiling and laughing. A few were even carrying musical instruments of some kind. There were several children, too, running around the adults, and sometimes ducking under the gate for a moment before returning to the other side.

A Caucasian man stood just inside the gate, facing them. His hands were empty, but Logan had no doubt he had a weapon hidden somewhere. Two others—the two who'd been on the train, Logan realized—were walking toward the gate from the main building. Suddenly, the refugee group broke into song.

"How long can they keep it up?" Logan asked.

"They can go all day if we want," Daeng said. "It's not like the *farang* are going to call the police."

Logan nodded. "I'm going over."

"Are you sure it's safe?"

Logan took a quick look around. There was no one in the back area. In fact, the only thing he could see that probably hadn't been there for a long time was a large, gray cargo van parked by the side of the building.

"I'll know soon enough."

If he had it figured correctly, and Bell had limited his group to the men he'd come to Thailand with, then there should have only been two people left in the building, not counting the possibility of Elyse.

As soon as Logan pulled himself over the wall, Daeng followed. Logan almost told him to stay where he was, but he knew Daeng wouldn't listen. So together they made their way across the junk-strewn lot to the back of the central building.

Like the rest of the property, it was run-down, with several windows broken and many of its bricks missing. Logan quickly figured out that they could use this to their advantage.

He whispered his idea to Daeng, then started up the side of the building, using the holes where bricks had been as a makeshift ladder. Soon he came up beside one of the broken second-floor windows, and peeked in. The room beyond looked like it hadn't been used in years.

He slipped his hand through the break, and undid the latch. A few seconds later, he was standing inside.

Except for several chairs piled up against one wall, the room was empty. The only exit was a closed door directly across from the window.

Stepping lightly, he made his way over to it, and inched it open. As he did, Daeng entered the room and came up behind him. Logan took a peek through the slit in the doorway. On the other side was a wide room that took up much of the rest of the floor. It, too, appeared empty.

The others had probably contained their activity to the ground floor, having no use for anything more. Logan led the way in, intending to find a staircase that could take them down.

"Wait," Daeng whispered. "What are those?"

Logan wasn't sure what he meant at first, but then he saw the holes. There were dozens of them, each about the size of a soda can, cut into the floor about every six feet. He guessed that the place had once been used for manufacturing of some kind, and the holes, though empty now, had served as conduits for cables and wires.

He knelt next to one, hoping he would be able to see down into the first floor. Unfortunately, the only thing he saw was darkness. He moved to the next one. Black again. He checked three more, all the same.

Standing up, he decided the stairs were still their best bet, but before he could start looking for them, Daeng motioned for him to come over.

Logan crouched beside him, next to another one of the holes.

"What is it?" he asked.

Daeng held a finger to his mouth, then pointed down.

Logan looked into the hole, and wasn't surprised to see it was dark like the others. He was about to say as much, when he realized that while it did look like the others, it didn't *sound* like the others. There were voices coming up through it.

He leaned down, turning his head so that his ear was only inches from the opening.

"...out of here," a male voice said.

"I tried to find out what they wanted, but I don't think any of them speaks English," a second replied.

"Find someone who does, and get rid of them!"

There was a lull, then a third voice spoke up. "Does it really matter? They're not doing anything. Just standing at the gate, playing a few songs. Have you tried giving them money? Maybe that's all they want."

"We tried that," the second voice said. "It just made them play more."

"I bet if we ignore them, they'll go away."

"They can't be there when we head out." This was the first voice again, the most authoritative of the three.

"That's not for another four hours. More, if we haven't heard from the woman by then. It'll be fine."

There was a pause, then the first voice said, "It better be."

Silence again. Logan looked at his watch. It was almost 11:00 a.m. If the four hours was an approximation, that meant they would probably be leaving between 2:30 and 3:30.

He had to assume the "where" was the location of the hand-off Aaron had mentioned. Time was rapidly running out. If Elyse was in the building, Logan needed to get her out now.

He pushed himself up.

"Where are you going?" Daeng whispered.

Instead of answering, Logan turned toward the back of the room. Along the far wall were several doors, including the one to the room they'd entered through. He figured the stairs would be at one end or the other, and since he was closer to the door on the right, he went there first.

Bingo.

Daeng caught up to him just as Logan entered the stairwell. "What are you doing?"

"If she's here, we have to get her."

"Are you kidding? You go downstairs, they'll catch you. That's not going to do anyone any good."

"It's the only way we can find out if she's here or not."

On that point, Daeng had no argument, and he knew it. "I'll go," he said. "If they catch me, I'm just an unlucky local who stumbled into something he shouldn't have."

"That's not going to make it any safer for you."

"Maybe not a lot, but it's better than them finding you. They've pretty much all seen your face now."

"Those two from the train know what *you* look like, too."

"I'm Thai, remember? There are millions of us here. They won't recognize me."

"You're Thai with a bandage on your ear," Logan said. "Besides, that whole we-all-look-the-same routine is never really true." He paused. "You can lead, but I'm still coming."

Daeng shook his head. "Your stubbornness is predictable."

"Yes, it is."

"I didn't mean it as a compliment."

Logan shrugged, then said, "Let's go."

They moved quietly down the stairs to the door at the bottom. Daeng then opened it just enough so that he could look through.

"Well?" Logan whispered.

"Hallway. Looks empty."

"No reason to stay here, then."

Not hiding his annoyance, Daeng pulled the door open.

The hallway was maybe fifteen feet long, with doors at either end. The one to their left would lead further into the building, and the one to their right, if Logan's sense of direction was still intact, would lead outside.

Daeng looked at him, asking which way he wanted to go.

Logan pointed at the door on the left first, then at the one on the right, marking them off in order.

The good news was that his sense of direction still worked, and the first door led to the outside. It would be handy if they needed a quick means of escape.

They moved down to the door at the other end of the hallway. If Tooney's granddaughter was in the building, she would be somewhere beyond it.

Daeng reached for the knob, but then paused and looked at Logan. "If someone sees me after I open this, I'll pull it shut and hold it while you get out, okay?"

Reluctantly, Logan nodded.

Daeng opened the door a crack. Immediately, they could both hear voices, but none distinct enough to make out what was being said.

Daeng eased it open wider, then stuck his head through the gap. Suddenly, he pulled back and closed the door. The only thing that kept Logan from heading for the exit was that Daeng hadn't slammed it.

"What?" Logan whispered.

"We need to leave."

"Did someone see you?"

Daeng shook his head. "No."

"Then what?"

Daeng hesitated, then said, "She's there, but there's no way we can get to her."

"Let me take a look." Logan tried to get by him, but Daeng pushed him back.

"She's tied in a chair, either unconscious or drugged. Maybe both." He paused. "There's blood on her shirt, too."

"Are you sure she's alive?"

"I think so," Daeng said. He held Logan's gaze for a moment. "Logan, you were wrong."

"About what?"

"This Mr. Bell isn't just working with the men who came with him. There are at least half a dozen others in there. All *farang*."

Logan couldn't believe it. Elyse was right beyond that door. If there had only been the two men he'd expected, he and Daeng would have had an excellent chance at getting her out. But the two of them against eight? The only chance now would be one of total failure. "I need to see."

Daeng hesitated a moment, then said, "There's an enclosed area just beyond the door. If you don't open it too wide, they shouldn't notice."

They switched places, then Logan slowly opened the door.

Beyond the enclosed space was a large room similar to the one upstairs, except this one had several tables and some chairs spread around. He spotted Elyse right away. Her chair was just within his line of sight, toward the center of the room. She was angled so that he could see mostly a front view of her. There was indeed blood on her shirt. Not as much as he feared, but more than he would have liked.

He stared at her until he saw her chest move up and down, glad for the confirmation that she was alive. It did nothing for his overall feeling of frustration, though.

He turned his attention to the rest of the room. Sitting just behind Elyse were two men he'd never seen before, and clear across the room near the corner were several others. Perhaps Bell had gotten scared when Ryan had disappeared, or when he was unable to contact Williams and Dean back in the States. Or perhaps he'd always planned on having extra help for the scheduled handoff.

Logan pulled back into the hallway and silently closed the door.

It didn't really matter what the reason was for the increase in manpower. It meant only one thing.

Logan's job had just become considerably more complicated.

38

LOGAN AND Daeng were back at the roadside restaurant. Across the street, everything at the compound had returned to normal, their diversionary group of Burmese refugees having walked off as soon as Daeng had given them the signal.

Four hours, Logan thought. Probably more like three and a half by that point.

They had to assume that was when Elyse was going to be turned over to someone else. Once she was in the others' hands, Logan's chances of getting her back dropped to near zero. So three and a half hours was all the time he had to free her.

Without a platoon of commandos, getting her out of the compound wasn't an option. And while Daeng had proven resourceful in obtaining help, access to elite soldiers was a little beyond his reach. So that left two options: grab her while she was being transported to the handoff point, or do it at the handoff point itself. While Logan didn't want it to come down to the last minute, he felt there were too many ways she could get injured or even killed if they made the attempt while she was riding in a car.

Like it or not, the handoff point was the most logical place to make their move. Or would have been if Logan had actually known where it was.

As he tossed around a few generic plans with Daeng, something in the back of his mind tugged at him, demanding attention.

He looked out at the road again, focusing on nothing as he attempted to let whatever was hovering back there come forward.

Slowly, he started to remember. It was something he'd heard. While he was…in the building across the street…when…

When I'd been listening at the hole. That was it.

He'd been listening to the conversation coming up through the first floor.

It wasn't the thing about the four hours. That, he hadn't forgotten.

It was after.

Right after.

…more, if we haven't heard from the woman by then….

The woman.

He'd assumed at the time the speaker was talking about whoever it was they were supposed to be meeting. But wasn't it possible it meant something else?

Something more straightforward? Like…

"No," he said softly to himself.

"What?" Daeng asked.

Logan stared into the distance for a moment longer, then glanced at Daeng. "Give me a minute." Pulling out his phone, he called his father.

"Hello?" his dad said.

"Is Tooney still staying with you?"

"Logan?"

"Dad, please. Is he?"

"Yeah. He's still here."

"I need to talk to him."

"He might be asleep."

"Now, Dad."

"Sure, sure. Hold on."

Logan looked down at the table, hoping that he was wrong.

"Yes, Logan?" Tooney's voice sounded old and resigned, like he was expecting bad news.

"When I talked to my father yesterday, he said your daughter was on her way to Thailand. Do you know if she made it yet?"

"Sein? I believe so."

"Do you know specifically where she was going?"

"Everything I find out from other daughter. Sein not talk to me again after she call about Elyse."

"Tooney, I need to know where she is."

Tooney paused. "Can you wait? I call Anka."

"I'll stay on the line."

Logan glanced at Daeng, and could see his new friend was putting the pieces together, too.

Less than a minute later, Tooney came back on. "Anka says Sein in Chiang Mai."

Logan closed his eyes. He was right. "Do you know where?"

"Hotel called NS Guest House."

"Do you have a cell number for her?"

Tooney gave it to him, then said, "Do you think…is Elyse…"

"I'm doing everything I can," Logan said.

A pause. "I know you are. Thank you. I wait to hear from you again." Tooney hung up.

Logan dialed Sein's number, but the call went directly to a voicemail message that merely restated the phone number. After the beep, but before he could even start leaving a message, a recorded voice cut in and told him, "Mailbox full."

"Dammit." He looked at Daeng. "Does your friend here know of a place in town called NS Guest House?"

Daeng spoke with the driver for a moment, then said, "He thinks he knows, but can make a phone call to be sure." He paused. "He can do that on the way."

As they headed back into town, Daeng asked, "Can I see those papers again?"

Logan had almost forgotten about the pages he'd taken from Aaron's bag. Earlier, he'd stuffed them into a mesh holder on the back of the seat in front of him. He pulled the packet out, and handed it to Daeng.

After Daeng read for a moment, he said, "The oil rights are for an area off the Burma coast. The payment for the rights is a little vague, though. Money, yes, but there is an extra condition. It's only alluded to, but not stated."

"Who's the contract between?" Logan asked.

"The Burmese company name isn't important. Ultimately, it has to be controlled by the Myanmar generals."

"But who's buying the rights?"

Daeng flipped through the pages.

"It should be right there on the front, shouldn't it?" Logan asked.

"I would think so, but the company's name isn't mentioned. There's a signature at the end, but I can't read it."

He held it up, but Logan couldn't read it, either.

"It must be this Lyon Exploratory place," Logan said. "They just don't want their name in print."

"Possibly."

Logan thought for a moment, then pulled out his cell phone, and opened the web browser. After several tries, he realized it wasn't working. Apparently he could get calls and texts, but no overseas Internet access.

"Can you get on the web on your phone?" he asked.

"Sure."

Logan held out his hand. "Do you mind?"

Daeng hesitated for only a second, then hit a couple of buttons on the screen of his phone, and put it in Logan's palm.

Logan brought up Google, and typed in Lyon Exploratory Research, then hit Search. The top result was the company's website. He went there.

The company's main focus seemed to be geological research—finding things like oil fields and mineral deposits, but not, as far as he could tell, actually pulling what they found out of the ground. He went back to the search results, and started scrolling through. He was halfway down the third page when a link jumped off the screen at him. He clicked on it, and read the accompanying article.

When he was through, he looked up. "Son of a bitch," he said under his breath. It all finally made sense.

By the time he finished telling Daeng what he'd discovered, they reached the small side street where the NS Guest House was located. Since the road was so narrow, it was easier for Logan and Daeng to get out and walk down.

As they headed over, Daeng said, "Those bastards."

"Yeah."

"We need to stop them."

"We do."

"We need people to know."

Logan nodded. "They will."

The hotel was a modest, four-story place squeezed between apartment buildings near the center of the city. There was an opening in the wall right in front, and a sign that read:

NS GUEST HOUSE
Welcome

They turned onto the walkway and found themselves under an L-shaped veranda that skirted around a swimming pool. Ahead of them was the reception desk, and under the veranda, where it jutted to the right beyond the pool, were several tables, three of which were occupied. At one was a young Caucasian couple eating a meal, at another a solitary Asian man reading a newspaper, and at the third, four larger Asian men, none of whom were drinking or eating or even talking. In fact, what they were doing was watching Logan and Daeng.

When the two of them reached the front desk, they were greeted by a casually dressed Thai man with shoulder-length hair, a goatee, and tattoos running up both arms. "Welcome NS Guest House. You need rooms? We have very nice ones."

"We're looking for one of your guests," Logan said.

If the man was disappointed, he didn't show it. "Sure. What is their name?"

"It's a woman. Sein Myat."

This time the man's smile faltered, and his eyes involuntarily flicked for a split second toward the four men sitting at the table. "Sorry. No guest with that name."

"You didn't check," Logan said.

"Didn't have to. I know all guests' names. It's my job."

Daeng said something to the man in Thai. Logan tried to read the body language as their conversation went back and forth. It was obvious the man was nervous. Then he stopped in what sounded like mid-sentence, and his gaze moved to something beyond Logan's shoulder. He gave a quick, tentative smile, bowed his head, then walked away from the counter.

When Logan turned, he expected to see the four big men standing behind him. Instead, he found the smaller man who'd been reading the newspaper.

"Can I help you?" the man said. His English was very clean and proper, but with the definite hint of an accent.

"I don't know. Can you?" Logan asked. He was feeling more than a little annoyed. He needed to talk to Elyse's mom as quickly as possible, not be delayed by a runaround.

The man smiled as if he were merely putting up with Logan. "You are looking for someone?"

"Yeah. We are."

Daeng said something to him, but he shook his head. "I'm sorry. I don't speak Thai."

Daeng spoke again in a language Logan was pretty sure *wasn't* Thai.

The man's eyes narrowed as he studied Daeng for a moment. Then he replied using the same language.

As they talked, the four men at the table rose and walked over.

After several moments, Daeng said something that made the man glance at Logan, then turn to the others and say something. With a nod, one of the big men walked over to the staircase at the back of the dining area, and went up.

"Perhaps you would like to join me for a drink while we wait," the smaller man said.

It seemed like more of an order than an invitation, but Logan wasn't in an obeying mood. "Wait for what?"

"It's okay," Daeng told him. "They're letting her know we're here."

As they sat down at the table, the man said, "You can call me Taw." He then looked at Logan expectantly.

"Logan. Logan Harper."

"Pleasure to meet you, Mr. Harper. You keep fine company."

Logan tried to figure out if he was being sarcastic, but the sentiment seemed sincere.

"Would you like something?" Taw asked. "A beer, perhaps? Maybe a soda?"

"I'm fine," Logan said.

Taw looked at Daeng.

"Nothing for me, either."

The man glanced toward reception. "A water, please," he called out. "Just one."

It turned out they didn't have time to have a drink anyway. The big man returned before the water got to the table, and they were immediately escorted upstairs by Taw.

He took them to a door at the end of the hall on the third floor. Another Asian man was standing beside it. He was big like the guys downstairs, and Logan would have laid money on the fact that he was armed. The man opened the door as soon as they arrived, and Taw led Daeng and Logan inside.

The NS Guest House was not the Ritz. Then again, it wasn't even close to the worst place Logan had ever stayed. The floor was tiled, nothing fancy, but durable. The furniture, too, looked more like it had been built to last than be pleasing to the eye. There was a window on the far wall, but the curtain was drawn across it.

Sitting on the bed was a tiny woman. Though Logan hadn't seen her in person in twenty years, he would have still recognized Sein even if he hadn't watched the videos he'd downloaded. She had the same beautiful yet slightly stern face, and eyes that seemed to see more than just the surface of things. The only change he could see was a maturity, not so much in looks, but in the way she carried herself. Perhaps it was the years of speaking out and educating the world, fighting what must have seemed like a never-ending battle. In this respect, she actually looked older than her years.

Beside her was an Asian man of average size. He wore glasses, and had flecks of gray in his hair. By the way his arm was draped around her shoulders, Logan knew he was once the young man from the refugee camp who'd come looking for Sein after he'd finished high school. Khin, Tooney had said his name was.

"This is Daeng, and this is Logan Harper," Taw said.

"It's an honor to met you, Daw Sein," Daeng said, bowing his head.

"I've heard of you, Daeng," she replied. "I know of the sacrifices you have made. The Burmese people are indeed lucky to have you on their side."

"I only do what I can."

Sein smiled briefly, then turned to Logan. "Why are you here, Mr. Harper?"

"Because Tooney asked for my help."

It took her a moment to realize what he'd said. When she spoke again, the sense of control she'd displayed a moment before slipped a little. "My…father?"

Logan nodded. "You don't remember me, but I remember you. I went to Cambria High School with your sister. Anka was a few years behind me, but we were there at the same time for a while. My father owns Dunn Right Auto Repair. Maybe you remember that. He and Tooney are best friends."

She stared at him. "I'm sorry. I don't…I don't remember you."

"It was a long time ago," he said, shrugging. "I was fifteen."

"I still don't understand why you are here."

"Elyse was supposed to visit your father several days go. When she didn't show up, he became concerned, and asked me to see if I could find her."

"You're a long way from California," Khin said.

"I haven't found her yet."

Sein frowned. "This only happened *because* of my father."

"How do you figure that?" Logan asked.

"Elyse wanted to go to school in Los Angeles. She wanted to be close to him. If she'd gone somewhere else this wouldn't have happened."

Her words took him by surprise. "Do you really think the reason she was taken was because she decided to live close to Tooney? They took her to silence *you*, not your father."

She pushed herself off the bed. "Are you trying to say it's my fault?"

Taw took a step forward. "I'm sorry. I should not have brought them up." He grabbed Logan's arm, intending to usher him out.

But Logan wasn't budging. "No. I'm not saying it's your fault at all. You're doing what needs to be done. I'm just saying that's what happened. It's not about blame." He paused. "You do know they almost killed your father because of this, right?"

She scoffed. "Is that what he told you? Another of his cowardly lies, I think."

Now Logan was pissed. "No, he didn't tell me. He didn't have to, because *I* was the one who walked in and saw the gun pointed at his head. *I* was the one who stopped it from happening. *I* was the one who made sure he got medical attention."

She hesitated, then said in a voice more tentative than before, "Why would they want to kill him?"

"Can't you see why? Because your daughter was going to visit him. If she didn't show up, he'd raise an alarm. But if he was dead, no one would know she was gone until well after they got her out of the country."

"But…but they still got her out."

"Yeah, that's true. But they brought me along. That, I guarantee you, is not something they planned on."

"What can you do?" she asked. "You're already too late. The only thing left is for me to trade myself for her."

"That's exactly what they've wanted from the beginning. Don't you see that?" When Harp had told him she was coming to Thailand, he realized the target had never really been Elyse at all. It had been her mother the whole time. The troublemaker.

"It doesn't matter what I see," she told him, power returning to her voice. "She's my *daughter*. I have no choice."

"I can get her free."

"How?"

"I just need to know where the trade is supposed to happen."

"And if I tell you this, what are you going to do?"

"Get her away from them."

"What if whatever you try goes wrong? What if they keep her? What if she *dies*?"

"You need to trust me."

Daeng began talking in the language he'd used with Taw. Burmese, Logan assumed. But he only got a few words out before Sein held up a hand, stopping him.

"I'm sorry," she said in English. "I can't take the chance." She nodded at Taw, and turned her back on Logan and Daeng.

"Please," Logan said. "At least tell us where it's supposed to happen."

Without turning, she said, "Tell my father you did everything you could. Goodbye, gentlemen."

Daeng and Logan continued to protest, but she said nothing more. Taw called out, and the man in the hallway came in. Between the two of them, they got Logan and Daeng outside, and forcibly guided them to the stairs.

Logan's mind was churning. The only choices left now were to follow either Sein or Bell's group to the meeting point, and hope an opportunity presented itself.

They'd only gone down a couple of steps when Taw paused. He looked back at Logan and Daeng, then whispered, "Wat Doi Suthep. Three forty-five." He immediately turned around and continued down the stairs.

Logan glanced at Daeng. "Do you know—"

"Go, go," Daeng whispered, cutting him off.

39

WAT MEANT temple in Thai. And Wat Doi Suthep was the most famous temple in the Chiang Mai area. It was located about twenty minutes outside of town, in the hills overlooking the city.

Logan and Daeng were able to get there by 1 p.m., a little more than two and a half hours prior to when Sein was supposed to exchange herself for her daughter.

The temple was not exactly streetside. After walking through a winding area packed with vendors selling food and souvenirs, they came to the foot of a three-hundred-step staircase that led up a steep hill to the actual *wat*. Lining both sides of the stairs were three-foot-high walls, each shaped in the form of a vibrant, snake-like dragon, colored by green and orange titles.

They passed dozens of people on the way up, an equal mix of tourists and Thais. At the top was a building with a wide passageway that ran underneath it into an open-air courtyard.

"Is this it?" Logan asked, once they were in the courtyard. If it was, he was underwhelmed.

"No. Over there."

Daeng pointed at another, considerably shorter set of stairs, this one only about twenty steps. There were dozens of pairs of shoes sitting on and below it.

"You need a ticket first," Daeng said.

"You don't need one?" Logan asked.

Daeng shook his head. "Only *farang*."

Once Logan had his ticket, they left their shoes at the bottom of the staircase and proceeded up to the main part of the temple.

This was more like what Logan expected. It, too, was basically a courtyard, but there, the similarities ended.

Everything here seemed to be covered in gold. There must have been a hundred Buddha statues in different sizes, standing and sitting and lying down. In addition, there were bells and elephants and latticework on the building, all of it in gold.

And then there was the stupa, or as Daeng called it, the *chedi*. This was the bell-shaped tower that rose into the sky in the middle of the temple. Logan had seen them in the other temples they'd passed. While this one wasn't the largest, it was definitely the most golden.

Daeng took him quickly around the grounds. It was basically a square. The stupa was in the middle, and had a narrow area directly surrounding it for devotees to circumnavigate in prayer. A few people were doing so, their hands clasped together in front of them and holding several sticks of burning incense. Outside this was a larger area that also went around the stupa. That's where the majority of the people were, the tourists in the crowd snapping pictures of almost everything in sight. Between this pathway and the walls containing the grounds were several enclosed areas. Some were small shrines, while others housed larger displays of Buddhas. As they walked around, Logan noted several doors that appeared to lead out from the temple, but all of them seemed closed to tourists.

The problem was he had no idea what mattered here, and what didn't.

For all he knew, Bell wasn't planning on coming all the way

up to the actual temple. Maybe the switch was going to happen in the area where Logan had bought his ticket. Or maybe down below before the steps, where the vendors were.

"We're going to need help," he told Daeng. "There're just too many places to watch on our own. Do you think your friends from earlier can give us a hand again, and be our eyes?"

"I have a better idea, but I need to check first," Daeng said. "Can you give me thirty minutes?"

"Help?"

"I hope so."

"Sure. Do it."

"I'll meet you at the bottom of the steps when I'm done. Near the food vendor selling the fried rice cakes."

With that Daeng was gone.

Logan spent fifteen more minutes familiarizing himself with the layout, and fixing the locations of every potential exit in his mind. As he walked back down the long stairway, he couldn't help but think that this was an odd place for a foreigner to choose. If he were Bell, he would have wanted a quiet place on some empty side street to exchange daughter for mother, not a crowded temple at the top of a mountain. Though there were several Western tourists around, if something happened, Bell and his men would stand out.

Unless...

...Bell wasn't the one who picked the location.

Logan stopped halfway down, his hand resting on the dragon's back.

What if this wasn't just where Bell planned to exchange Elyse for Sein? What if this was also the place he was supposed to deliver Sein to the ultimate interested party? Which, Logan was confident, had to be a representative of the Myanmar generals.

It was brilliant. This way Bell not only avoided detaining a known public figure in Sein, he also bypassed the even trickier proposition of having to transport her internationally. Instead, he had made her come to Chiang Mai on her own. All he had to do was grab her considerably lower-profile daughter. It was much easier to make sure Elyse's disappearance wouldn't be noticed for days. If Logan hadn't walked into the back of the Coffee Time when he had, that's exactly what would have happened. Tooney would have been dead, and no one would have known a thing. Still, as Sein had pointed out, even with that foul-up, Bell had managed to get both of the Myat women to Chiang Mai.

And as far as choosing the temple?

Chiang Mai *was* only a fifty-mile helicopter flight from the Burmese border. And the temple itself would provide camouflage and confusion. If trouble occurred, the Myanmar contingent could easily blend in with the crowd, and disappear with their prize, not caring at all what happened to their Western counterparts.

There was no way to know for sure if Logan was right, but he felt like he was. And it certainly fit with everything else he now knew.

He finished the steps, then found a spot near the rice cake vendor to wait.

When Daeng showed up, the first thing Logan did was tell him his theory. Daeng was nodding by the time he was done.

"That fits with something I heard," Daeng said.

"What?"

"There were some men here yesterday and again this morning. They spoke Thai fluently, but their accents were a little off. They claimed to be from the government in Bangkok, and were given a full tour of the *wat*."

"Why would they be given a tour if they weren't who they said they were?"

"The *wat* is a Buddhist Temple. It's the people's place. Even if they weren't from the government there was no reason not to show them around."

"So you think these men were from the generals?"

"Probably secret police," Daeng said, nodding. "They're the only ones the generals would trust to send out of the country." He paused. "I was told they were particularly interested in the different ways to get into and out of the central temple grounds."

Of course they were. "Were you able to arrange for any help?"

"I was."

"Enough?"

"More than."

"Really? Who are they?"

When Daeng told him, the first thing Logan said was, "You've got to be kidding me." The second was, "I know what we're going to do."

40

GIVEN THE interest the men from Myanmar had shown in the actual temple grounds, Logan decided that it was the most likely spot for the handoff to occur. So the plan was for both him and Daeng to be in the *wat* prior to 3:30, in case things started early.

Some of Daeng's arranged help would be around, too, while a few others would be at the bottom of the steps with instructions to both tell Daeng when Bell and his team arrived, and to delay Sein as soon as they spotted her.

Right after Logan and Daeng worked all this out, they sent Daeng's driver into town to purchase several cheap digital video cameras. He got back just after 3:00 p.m., and they passed the cameras out to several of Daeng's contacts both at the top and at the bottom, keeping one camera each for themselves. The idea was that if they could videotape as much of the—hopefully unsuccessful—handover as possible, it would be damning evidence that could be released later.

As a final precaution, Logan had asked Daeng to contact the Burmese refugees they used at the compound, and have them waiting in a couple of cars at the bottom of the hill.

Having done everything they could to prepare, he and Daeng headed back up the steps, then staggered their return into the temple so that they didn't arrive together.

Logan felt anxious. He knew they'd done all that they could, but he couldn't help worrying that it wasn't enough. Consumed with these thoughts, he barely heard a voice behind him say, "Hey, it's the train walker."

"It is, isn't it?" a second voice said, this one belonging to a girl. Like the guy, her accent was Irish. "Hey, train walker. Enjoying Chiang Mai, are you?"

Logan forced a smile and looked over his shoulder. Sure enough, standing off to the side were Barry and Saoirse, two thirds of the Irish backpacking trio he'd hung out with on the train the night before.

"Having a good time so far," he said. "How about you guys?"

"Yeah, great," Barry said. "This is our fourth temple already."

"But the best," Saoirse added. "It's gorgeous, isn't it?"

"Definitely. Where's your other friend?" Logan asked.

"Who? Brian?" Barry said. "He saw all those steps and decided to stay at the bottom and get something to eat."

"Can't believe he's missing out on this," the girl said.

Logan made a face like he couldn't believe it either, then said, "You know, there is a tram hidden around the side, too, for those who don't want to do the stairs."

Barry laughed. "Yeah, we didn't tell him about that. Thought the exercise would do him good. But when he saw the stairs, he said, 'No way.' His loss."

"Definitely is." Logan smiled again. "Well, my friend's in here somewhere, so…"

"Sure. Of course," Barry said. "Have a good time. Maybe we'll see you around town."

Logan gave them a wave, then headed toward the stupa.

There were a lot more people there now than when they'd done their earlier walk-through. He wasn't sure if that was a good thing or bad. It would certainly be easier to lose people this way, but he also thought it might make the others think twice before resorting to deadly force.

He spotted Daeng standing next to an altar in the wide aisle. Nearby a smiling monk chatted away with an elderly Asian couple. Daeng had a Bluetooth receiver tucked in his ear, but didn't appear to be talking to anyone at the moment, so Logan moved in next to him.

"Anything?" he whispered.

"The murderers from the secret police are here already. Six total. Two in white shirts and khaki pants off to my left. Three on the far side, one in a tropical shirt, one in a brown, and one in a blue. You passed the last guy when you walked in. Wearing a brown T-shirt. He was interested in you until you talked to your friends over there."

"Anyone else?"

"No sign of Daw Myat, and no sign of Bell and Elyse. But if we're going by the time Taw told us, we still have more than ten minutes."

"Those stairs will take them that long, so they'll take the tram for sure."

Logan made a quick circuit of the stupa to get a look at the generals' team. The common terms he would have used to describe them were focused and tough. He guessed it would have been a little too much to expect them to be disinterested and out of shape.

A group of monks in bright saffron robes entered through a back door, then walked over to one of the roof-covered shrines. As they passed Logan, he bowed like the other people around him were doing. Once the monks moved on, he worked his way back around to where he started.

That's when Daeng caught his eye, then scratched his temple

with two fingers—their sign that Elyse and her kidnappers were on their way up.

That left only Sein, but it made sense that she'd be last. Bell definitely wouldn't want her to show up before he did. Too much of a chance the generals' men would grab her and leave. That, no doubt, would negate the contract.

As expected, Bell and his team took the tram to the top. The second Logan saw Elyse he could tell she was still drugged. She was leaning heavily against Bell, her eyes barely open. He, in turn, had his arm around her, propping her up.

They were loosely surrounded by six of Bell's men. Two were the men Logan had seen on the train, and one was the jerk who chased him and Angie on the L.A. freeways. But the guy who tried to kill Tooney wasn't there, and there were at least three others missing.

Waiting at the bottom? Logan wondered. Or were they already up here and he hadn't seen them?

He stepped over to Daeng and told him about the missing men. Daeng nodded, then quickly moved away to a less crowded area, and touched the Bluetooth device in his ear.

Logan looked back at Bell and Elyse. They were walking toward the stupa with the man from Myanmar in the brown T-shirt following not far behind them.

Near Logan was a row of beautiful Buddha statues, each with a pot of sand in front for sticking incense sticks into. He kept his eyes focused on these as he worked his way from one to the other, trying to get as close as he could to Elyse without attracting attention.

Drawing nearer, he heard a heavily accented voice say, "Good afternoon, Mr. Andrews."

"How are you, sir?" Bell's voice, the same voice that had been giving orders back in the building outside of town.

"This is not what was agreed to."

"Don't worry. It'll be just a couple more minutes."

"Then who is this?"

"No one important," Bell said. "I have the signed contract. One copy I'm afraid."

"There was supposed to be two."

"And you *will* get the second. But you have a signed one. So that should be everything."

"Except the payment."

"Which will happen momentarily."

Logan glanced over at Daeng, and gave him a single nod. It was time to make their move.

"You know what the problem is, it's all so beautiful you begin taking it for granted, and start calling it 'just another Buddha statue.'" Saoirse had walked up beside Logan. She smiled. "Find your friend?"

"He's on the other side," Logan said quickly.

"Ah, good."

He tried to listen to what was going on behind him, but Saoirse's voice drowned it out.

"Me and the boys found a great pub down by the wall in town. You've seen it, haven't you? The wall. The guidebook says it used to go all the way around the old part of the city. Anyway, thought maybe you and your friend might want to join us for a drink this evening. They've got some pool tables. Might get in a few games. What do you say?"

"Uh, maybe. Why not?"

He saw movement out the corner of his eye, and turned. Daeng was looking directly at him, waving an arm. Once he saw he had Logan's attention, he held up one finger, then collapsed it into his fist so that none were showing.

Sein had arrived, and the clenched fist meant she was with Daeng's people.

"The place is called The Hitch," Saoirse said. "Near the east wall, on the old town side. Don't know the name of the street, though."

"It's okay," Logan said. "I'll find it." Having no choice, he looked over his shoulder at Bell.

The man was smiling and definitely looking confident. Logan locked eyes with Daeng, and gave him a second nod.

"It would be great if you can make it. I love Barry, and Brian's a lot of fun, but we've been traveling together for about a month now, and sometimes it's nice to talk—"

"I'm sorry. You'll have to excuse me."

He didn't wait for a reply.

41

LOGAN TRIED to make it look like he was just another tourist taking in all the sights as he walked casually toward Elyse and Bell. But as he took another step, a hand suddenly grabbed his shoulder from behind.

"Hey. I think you need to apologize."

It was Barry, and he didn't look happy.

Why, Logan had no idea, but he didn't have time to care. "Sure. Sorry." He glanced back at Bell.

The guy was now holding a phone to his ear, but was leaning down and saying something to the secret policeman.

Barry suddenly moved in front of Logan. "Really? That's pretty damn rude, don't you think?"

Logan took a breath. "Look, I don't know what you're talking about, but I'm sorry, okay? I've gotta go."

"I'm not the one you need to apologize to. It's Saoirse." Barry looked past Logan's shoulder.

Logan followed his gaze, and could see Barry's girlfriend standing pretty much where Logan had left her. He wasn't sure if she was feeling hurt, or just embarrassed that her boyfriend was making a scene, but he didn't care. "I apologize," he said to her. "I didn't mean to be rude. I'm just in a hurry." He turned back around, but Barry was still standing there. "You need to get out of my way."

He could see something was happening ahead. Bell, with Elyse still under his arm, and the Myanmar man next to him were heading toward the exit, Bell's men loosely surrounding them.

As Logan started to weave around Barry, the Irishman reached out and grabbed Logan's arm. "Who the hell do you think—"

Before he could finish, Logan grabbed his arm, swept his feet out from under him, and lowered the Irishman quickly to the ground. The anger that had been in Barry's face disappeared. There was nothing but surprise in his eyes.

"I said I'm sorry," Logan told him.

"Yeah, sure. No problem."

When he looked back up, the others were more than halfway to the exit. They were going to get away if he didn't move fast. He started dodging through the crowd, trying to convince himself he hadn't missed his chance.

Then everything turned chaotic.

Monks started appearing through doorways, up through the main entrance, and even seemingly materializing out of the crowd.

This was Daeng's doing, the extra help he had enlisted. Only the plan had been that the sudden influx of monks would confuse Bell, and create movement problems for his men, allowing Logan to grab Elyse.

But Logan was nowhere near Elyse. And while the tactic was definitely slowing the others' escape, the flash mob created by the monks was also blocking Logan from getting closer to Tooney's granddaughter.

He continued to push his way into the crowd, trying to squeeze through any seam that he could find.

"We have a problem."

Logan looked over. Daeng had somehow caught up with him.

"Yeah. I noticed," Logan said as he kept shoving his way forward.

"It's the mother," Daeng told him. "The monks tried to detain her, but she wouldn't stay. Then some of your *farang* friends grabbed her as she was about to start up the stairs."

Bell's other men, Logan thought. The ones that were missing.

Daeng must have read Logan's silence as displeasure, because he said, "The monks did all they could, but they weren't going to hold her by force."

"I know," Logan told him. "It's okay."

It wasn't okay, but it wasn't their fault, either. He should have given Daeng the signal as soon as Bell had stepped onto the temple grounds. They would have had Elyse by now, and they could have communicated that down to the monks who'd been with Sein. But he'd wanted to make sure he had accounted for everyone, and had gotten in as close as he could first.

Once more his delayed action had caused a mistake.

Get the girl. Carl's voice whispered in his mind.

As they got closer to the exit, Logan could see that some of Bell's men had been forced off to the side, and were being surrounded by monks. One of them stared at Logan across the crowd. It was the guy who had the beers on the train. Logan could see the light bulb go on as he suddenly realized Logan must have had something to do with all this.

The man shoved one of the monks out of his way. Only he didn't get very far. Laying a violent hand on a monk was unheard of. Several Thais had seen the shove and were pulling the man back. More quickly joined in.

Logan craned his neck, looking ahead and hoping other monks had been able to corner Bell and Elyse, too, but no such luck. Bell was leading her and the Myanmar man down the short steps to the courtyard, with one of his men still with him.

"Excuse me!" Logan said loudly. "Excuse me!"

Daeng was shouting something in Thai next to him that he assumed was the equivalent.

It was working, at least a little. Some of the monks looked at them, then stepped out of the way once they saw Daeng. The biggest problem was the tourists. The sudden appearance of all the monks confused them, and they didn't seem to know what to do, so they just stood in the way, taking pictures.

Finally, Logan and Daeng reached the exit steps. They raced down into the courtyard, not even worrying about grabbing their shoes.

"What about the generals' men?" Logan asked. "One of them's with Bell, but the others are going to get away."

"No," Daeng said. "They've been taken care of."

"What do you mean?"

"The monks."

"I thought you said they wouldn't hold anyone by force."

"I said they wouldn't hold Sein by force. Elyse's mother has done nothing wrong."

Logan had a quick vision of the temple in Rangoon, and monks being beaten by the secret police. There would be no love lost here for those associated with that inhumane act.

They reached the top of the long, dragon-lined staircase. Logan took two seconds to pull off his socks so he wouldn't slip, then kept moving. The others were about two-thirds of the way down, and he could see they'd taken a moment to put on their shoes. Bell's man was carrying Elyse over his shoulder. It would have been nice if that had slowed him down, but he was moving as quickly as the others.

Daeng's hand flew up, and he touched the Bluetooth receiver in his ear.

"They have Sein…in a van," he said, his voice punctuated by the steps and the rhythm of his breath. "It's waiting at the bottom."

Bell was going to get away before they got there.

No! Logan thought. *No! No! No!*

He couldn't fail again. He just couldn't.

He increased his speed, knowing he might end up tumbling all the way down, but he didn't care.

Not only was Elyse still in danger, her mother was in trouble, too. The only way to make this right was if he could get both women free.

When he jumped off the final step, he estimated that the others had about a thirty-second lead. With Daeng not far behind him, he sprinted down the looping path through the vending area, and toward the street.

But as he took the final turn, he stumbled to a halt.

He was too late.

The same gray cargo van that had been parked by Bell's building in the outskirts of the city was now pulling away from the curb.

"No!" he yelled.

He whipped his head around, looking up and down the road. There were several taxis parked off to the right, but a four-wheeled taxi wouldn't do him any good. What he wanted was—

—a motorcycle.

It was parked at the side of the road. Its owner was sitting on the curb, eating. The guy wasn't wearing one of the familiar orange vests, though, so it was a pretty good bet his ride wasn't a motorcycle taxi.

Logan sprinted over to him. "Speak English?"

"Yeah," the guy said. "I speak."

"I need to use your bike."

He laughed. "You kidding? No way."

Logan pulled out a thousand *baht* note and held it out to him. "You can drive." With his other hand he pointed at the rapidly receding gray cargo van. "They took my friend!"

The guy looked at the van, then back at Logan. "Serious?"

"Yes."

As Logan got onto the back of his bike, Daeng ran up. "Let your friends at the bottom know we're going to need them," Logan said.

He nodded, then pulled out his phone.

"What's you name?" Logan asked his new driver.

"Kai."

"Okay, Kai. Let's go!"

42

THE ROAD between Wat Doi Suthep and Chiang Mai followed the contours of the mountain down to the plateau where the city lay. The hillside was covered with tropical vegetation. With the exception of where there was a roadside business or home, the plants and trees came right up to the edge of the road, sometimes even creating a partial canopy over the top.

It would have been beautiful if Logan had time to pay attention, but his focus was on spotting the van that was somewhere ahead of them, not on the local flora. He kept his eyes glued over Kai's shoulder at the asphalt ahead. If this had been a straight road through a flat countryside he would have seen them right away. But the curves severely shortened his visual range.

Finally, after another sharp turn to the left, he saw the van, then pointed at it.

Kai said something.

"What?" Logan asked, unable to understand.

"What you want do?" Kai yelled.

"Go around him," Logan said. "And keep going fast all the way to the bottom."

"Why bottom?"

"I have friends waiting there."

"Okay."

Kai gunned the engine, and within seconds they were whipping past the van. Logan made sure not to look at it as they went by, so that those inside wouldn't know he was interested in them. Soon the van disappeared behind them, swallowed up by the bends in the road.

It had taken Logan and Daeng twenty minutes to climb the mountain to the temple earlier, but the trip down on Kai's motorcycle took no more than five.

"There," Logan said, pointing to a wide spot on the side of the road that Daeng had described to him earlier.

They pulled over, and Logan immediately hopped off. He then pulled out another thousand *baht* note from this pocket gave it to Kai.

"Thanks," Logan said.

"You need more help?"

Logan shook his head. "Trust me. You've done more than enough."

"Okay, if you sure. Good luck," Kai said, then took off.

Daeng had told Logan there would be five of his Burmese refugee contacts waiting at the wide spot if they ended up needing them. So Logan was a little surprised to find nine of them there. It seemed the only ones missing were the kids and a couple of the others.

 He pointed at the two cars parked nearby. "Yours?"

"Yes," one of the man said.

"Who's driving them?"

He signaled for a couple of the other men to join them, and Logan quickly explained what he wanted to do. The main guy had to do a little translating for him, but they all got the gist of it.

"You guys okay with this plan?" Logan asked when he was through.

"Okay," the main guy said. "No problem."

"Excellent. Then they should get ready. It's almost time."

The two drivers got into their cars, and started their engines.

"Just tell me when you want them to go," the headman said.

Logan nodded, then, after a moment, said, "Daeng said you might have a gun I can use."

"You sure you want?"

"Better to have it than not."

The man retrieved a pistol from the back of the closest car, and gave it to Logan. "Police catch you, not good."

"I'll remember that," Logan said.

He quickly found a good spot, then looked up the hill. Through the trees, he could see a small stretch of the road that was beyond the curve just up from their position. He kept his eye on it, waiting for the van to appear. Finally, the gray van moved by, then passed out of sight.

Forty-five seconds tops and they'd be here.

"Now," Logan said.

The headman waved at the two parked cars. Instantly, they pulled into the street. Only instead of merging with traffic, they drove across the lanes, and halted, creating a roadblock. The lead car was all the way on the road, while the second car hung partially over the shoulder.

Immediately cars slowed to a stop and began honking, but the Burmese drivers didn't move.

The van appeared around the curve only a few seconds later than Logan thought it would. A quick calculation told him that it would be about six cars back in the jam. Other cars were still coming around the bend after the van, so it would immediately be hemmed in.

"Stay in the outside lane," Logan whispered to himself, as he backed into the cover of the bushes. "Stay in the outside lane."

It did.

Then, as it came down the final part of the hill, it slowed to a crawl, and finally to a stop at the back of the traffic jam.

"Okay," he said to the headman, then pointed at the line of traffic. "Start them moving around."

The man nodded, then he and several of his men ran over to the car that was sitting halfway in the wide area. Together they pushed it all the way onto the road, as if it were stalled. Then the headman got the attention of the driver of the first car in the outside lane, moving his hand in an arc, directing the guy into the wide area so he could drive around the blockage.

Soon the next car in line was following suit.

Then the third. And the fourth. And the fifth.

Finally it was the van's turn.

Logan gave the blockade driver a wave, and the guy acknowledged with a quick nod.

The van turned cautiously off the road, rocking a little on the uneven shoulder, but not stopping. Then, just as it pulled abreast of the roadblock, the blockade car shot backwards, slamming into the van's front wheel well.

There was a crunch and a rip and an expulsion of air as the van's tire went flat. It was better than Logan could have hoped for.

Quickly, he stepped out from the bushes and over to the back of the van.

As he was sure would happen, someone on the inside turned the handle and pushed one of the back doors open. Logan slipped around the side, out of view, not worried about being seen in the side mirror. He could hear one of the Burmese men arguing with the van's driver up front on the other side, keeping him busy.

The van rocked, and three people stepped out. Whoever they were, they headed around to see the damage, and deal with the problem.

If Logan hadn't miscounted, the only ones left inside would be Bell, his Myanmar client, Elyse, and Sein. There was also the driver, of course, if he had access to the back area. But he was currently preoccupied.

On hands and knees, Logan crawled past the open back door so as not to be seen. Once he was clear, he got up, and peeked around the other side. There were five of the refugees there now, one talking to the driver, while the other four talked with the three men who'd gotten out to see what was going on.

When Logan was sure the only people who were able to see him were the refugees, he took a step out, and gave them a quick wave. The one who saw him first said something to his friends.

Suddenly there were guns in their hands pointed at Bell's men. Logan held a finger to his mouth, reminding them they all had to stay quiet, then turned toward the back doors.

Before he entered, he pulled out the small, palm-sized digital video camera. This would be the cherry on top of the other footage Daeng's friends had taken. He turned the camera on, and stuck it in the front pocket of his pants so that only the portion with the lens and the microphone were exposed.

He then took two deep breaths, gripped his gun, and jumped into the back of the van.

43

"EVERYONE STAY where you are," Logan said, sweeping the interior with the barrel of his gun.

Immediately, he saw he'd made a miscalculation. Instead of the four people he expected to find, there were five.

Sitting on the bench that ran along the right were Bell, Elyse and the guy from Myanmar. On the bench to the left were Sein, and the man who'd been sent to kill Tooney.

Tooney's attacker stared at Logan, shocked.

"Nice to know you remember me," Logan said.

"Remember you?" Bell asked. He looked at his man. "Who the hell is he?"

But the guy seemed too stunned to speak, so Logan explained for him. "We met last week in a refrigerator in Cambria."

"Cambria? Wait. You've got to be kidding me, right?" He looked at his man sitting next to Sein. "This is the guy who screwed you up? What the hell's he doing here?" He turned back to Logan. "Hey, what the hell are you doing here?"

"All of you. Toss your weapons over here," Logan told them.

"I asked you a question," Bell said.

"And I gave you an order," Logan told him."

Bell smiled and shook his head. "You have no idea who you're dealing with, do you? If I were you, I'd back right out that door, and get the hell out of here."

"Is that right? Well, I've recently been told I'm stubborn, so that's probably not going to happen."

"If you're still here when my men come back, I'm not going to be able to let you go. But I'll tell you what, if you leave now, I'm willing to forget about it."

"You'd do that? You're a real generous man, Mr. Andrews." Logan paused, then said, "Oh, sorry. I should probably call you by your real name. Mr. Bell."

Bell's smile faltered.

"Yeah, I *do* know who I'm dealing with," Logan told him. "I also know your friend here is with the Myanmar secret police. And, if I'm not mistaken, you were planning on transferring these two ladies to him. Now, I'm not a lawyer, nor do I work for one like you do…what's that firm's name? Bracher Schwartz? Anyway, this looks a lot like human trafficking to me."

"What's your name?"

"Logan Harper."

"You are *so* out of your depth, Mr. Harper. This is not going to end well for you."

"Are you threatening me?"

"Absolutely."

"How, exactly, do you think you're going to pull that off?"

"My reach is a hell of a lot longer than yours."

"Oh, that's right. You're the guy who makes things happen, aren't you? Like this business deal? Sein, here, for Burmese off-shore oil rights? I'm pretty sure LRB Oil's shareholders aren't going to be too happy when news of this transaction comes out." That had been the connection Logan found during his web search on Daeng's phone, a direct link between LRB Oil and Lyon Exploratory Research.

Bell glanced at his man. "Perry, shoot him. Now."

Perry fumbled with his coat, then started pulling a gun out from under it.

"Don't do it, Perry," Logan told him.

But he didn't listen. As soon as Logan saw the handle of the man's pistol, he pulled his own trigger.

Logan had killed two men before that moment, including the man who shot Carl. Perry was his third.

In the distance, he could hear sirens. They weren't the same rhythms and tones he was used to from the States, but there was no mistaking the police were on the way.

"Either of you two armed?" he asked Bell and his client.

Bell shook his head, while the Myanmar man reluctantly pulled a gun out of his pocket, and tossed it on the floor.

"Good. So, shall we just sit and wait?" Logan asked.

"Do something," the man from the secret police said to Bell.

"You can have the women," Bell told Logan. "Just let us go."

"No!" the other man blurted out. "That woman is traitor to her country." He shot up from the bench, and stepped towards Sein. "She commit crime against my government. She tell lies everywhere she go. She come with me."

As he reached out to grab her arm, Logan said, "You don't want to touch her!"

But he did it anyway, or at least he tried. As his fingers brushed against her arm, Logan pulled his trigger again. The only difference this time was that he wanted this guy to live. The bullet hit the man just below his knee, and he collapsed screaming onto the floor of the truck.

Bell, who had been keeping Elyse close to him, suddenly let her go. "She's all yours. Please, I'm not going to do anything."

Sein immediately rushed over to her daughter, and threw her arms around her.

"Take her outside," Logan said. "And shut the door."

Sein looked at him for a moment, then nodded, and helped

Elyse to her feet. As they passed, she whispered, "I'm sorry I didn't trust you."

"Don't even worry about it. Just get her out."

As soon as the door was closed, Bell said, "What are you? Some kind of mercenary?"

"No. Auto mechanic."

Logan pulled the camera out of his pocket. He stopped the recording, then started it again so he'd have a new file, and then pointed it at Bell.

"Let's you and I have a little talk."

44

TO SAY it was a bit of a diplomatic mess was probably an understatement.

The only way to stem the fallout on the U.S. side was to swiftly move to arrest those suspected of being involved in the "Kidnapping for Oil Scheme," as it was soon labeled by cable news.

Within 24 hours, Charles Bracher, Samuel Schwartz, David Lyons—the CEO of Lyon Exploratory Research and the "L" of LRB Oil—and several other employees of all three companies were behind bars. The government had also filed extradition papers for Scott Bell, Aaron Hughes, and the remaining members of Bell's team with the Thai government.

As for the secret police team from Myanmar, Logan was never really sure what happened to them. But he had a feeling that even if they were sent back to Burma, things weren't going to go very well for them.

He heard later there was a little bit of confusion when five Vietnam vets showed up at the Federal Building in West Los Angeles with three people they claimed were connected to the matter. But it was soon cleared up, and Elyse's former roommate

Angie, along with a Mr. Williams and a Mr. Dean, were turned over to the FBI.

Logan was a big part of the mess. He had actually killed someone, *and* shot a member of the Myanmar secret police. For those reasons, it had been decided early on that his name wasn't to be mentioned in connection at all with the case. Like what his father and the rest of the WAMO gang had decided about the attack on Tooney, Logan was apparently not involved in this incident either. That was okay with him. He wasn't interested in the publicity.

Still, the authorities didn't know what to do with him, so he was detained for nearly a week, talking only to governmental representatives of the U.S. and Thailand.

It was Sein who finally got him out.

They were all in a room somewhere in Bangkok—Sein, two men from the U.S. embassy, three from the Thai government, and Logan. After they'd gone on for a half hour about how it was impossible for Logan to just walk away without paying some kind of price, Sein reached into her bag, and pulled out a laptop. Setting it on the table, she turned it so everyone could see the screen.

"One," she began. "Mr. Harper is to be release *today*, within the hour, with no charges made against him." She looked at the representatives from the U.S. "This includes anything that may have happened in California before he left for Thailand."

Detective Baker was not going to be happy to hear that, Logan thought.

"Two, if anything happens to Mr. Harper, now or in the future, and I mean *anything*, I will make a point of including both of your governments' involvement in the blame when I talk about what happened here. And then I will show this."

She tapped the spacebar, and a movie began to play on the screen.

As Logan watched, a smile grew on his face. Someone had

done a pretty damn good job of cutting together all the footage that had been shot at Doi Suthep. Logan's footage was there, too, because he made sure to slip his camera to one of Daeng's refugee friends before the police had taken him in. But there was more than just what they had shot. Intercut at strategic points was news footage and stills showing prominent leaders from both the U.S. and Thailand in the company of Mr. Bracher and Mr. Schwartz and Mr. Lyon.

Logan was released the moment the meeting was over, and was even given a free flight home, courtesy of the Thai government.

He did get to see Daeng one more time, though. They had lunch in Bangkok the afternoon before his flight left. Daeng seemed energized and more focused than ever.

"Word of our…*work* is spreading in Burma. More and more people know what happened to Sein Myat and her family, and that she survived to continue working for their freedom."

"If it helps, I'm glad to hear it," Logan said.

"I told you, it's a long fight for us. Years, decades, whatever it takes. At some point my mother's people will be free again. And you. They know about you, too, and the part you played."

"Yours is the one they need to know about. Without you, I wouldn't have gotten anywhere. And you're still here helping them."

"Of course they know my name. I'm not stupid."

They both laughed.

"If you're ever looking for a change of scenery, you'll always be welcome to come here and work with me," Daeng said.

"Thanks," Logan told him. "And if you're ever back in L.A., give me a call, and I'll drive down."

Daeng smiled. "I've been craving a little bit of that mild weather, so I'm sure I'll make the trip soon enough."

"Please tell Christina thank you for introducing us."

"I will."

The funny thing was, the only person Logan didn't talk to was Elyse. She was still heavily drugged when the ambulance took her and Sein away in Chiang Mai, and Sein told him at the meeting that her husband and Elyse had flown home several days earlier. Logan was actually glad to hear it. It meant he'd accomplished what he set out to do, to see that Elyse got safely home.

Thailand not only paid his flight to LAX, they also threw in the commuter hop from there to San Luis Obispo. When he got off the plane, he thought he'd have to rent a car to get back to Cambria, but waiting for him in the lobby was the entire membership of WAMO.

Logan got handshakes and backslaps and "well dones" all around. When Tooney's turn came, he shook Logan's hand first, then threw his arms around him. "Thank you," he whispered.

"I was lucky," Logan said.

"No, *I* was lucky," Tooney told him. "Lucky your father convince me to trust you."

"I had a lot of help. So it wasn't just me."

"Yes, yes, yes. I know. But you, you make everything happen. You brought her back."

Logan mumbled a reply, then headed outside with his dad and the others.

It was a beautiful, mild day, the humidity of Thailand suddenly a distant memory.

They were almost to Jerry's Cadillac when Harp pulled Logan to the left. "Our ride's over here."

Parked in the next aisle was Logan's El Camino, its back end facing them. It took Logan a few seconds before he realized the damage was all gone.

He leaned down for a closer look.

"I figured since you weren't using it, I'd have the guys over at Floyd's Body Shop see what they could do. They took care of the front, too."

It looked good as new to Logan. "Thanks, Dad."

Harp was silent for a moment. "I owe you at least that much. For what you did for Tooney."

"No, you don't."

"I do." He hesitated, then said, "I know there's a lot going on in that head of yours, but you did good. Real good. I couldn't be more proud."

Logan had no response for that. There were so many times he'd almost failed since that morning Tooney had been attacked, he wasn't ready to pat himself on the back.

He dropped his dad off at his home, then headed to his apartment in West Village. It was dark by the time he parked around back. He grabbed his backpack, then walked over to the stairs that led to his front door. But he didn't go up.

Elyse was sitting in his way.

She stared at him for several seconds, then said, "I just wanted to get a look at you."

"Um, okay."

"I hear you saved my life."

"I was just one of many."

"That's not what I was told."

"Doesn't really matter. The important thing is that you're home."

After several seconds, she said, "I don't remember most of it. Not well, anyway. After they grabbed me outside Anthony's place…" She paused. "Grandpa told me you were the one who found him."

Logan took a breath. "Yes."

Silence.

"If Anthony didn't know me, he'd still be alive."

"You can't think that way," he told her.

"But it's true."

"It doesn't matter. It wasn't your fault. Not even a little."

"How can I be friends with anyone now? How can I trust

the same thing won't happen to someone else?"

He knew telling her it wasn't her fault again wouldn't help, so he said what he thought she really needed to hear. "You'll find a way."

Neither of them said anything for a moment.

Then she said, "I…I know I need to thank you, but I don't know how. Just saying it doesn't seem like it would be enough."

"You don't need to thank me at all."

"I don't think I could even if I tried." She picked up something that was lying on the step behind her. "Here. It's the best I can do for now."

What she handed him was a small painting in a dark green wooden frame—a painting of a young girl with wings and a mischievous smile.

"You?" he asked.

She shrugged. "I painted it."

"No, I mean the girl. Is it you?"

She walked down the steps, stopped in front of him, then raised up on her toes and kissed him on the cheek. "Grandpa says you get free coffee for life."

She stepped around him, and started walking away.

Did you get her? Carl asked.

Did you get her?

Logan looked down at the picture, then back at Elyse as she disappeared into the night.

"Yes," he said. "I got her."

Made in the USA
Lexington, KY
03 October 2011